"Combining elements of Harry Potter and The Hunger Games, fantasy readers will be drawn to this plot. . . . Don't expect this to stay long on your library shelves."
—*Library Media Connection*

"McMann has created a world of magical whimsy."
—*School Library Journal*

"Imagination runs wild in this creative adventure."
—#1 *New York Times* bestselling author Brandon Mull

"Reading *The Unwanteds* was like discovering a brilliant, lost children's classic—except it's never going to be lost, because the readers will never, ever forget the magic they'll experience in its pages."
—James A. Owen, author and illustrator of *Here, There Be Dragons.*

LISA McMANN

THE UNWANTEDS

Aladdin

NEW YORK LONDON TORONTO SYDNEY NEW DELHI

For Kilian

» » « «

ALADDIN
An imprint of Simon & Schuster Children's Publishing Division
1230 Avenue of the Americas, New York, NY 10020
First Aladdin paperback edition July 2012
Text copyright © 2011 by Lisa McMann
All rights reserved, including the right of reproduction in whole or in part in any form.
ALADDIN is a trademark of Simon & Schuster, Inc.,
and related logo is a registered trademark of Simon & Schuster, Inc.
Also available in an Aladdin hardcover edition.
For information about special discounts for bulk purchases,
please contact Simon & Schuster Special Sales at 1-866-506-1949 or business@simonandschuster.com.
The Simon & Schuster Speakers Bureau can bring authors to your live event.
For more information or to book an event contact the Simon & Schuster Speakers Bureau at 1-866-248-3049
or visit our website at www.simonspeakers.com.
Designed by Karin Paprocki
The text of this book was set in Truesdell Regular.
Manufactured in the United States of America 0613 OFF
8 10 9 7
The Library of Congress has cataloged the hardcover edition as follows:

McMann, Lisa. The Unwanteds / by Lisa McMann. — 1st Aladdin hardcover ed. p. cm.

Summary: In a society that purges thirteen-year-olds who are creative, identical twins Aaron and Alex are separated, one to attend University and the other, supposedly Eliminated, finds himself in a wondrous place where youths hone their abilities and learn magic.

ISBN 978-1-4424-0768-8 (hardcover) ISBN 978-1-4424-0770-1 (eBook)

[1. Fantasy. 2. Creative ability—Fiction. 3. Magic—Fiction. 4. Brothers—Fiction.

5. Twins—Fiction.] I. Title. PZ7.M478757Unw 2011 [Fic]—dc22 2010043836
ISBN 978-1-4424-0769-5 (pbk)

Acknowledgments

There would be no scatterclips and no "to the death!" without my creative son, Kilian, who was there when the idea for *The Unwanteds* came to life. You'll find my token of thanks in your college fund, kid. Great thanks also to my dear husband, Matt, fantasy expert extraordinaire, and daughter, Kennedy, one of the earliest and most important readers—she knows why.

Many heartfelt thanks to all the other early readers of *The Unwanteds*: Diane Blake Harper, Andy Marshall, Erica Reynolds, Kate Reynolds, Greg Bouman, Tricia Kiepert, Joanne Levy, Lynn Sinclair, Richard Lewis, and Cathy Sproul. Your feedback and encouragement was invaluable and the book is better for it. And to my dear friend Lou, former artistic magician in our world, now inspiring others beyond.

Thanks also to the entire team at Aladdin, most especially my editor, Liesa Abrams, who has an uncanny ability to take a flawed manuscript and coax it into behaving. From the first round of edits to cover design (Karin Paprocki, your amazing creativity would deem you Unwanted at birth!), and through all the nitpicky details required to make the book shine (I'm looking at you, Lauren Forte), this was such a tremendous and enjoyable process. I look forward to making more books with you.

To my agent, Michael Bourret—it's hard to find words. I'm just so grateful. I get all sappy when I think about our journey together, and before you know it I'll be spouting off some cheesy line from *Jerry Maguire*, so let's just end it here: thank you.

And finally, to all of you artists out there: keep creating. Don't give up.

Contents

The Purge

There was a hint of wind coming over the top of the stone walls and through the barbed-wire sky on the day Alexander Stowe was to be Purged. Alex waited in the dusty Commons of Quill and felt the light breeze cooling the sweat on his upper lip. His twin brother, Aaron, stood beside him; their parents, behind. And all around, the entire community of Quill watched and waited, the bland looks of sleeping fish on their faces.

Mr. Stowe pressed his finger hard into Alex's back. A final poke in the kidneys, a last good-bye, Alex thought. Or a warning not to run. Alex glanced at Aaron, whose face showed

LISA McMANN

the tiniest emotion. Scared, was it? Or sad? Alex didn't know.

The High Priest Justine, her long white hair undisturbed despite the breeze, rose to her full height and observed the silent crowd. She began without introduction or ado, for a Purge was neither exciting nor boring; it just was, as many things just were in Quill.

There were nearly fifty thirteen-year-olds this year. The people of Quill waited to hear which of these teenagers had been marked as Wanted or Necessary, and, by process of elimination, which of them remained to be Purged.

Alex scanned the group and their families around the giant half circle of the amphitheater. He knew some of them, not all. Alex's mind wandered as the High Priest Justine announced first the names of the Wanteds, and he startled only slightly as the high priest spoke Aaron's name. Aaron, who'd had nothing to worry about, sighed anyway in relief when he was among the fifteen names called.

The Necessaries were next. Thirteen names were read. Alexander Stowe was not one of those, either. Even though Alex knew that he was Unwanted, and had known ever since his parents had told him over breakfast when he was ten, the knowledge and three years of preparation weren't enough to stop the sweat that pricked his armpits now.

It was down to a mere formality unless there was a surprise, which there sometimes was, but it didn't matter. Everyone stood motionless until the final twenty names were called. Among the Unwanted, Alexander Stowe.

Alex didn't move, though his heart fell like a cement block into his gut. He stared straight ahead as he'd seen the other Unwanteds do in past years. His lip quivered for a moment, but he fought to still it. When the governors came over to him, he put his arms out for them to shackle with rusty iron bands. He made his eyes icy cool before he glanced over his shoulder at his parents, who remained unemotional. His father nodded slightly, and finally took his finger out of Alex's back after the shackles were secure. That was a minor relief, but what did it matter now?

Aaron sniffed once quietly, catching Alex's attention in the silent amphitheater. The identical boys held a glance for a moment. Something, like a jolt of energy, passed between them. And then it was gone.

"Good-bye," Aaron whispered.

Alex swallowed hard, held the stare a second more as the governors tugged at him to follow, and then broke the connection and went with the governors to the waiting bus that would take him to his death.

Wanted

Aaron Stowe, the Wanted, watched his brother, Alex, board the rusty box of a bus, and then he turned his eyes to the formidable High Priest Justine. She retreated to her aging Jeep-like vehicle, flanked by two guards and her secretary, and they began the drive back up the dusty hill to the palace, leaving a trail of gray smoke and a sharp odor to linger in the heavy air. The rest of Quill slowly dispersed on foot.

Murmurs surfaced and drifted through the crowd. Not about the Purge, of course. That was already a cloudy memory for some. Instead they spoke of their plans for the rest of the day, for the day of the Purge was Quill's one holiday each year. All of the Wanteds and most of the Necessaries, except those who tended to the farm animals, were free to do as they pleased for the rest of it.

Aaron knew what he would be doing. He turned to his mother and father and said with a decisive air, "All set, then?"

Mrs. Stowe nodded primly, and the three of them followed the crowd down the dusty path that led to Quadrant Four, where they lived. "We'll finish making your uniform and get your things packed for university," she said. "Cut your hair, too." She looked at Mr. Stowe and asked, "I don't suppose we'll get the Unwanted boy's clothes and shoes back, will we?"

Mr. Stowe, who had once been quite handsome but now had curled up a bit from years of backbreaking work as a burier, shook his head. "No."

"Well, that's a waste. Aaron could use them. The shoes, at least. Wish I'd thought to take them before he left."

"I wouldn't want to wear them," Aaron said, and then he pinched his lips together before he said more.

Still, his mother narrowed her eyes and spoke softly, almost fearfully. "You'll do well to forget about him."

Aaron kept silent for a moment, thinking. "You're right," he said finally. "It won't happen again."

"See to it," said Mr. Stowe.

After fifteen minutes they had reached Quadrant Four, a residential square mile of tiny, identical houses planted closely together like rows of sweet corn, each house the color of the dry, cracked desert that surrounded it. The crowd of people split up now and weaved their way between the structures until they reached their own individual homes.

Aaron and his parents nodded politely to their neighbors as they walked along. When Aaron saw a familiar couple around the same age as his parents, walking alone, he touched his mother's sleeve. "How odd," he said. "Isn't Mr. Ranger a milker?"

"Yes," she said.

"Why's he out and about instead of doing his job?" Aaron's eyes narrowed.

"He must have been given the day off this year because of the Unwanted daughter. Did they know in advance, I wonder?" She turned to Mr. Stowe.

"Not that I heard. That's a blow," Mr. Stowe said. He

LISA McMANN

7 « The Unwanteds

yawned as they neared their house, number 54-43. "They'll be cut off from reproducing now—this was their second offense." Mr. Stowe wrinkled his nose. "They'll be completely ridiculed by the Wanteds for poor production."

Mrs. Stowe gave her husband a disapproving glance. "You'll be careful what you say," she snapped. "Lest you forget, we've a Wanted in our presence now."

Aaron raised his chin slightly as his parents stood aside at the front door, allowing the boy to enter before them for the first time. "Yes, be careful, Father," Aaron said coolly, "or I'll have to report your insubordination for a comment like that."

Aaron took on a dignified stride as he made his way through the tiny kitchen to the even tinier bedroom that he no longer had to share. *It's true*, he thought. *Enough mourning. Alex has likely been eliminated by now.* The twinge in his gut was soon dulled by thoughts of his now-secured future, and a tiny surge of power. He was Aaron Stowe, the Wanted. And he had a lot more to prove than most, having been born of two Necessaries. Not to mention overcoming the stigma of a worthless twin brother. It was, Aaron knew, a huge accomplishment to have made it to the top like this.

He began to pack his suitcase, a satisfied feeling growing inside him, for tonight would be his last night living with his Necessary parents. Tomorrow he would go to university to be with the others of his elevated status.

The Death Farm

o one spoke during the fifteen-minute bus ride to the Death Farm. It was stiflingly hot. Flies buzzed and darted at the closed windows, unable to escape. When Alex pulled out of his deep daze, he wiped the sweat off his forehead with his upper arm and looked around the bus.

In front of Alex, connected to him by a long chain over the high-backed bus seat, was his neighbor and friend, Meghan Ranger. It was a bit of a shock to see her in this group—she'd had only one infraction, as far as he knew, but it was a double. Singing and dancing. Alex had witnessed it, but it wasn't he who had reported her. She'd had a pretty voice, too, but Alex was not permitted to think about that. Despite the heat Meghan's face was white as the moon.

Across the bus aisle was Samheed Burkesh, who was well known to Alex but not necessarily well liked by him. Alex was surprised to see him here too, since the boy had privately boasted to Alex and Aaron only last week that he was going to be in the Quillitary. Samheed was obviously fighting tears and glared furiously when Alex's eyes landed on him.

"What are you looking at?" Samheed said. But one of the younger governors gave Samheed a warning look. Unwanteds were not allowed to speak—their last words had already been uttered before the Purge.

Alex dropped his eyes and took in a few breaths, vowing silently not to look at Samheed again until . . . well, ever. Instead he turned his gaze to the seat behind his own, not having noted in the shock of it all who was attached to his other arm. He nearly had to stand in order to see over the high seat back to where the chain led, but he didn't, since the governors were watching. All he could see was the straight jet-black hair and big, watery blue eyes of someone he was sure had to be a girl, but a tiny girl for thirteen, he thought. She didn't turn away. Instead she held his gaze, blinking away her tears only once during the long moment.

Her eyes were deep and soulful, with wet black lashes all clumped together from crying. After a moment Alex attempted a half smile. He doubted that she could see his mouth if he couldn't see hers. But her eyes crinkled the tiniest bit in response, and for some reason it made Alex feel just a little bit good.

There was no one else on the rickety old bus that Alex knew. He thought for a moment about being here alone with the governors. And for some selfish reason he couldn't quite explain, he felt a rush of something glad, knowing Meghan and the others were there with him. That he wasn't the only Unwanted in the entire land of Quill.

The bus chugged past the nursery where all of Quill's trees stood, past the cattle ranch on the way out of town, and along the stark, dingy, gray south wall of Quill for several minutes before the equally bland houses disappeared and the land grew untended and desolate.

Alex's stomach churned when the driver braked and the

bus slowly groaned to a stop in front of the black, solid iron gates of what the people of Quill called the Death Farm.

None but the High Priest Justine and the governors had ever been inside the gates and returned alive, and they didn't speak of it. Only the people of Quill, in hushed voices, would talk about it now and then, and speculate about how long you might be held there before the Eliminators disposed of you. And just how did they do it? Was it painful? Did they sedate you before tossing you into the Great Lake of Boiling Oil? Alex tried hard not to think of these things, but the harder he tried, the more he thought of them. And so it was almost with relief that he heard the bus door creak open and the governors tell all of the Unwanteds to stand and disembark.

There was a distinct smell—pungent—when the children walked off the bus and gathered along the black gate that led to the farm. It was an uncommon odor, different from the fried smells that came from the Quillitary vehicles. Alex assumed it was burning oil wafting off the nearby lake. He had never been this close to it before, since no one was allowed near it. No one could even *see* the lake, because the towering cement-block walls that surrounded the land reached all the way up to the barbed-wire ceiling, forty feet above. No one, that is, except the Unwanteds.

Alex glanced at the black-haired, blue-eyed girl next to him. The protective barbed-wire ceiling that crisscrossed and covered the entire land of Quill made a shadow box on her face, capturing a tear. She shook silently. She was not thirteen, Alex decided. In a brave moment, with nothing to lose, he whispered, "I'm Alex. It'll go quickly." He wasn't sure why he said that. It was the only comforting thing he could think of.

She blinked and turned her face up at him, making the shadow boxes race across her face like they did across everything, everywhere. "Lani," she whispered back, and shook her head. "And no. It won't."

Alex didn't know what to say. He stood at attention as a governor took a key from a string around her neck and unlocked the gate. "Summon the Eliminators," the woman said.

Another governor obliged by pounding on the gate. When the enormous gate creaked open, the governors stepped away and began boarding the bus again.

Lani watched them go, tears streaming down her face. "Good-bye, Father," she said as a slight, gray-haired man boarded.

The senior governor paused in the doorway for a split second and then, perhaps heavily, continued up the steps without looking back. He took a seat on the opposite side of the bus. Lani turned away and roughly whisked the tears from her cheeks. The bus drove off as the giant black iron door to the Death Farm widened enough for the chained children to enter single file.

Inside were four enormous Eliminators robed in black. Their heads were covered in cloth, but their beady red eyes pierced into the already frightened souls of the children. Lani now appeared to be the only calm one. She held her head high as the long chain of children walked inside.

"What are they?" Meghan gasped, and reached awkwardly for Alex's hand.

Alex grasped Meghan's hand and gave it a frightened squeeze. "I don't know," he whispered. He felt like his chest was going to collapse. Breathing in and out slowly, Alex closed his eyes for a moment and shivered as the gate groaned and closed with a loud clang, the lock clicking automatically on the other side, separating them from Quill forever. The Eliminators took the ends of the chains and trudged slowly, the children following.

LISA McMANN

They were in a small, cement yard. A gray stone building stood before them, and a steaming black lake boiled beyond it. Alex shuddered. *That's where they'll do it to us.* The oily stench seemed to grow stronger as they shuffled across broken cement, past bundles of burned-looking weeds, toward the building. It was more desolate than the most wasted section of Quill. Even the sky was clouded and gray here, although there was no barbed wire—just open sky. None of them had ever seen an uninterrupted sky before.

Everything was eerily silent but for the clanking of the chains and the scuffle of shoes as the Unwanteds moved forward. The seconds felt like hours. When the Eliminators stopped walking and turned their eyes to the sky, Alex followed their gaze.

The other children looked up too. From the sky over the boiling black lake, a large bird—or something—slowly approached. The Eliminators seemed to be waiting for it, and they stood, huge, hulking, silent, as a four-legged winged creature landed with an ominous thud directly in front of them.

Elimination

The creature was an extraordinarily beautiful yet frightening tortoise with long wings that were covered with glistening white feathers, tipped in black. The mosaic-shelled beast stood on all four legs, stretching out its neck to view its audience, and, even on all fours, was more than half as tall as the smallest child, Lani. The spectacular creature bobbed its head to the Eliminators, and then it looked each Unwanted in the eye. In turn, each dropped his gaze and instinctively drew back as far as his chains would allow.

After a few moments the tortoise appeared satisfied. When

it spoke—to the utter shock of the children—it was in a deep, agonizingly slow voice.

"Wel . . . come," the tortoise said, low and grim, and the word caused a chill to run up Alex's spine. "We've been"— it paused for a breath—"ex . . . pect . . . ing you."

Samheed, the glaring boy from the bus who had been silent all this time, muttered an oath under his breath and raised his fists, ready to fight, but Alex and the others were fearfully mesmerized by the odd creature that stood before them.

What was this thing? Was it going to attack? What did it have to do with this decrepit farm that contained nothing but the smell of death? They watched the tortoise, almost afraid to look at its grim face, but not quite able to look away, either.

The tortoise blinked a long, slow blink. Craning its long neck to look behind it, it lifted its round front leg and held it next to its mouth, as if to cup its words. "Mar . . . cus," it called out in its slow, grim voice. "It's time."

What in the name of Quill is it doing? Alex wondered. A moment later a tall, thin figure emerged from the gray building and lifted his hand.

All at once, Alex felt dizzy, as the space around him seemed to swirl, the oily lake whirling with the gray building and the wall behind them until everything was a spinning charcoal haze. He blinked rapidly and wondered if he and all the children had already been eliminated—if it was over. Nothing on his body hurt, yet the charcoal blur of everything around him now faded, softened, cooled to white, and then grew steadily brighter, nearly blinding him. This was nothing at all like what Alex expected to feel when immersed in the Great Lake of Boiling Oil.

Meghan, who could not help herself, cried out, "What's happening?"

Alex squeezed her fingers, more to assure himself than her that they were still together. He sucked in a breath but couldn't answer.

Another moment later the white melted and color emerged. The small, desolate lot had transformed into a huge world so full of color, Alex could hardly see.

The sun shone in a cerulean sky. The cement turned to a lush carpet of grass, and water fountains emerged from the earth. A thousand trees sprouted and grew to full height, scattered far and wide. The boiling lake softened into a calm sea of

LISA McMANN

blues and greens, and the single gray building expanded into an enormous, sprawling fieldstone mansion. The gnarled weeds at the children's feet wavered and transformed into wide-eyed animals, both common and fantastic.

Even the Eliminators transformed. Their black cloth coverings disappeared, and all four grew even taller, with animal-like heads and sleek, long necks that melded into huge, stout, strong bodies like the Unwanteds had never seen. The newly transformed Eliminators were covered in a fine layer of shimmering black hair that reflected the sunlight, and their previously frightening red eyes grew kind and intelligent, a rich amber-brown.

As the Unwanteds gawked, the shackles on their arms unbuckled and fell to the ground. They took in a collective, awed breath, rubbed their sore wrists, and checked to see if the others were all still there.

The tall, thin figure that had emerged from the gray building—now mansion—was a man dressed in a flowing multicolored robe. He strolled toward them. A fluffy shock of white hair stood up on his head as if he had just been struck by lightning.

"Greetings, friends," said the man. His voice, warm and clear, pealed like a pleasant-sounding bell. He opened his arms wide. "I am Marcus Today. Welcome to Artimé." He paused, touching a finger to his lips, and then he smiled brightly. "Tell me, children. How does it feel to be eliminated?"

Mr. Today

It was as if Alex and the others were mute. And indeed the colors of this magical place alone would have been enough to shock any Quillen, for Quill was a bland world whose brightest color was the green of the leafy trees in the nursery. In Quill all the trees were confined to one place so that no one would get notions about introducing such a bright color into the housing quadrants.

But here in Artimé, all of the colors felt warm, from the deep, foresty greens of plants to the soothing blues of the sky and sea. The strand of beach was not a dingy gray like the cement walls around Quill—it was clean and white with tiny bits of silver and gold sparkling in the sunshine.

A cool breeze whisked away the odor of burning oil from the children's noses and replaced it with the musky fragrance of the sea and the woods. The children breathed the wonderful scent, hesitating at first at its strangeness, and then nearly gulping it in, for several of them had been holding their breath for quite some time.

Not one of the Unwanteds could even look around and ask, "Is this a joke?" because Quill was a serious place, and it was doubtful that any of the twenty even thought a joke possible. Most likely nineteen of them had never known the word "joke," and the one that had known it most surely had been reported to the governors and thus ended up here. Whatever "here" was, if not the Death Farm.

Puzzled, Alex and the others could only stare at this man so brightly adorned. And some were frightened, perhaps, not of Mr. Today himself, but rather *for* him, since his smile was so animated, his delight so obvious, that it surely meant he would be reported to the governors and sent to the . . . well. Sent to here.

But beyond all of that was the pure shock of seeing a winged tortoise (which at the moment sported a droll smile), the transformation of the land and lake (so inviting that in a different situation one might entertain a thought of a swim on such a warm day, even though such imaginative thoughts were not allowed), and the—what would the Eliminators be called? No one had ever seen a creature like them. Whatever they were, their deep, heavy breaths made up the bulk of the noise for the moment. It was all so stunning that it was almost, nearly but not quite, uncomfortable.

And so the Unwanteds stood blinking, and the man called Mr. Today stood smiling, and the Eliminators stood panting, and the winged tortoise stood drolling, all of them in a sort of lumpy circle.

When they began to walk about the property, Mr. Today pointed out little fanciful combinations of creatures—rabbitkeys and beavops and squirrelicorns and owlbats—which hopped about the grounds looking for a snack, or strolled down footpaths together deep in conversation, or hung upside down from trees, twisting their necks about this way and that. Soon a queue of humans and creatures streamed from the mansion and appeared to go about business as usual, which was all the more shocking.

For a child of Quill, who might have been sent to his death for merely drawing something completely ordinary with a twig in the dirt—like a square, perhaps, or, good heavens, a *rhombus*—the shock of it all felt a little bit like a form of torture. And truly, more than half of the Unwanteds thought, *We are all still about to die.*

The tortoise cleared its throat and spoke to Mr. Today. "You may," it said slowly, "re . . . mem . . . ber, Marcus, what happens"—it yawned—"ev . . . er . . . y year."

Mr. Today, who had been gazing and smiling and taking in the sights of these new and wonderful people, watching their faces and eyes and noticing if they had long fingers or short ones, and taking note of how each one stood exactly so, startled when the tortoise spoke. And he jumped, quite, making everyone else just that much more edgy.

"Good heavens, Jim, you're right." Mr. Today stood up quite tall and announced in somewhat of a rushed voice, "Jim is correct, children. I generally forget from year to year what a terribly shocking experience this is for the Unwanteds. And let me assure you before you follow me around all day—this happened last year and I'll never forgive myself; those poor, sweet children agonized half the morning—that this is not a sort of torture-before-I-eliminate-you ordeal, this world and the shock of it. What I've done here, you see, is . . . well . . ." He gave a small smile. "I've saved you. That is, if you want saving."

His audience stared.

"Let me ask you this," the man continued, more slowly, trying to rein in his excitement for the sake of the bewildered Unwanteds. "Does anyone wish to be eliminated right now?" Mr. Today waited politely for ten seconds or so to see if there were volunteers. When he saw there were none, he nodded and smiled as the children uttered short gasps of acknowledgment to each other at the realization of their new fate, such as, "We're saved?" and "Wow!" and "Unreal!"

Mr. Today remained still and smiling until they were quite finished, and then he said, "Oh, splendid. Well, then. Let's have a tour."

Mr. Today dismissed the hefty, long-necked Eliminators— the girrinos, he called them—with a kindly, "Thank you, Arija. Ladies." And the four girrinos responded pleasantly, in melodious voices, "Pleasure, Marcus dear," before lumbering back to the gate to stand guard. Meanwhile Jim lifted a front leg in salute, turned away from the circle, broke into a staggering walk for momentum, and flapped his wings mightily. Slowly, very very slowly, he ascended and flew over the property this time, narrowly shaving the top of a particularly tall tree on the lawn, toward what looked to be a jungle in the far-off distance, just beyond the edge of the grass.

Mr. Today turned back to the children, who had moved very little all this time, and beckoned with his hand. "Walk with me," he urged, and with that he strode sprightly across the lawn, pointing out the flowers and various creatures like a tour guide, and pretending there was nothing at all unusual about twenty seemingly mute children stumbling after him.

Quill Prevails When the Strong Survive

After the Purge, the High Priest Justine gazed pointedly out the window of the ancient Quillitary jalopy in which she rode. Next to her sat the secretary to the high priest, a prune of a woman who had served the land of Quill since Justine had become ruler fifty years before. While the secretary was not a forgetful woman, she had somehow managed to disremember her own name decades ago, and no one else could recall it either. Now she simply answered to Secretary.

Normally, the High Priest Justine was accompanied by at least one governor as well, but on the day of the Purge all of the governors were busy delivering the Unwanteds to their deaths, and so it was just the two women in the backseat of the vehicle today.

"Secretary," Justine said evenly. "I've decided that this will be your last year."

Secretary stared straight ahead at the back of the driver's head. She nodded slowly.

The high priest continued. "I'll choose your successor from the university. You'll train him as your assistant. When he's ready, we'll send you on to the Ancients Sector to be put to sleep."

"Quill prevails when the strong survive," murmured Secretary. Her voice showed no emotion.

It was a matter of usefulness, of course. Until this year, when Secretary's eyesight had begun to grow fuzzy, there would have been no reason to eliminate her, though recently she seemed to be moving a little more slowly, too. Her time had come. And the last thing Secretary wanted was to bring shame to the High Priest Justine or the land of Quill for not emanating perfect strength. Secretary nodded her head slowly and watched the dizzying blur of checkerboard shadows that

LISA McMANN

rushed over the vehicle from the barbed wire overhead. The shadows did not make her feel secure today.

When they arrived at the palace, the High Priest Justine and Secretary made their way to the dining room for the annual steak luncheon feast, this year celebrating the largest Purge of Unwanteds Quill had ever seen. A moment later Quillitary General Blair arrived, greeted the high priest, and took his place at the far end of the table.

The three waited in silence until the governors returned from the Death Farm. Justine's eyes gleamed when finally they appeared. "Greetings, Governors. The Unwanteds have been disposed of, I presume?" she asked as the palace servants served the meal.

Senior Governor Haluki nodded curtly and handed the Death Farm's gate key to the High Priest Justine. "It's done," he said. He was one of two middle-aged governors. The other four were young and fairly new to their posts over the past five years—all recent graduates from Wanted University. They had replaced Justine's elderly governors, who'd had to be put to sleep once they'd lost their edge.

The high priest nodded to Haluki, satisfied. "A record year," she said. She became preoccupied with working her dull knife like a saw across the steak. After an unsuccessful bout, she glanced up. "It was the first year that the Unwanteds out-numbered our Wanteds."

Haluki grunted as he attacked his steak. "Even so, we've been too lenient in past years," he said gruffly. "Quill feels richer without them already."

"Indeed it does, quite right," Justine muttered, still struggling with the steak. Finally frustrated, she slammed the knife on the table. "Cook!" she bellowed to the empty doorway, and then she turned to the senior governor. "Great Land of Quill, Haluki. Find me a university student who can solve the beef problem, will you? This steak is nowhere near first-rate."

"Of course," Haluki said, nodding to young Governor Strang, who made a mental note of the assignment.

At the high priest's call, the palace cook rushed into the dining room and bowed deeply. His body trembled, though his face was dull and lifeless.

Justine glared at the cook. "Clean up the kitchen. When you are finished, find me a replacement cook—one who actually knows something about cooking—to serve in your stead."

The cook's eyes grew wide. "But the meat—," he began.

"Silence!" Justine hissed. "By dusk I want you to make your way to the Ancients Home. You have outlived your usefulness. How you made it past me when you were thirteen, I know not. You should have been an Unwanted."

"Yes, High Priest Justine," whispered the cook. His face was now struck with the realization that he would die that night. He knew better than to ask if he could stop at his house in Quadrant Three to say good-bye to his wife.

Justine dismissed the cook with a wave, and he disappeared. "Haluki," Justine continued, "you are right. I've been far too lenient, letting some slip by as Necessaries when they should have been eliminated. From now on, one reported infraction is one too many. There should be no room for mistakes in Quill!"

Loud cheers echoed all the way down the table to General Blair, who shouted, "Quill prevails when the strong survive!" Five governors echoed the sentiment. Senior Governor Haluki, gnawing wildly at his steak bone, eyed the elderly high priest. "Hear, hear," he said.

LISA McMANN

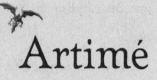

Artimé

I t took a good deal of the afternoon for the children to thaw. Alex had a small headache, but it seemed to go away once a group of teenagers, who were slightly older-looking than the group of Unwanteds, delivered to them a delicious picnic supper on the lawn by the shore. As the children ate, the teenagers formed two rows facing them. A rousing but pleasant noise burst from the nearby bushes, and the group stated words of welcome in a most peculiar way. The tops of nearby trees seemed to swish in the breeze like pom-poms. The Unwanteds had no idea what it all was, as they had never seen nor heard anything like it ever before.

LISA McMANN

33 « The Unwanteds

Alex could guess, though, since he had witnessed Meghan's very serious infraction, that what the teenagers were doing was called singing. And though the noise was very fast and loud, it was exciting, and it sounded good to his ears. He looked at Meghan, concerned, knowing how wrong this sort of thing was. But Meghan was enraptured by the performers and didn't notice.

When the song ended, the choir bowed politely while Mr. Today applauded loudly. "Clap for them!" he said to the new Unwanteds. "Like this—hands together! Applause! It tells them that you liked it," he explained as the choir dissipated. "You did like it, didn't you? Meghan, I'll bet you did."

Meghan's eyes grew wide. She glanced in each direction uneasily, perhaps out of habit, and cleared her throat. "Yes, very much, sir." And then, when Mr. Today chuckled merrily, she added, "Thank you," and tried to smile.

He nodded encouragingly to her, and to all the children, and then his face grew sober. "You may express your feelings and say what you are thinking here in Artimé," he said in a soft voice. "It will be hard, at first. But you are safe to speak your mind. All of you." His eyes grew misty for a moment, and then he clasped his hands in his lap. "There are some things we should talk about," he said.

Everyone stopped what they were doing, and all eyes focused on Mr. Today, who continued. "You already know that your parents and the government of Quill believe you to be eliminated by now. You know they are not mourning for you. They're doing what they do every day, which is to work to build Quill into a place of extreme power and super intelligence. You, dear children, are what they call creative. Imaginative. The government, and especially High Priest Justine, wants to eliminate creative thinkers like you—they see creativity as a weakness. After all, it could lead to something horrible . . . like magic." He afforded a small smile, picked a flower, and handed it to Meghan. She hesitated and then took it, and in her hand it turned into a small silver music box.

Meghan jumped and sucked in a startled breath.

"Music," Mr. Today said. "When you wind the little key, the music box will play a song. Sometimes you'll hear a song with voices saying something, like we just witnessed here a moment ago."

Meghan nodded. "Singing," she said. She turned the key

LISA McMANN

tentatively, and a few wondrous notes sprang from the box. She startled, and then her shock melted into a grin.

"Indeed," Mr. Today replied, peering at the others to see if they understood. "Singing and dancing. Painting, sculpting, telling wild tales," he said, glancing at Lani, who blushed. "Theater, playing instruments, writing stories and poems," he continued, glancing at various others at each word. "That is what you are now free to do." He noticed their puzzled looks. "Ah, but I'm getting ahead of myself."

He paused and tapped a finger on his lips as if he were thinking carefully. "I have two very serious requests. Because of your creative minds, you have been eliminated, or so think the people of Quill. My first request is this: Please consider the ramifications if you ever decide you want to go back to Quill."

The group of children blinked, hanging on to every word.

"If you ever go back, if you ever contact anyone there in any way, your parents or your siblings," he said, glancing at Alex, "the governors, or anyone, you risk exposing us all. You take the lives of everyone here in Artimé into your own hands. If discovered, this place, and everyone in it, will be destroyed.

Alex shivered, even though the day was still warm. He thought about his twin brother, Aaron, and felt a sharp pain run through him, as if half of his own body had been severed from the rest. But he knew that Mr. Today was right. And there was no way he would jeopardize the life of the man who had saved him, or the lives of the others here. Alex nodded very seriously along with the rest of the group. But part of Alex wished that Aaron could have shared in this good fortune.

"My second request," Mr. Today said, "is this: Please take the classes I offer. Train with my warriors and learn how to fight. Because if the High Priest Justine, the governors, or the Quillitary *does* discover that you have not been eliminated," he paused, letting the words sink in, "they will kill me for deceiving them. And then they will kill you once and for all. And if that happens, Artimé will disappear."

Samheed, who had been silent ever since his whispered oath, now stiffened. "Fight against the Quillitary?" he sneered. "Impossible."

Mr. Today cocked his head. "Ah, Samheed," he said. "The realm of possibility here in Artimé is only limited by our imaginations. You'll get used to it after a time. But you seem quite disturbed, my friend. Why is it that you think fighting is impossible?"

"Look at us!" Samheed waved his hand around at the group. He stopped and pointed at Alex, glaring. "In case you don't know, we're the rejects from Quill. We're not strong or intelligent. We're not capable of fighting. We're worthless! And you think we stand a chance against the Quillitary?" Samheed rose to his feet. "What you have here is all really impressive, Mr. Today, but come on! You don't seem to have any soldiers except for that group of oversized animals at the gate. No tanks, no weapons—they'll destroy us in about one minute!"

Alex shifted uncomfortably and looked down.

The small smile on Mr. Today's face remained hidden by his hand as he stroked his chin and grew thoughtful. "Hmm," he said, almost as if he expected Samheed to say more.

And the boy did. "This place is ridiculous. I'm not taking your stupid classes."

At the word "stupid," and all the words around it, the other children's eyes widened in fear. In Quill an outburst like this was against the law and a most egregious infraction that would seal a child's fate, with no exception.

"It's *not* stupid," Lani burst out, without meaning to. She clapped her hand over her mouth.

Alex, feeling both a bit protective of Lani and a bit miffed at Samheed for always glaring at him, shifted on the picnic blanket in case he had to do something—although he had no idea what "something" might be—and shot a look of support at Lani.

Samheed laughed sarcastically. "Not for a baby, maybe." He looked Mr. Today in the eye and said, "I think you are a complete lunatic." And then, as if he knew where he was going, he stalked off down the lawn to the seashore and kept walking along its edge.

The Unwanteds watched, stunned. Every one of the children knew that people in Quill were not allowed to argue or become angry with other Quillens. They were taught to bank their rage and keep it somewhere deep inside, so that in case of attack they would, with one unified surge, pour the rage out upon the heads of their enemies. Of course, Quill had quite a lot of rage saved up, since there had been no sign of enemies in the entire fifty years of High Priest Justine's reign. Yet the government instilled much fear into the people about evil foreign lands beyond the protective walls of Quill—unimaginable places like the great

LISA McMANN

desert and the dark forest—as if an attack were imminent. And who were the people of Quill to question the rulers who had kept them safe all this time?

But here in Artimé, nothing was as the Unwanteds expected.

The other children began chattering, shocked at Samheed's actions and words. "What is he doing?" "Is he allowed to go off like that?" "Isn't someone going to stop him?" "Why does he have to be so mean?" This last one from Lani, who felt wounded, having just been called a baby.

Samheed's outburst was foreign to the Unwanteds, and they watched Mr. Today, waiting for him to punish Samheed for the infraction. But to their great puzzlement Mr. Today did nothing.

As the old man watched the children react to the scene, it was hard for him to hide the mirth that crinkled around his eyes. "Bravo! Bravo, my dear boy!" he called in the direction of Samheed. "That's the way!" *Perfect*, he thought. Even better than he had hoped for the first day. He put his hands together and began clapping and shouting.

Samheed flung up his hand in disgust and continued walking.

The others, startled, had no idea what to think, but after a moment Meghan began to clap too, for there was something inside her churning mind that just about, but not quite, understood why. Soon Alex joined in as if he almost understood it too, and a curious look passed between Meghan and him, one that made them both want to laugh out loud.

Home in the Stone Mansion

I t was near dusk when the Unwanteds followed Mr. Today toward the mansion. Samheed had not rejoined them. Some of the children murmured their concerns.

Mr. Today smiled. "He'll be fine; there's no need to worry. He needs to think and walk, and that is a good thing for a strong, angry fighter like him."

"But what if he gets lost?" Lani asked, feeling quite comfortable in her new surroundings already. And though she was curious, she didn't particularly care whether the sullen Samheed ever returned.

"He can't get lost," Mr. Today assured the children. "I've

put the scroll feature into effect. Once he reaches the end of Artimé, just beyond the mansion, he'll slip through and come out the opposite side, at the edge of the jungle where it meets the shore. He'll simply need to walk a bit farther to get back to where he started."

Alex gave Mr. Today a quizzical look. "Scroll feature? So there is no jungle? It's just a . . . a . . ." He struggled for the word.

"A picture? More like a giant window at the moment, actually. And yes, the jungle is really there—good heavens, where would all the animals go if it weren't? You just can't get to it at the moment." His eyes twinkled. "But when you are all sure of me, and I am sure of you, and I know you have found your bearings quite satisfactorily, I'll remove the giant window and the scroll feature, and you'll find that the jungle is quite lovely." The old man paused thoughtfully. "Though it can be frightening and dangerous. Lots of fascinating things to see there too. But that's for another day."

Alex didn't understand, but he nodded anyway, and soon they reached the walkway to the mansion. As they drew near, a pleasant-sounding noise could be heard coming from the shrubs. "Music in the bushes," Mr. Today said.

He climbed the steps. "This is our home. You may come and go as you please and even stay out all night if you wish."

Lani's eyes opened wide. *That's a bit of a shock,* she thought. But what so far this day *wasn't?*

The old magician then opened the enormous wooden door to the mansion and walked inside, the children following.

Before them was a stunning, massive marble entryway flanked by two statues standing upright on pedestals. The pedestals alone were as tall as Alex, and the statues on top of them reached twenty-five feet off the floor, yet they nowhere nearly approached the ceiling. On the left stood a towering winged cheetah made of sand-colored stone, with sharp ivory teeth thicker and longer than the children's fingers. He stood poised to attack, reared up on his hind legs, his wings widespread, frozen in mid-flap. On the right, carved from ebony, was an enormous, sleek woman with long, flowing hair and bulging muscles, a quiver of arrows and a bow slung over her shoulder.

Mr. Today looked up. "Hello, Simber. Good evening, Florence," he said.

The statues nodded stiffly.

"There ought to be one more boy coming along presently,

so be aware. Probably shouldn't eat him, all right, Simber?"

The winged cheetah purr-growled in response and fluidly lowered himself to all fours on the pedestal, his huge paws with gleaming claws hanging off the edge within inches of Alex's face. Slowly the boy slid away from the stony beast.

"Wow," Lani breathed, and the others followed her gaze from the statues to the rest of the great foyer. Beyond the entrance the marble floor led to an extremely wide marble staircase whose steps split halfway up and wound around to meet again in an incredible expanse of balcony. They could see several hallways branching off the overlook.

The children's voices grew loud as they exclaimed or noted things to each other about the mansion from their viewpoint in the entryway.

Mr. Today strolled past the staircase. "We'll visit up there in a moment," he said. Instead he led the children behind the staircase to a hallway and showed them past several doors— classrooms, he said—and to the back of the mansion, to a kitchen the size of six Quill houses put together. At a long counter bar off to the left sat a dozen or fifteen older teenagers all laughing and snacking on popcorn and sodas as a brilliant pink ball of fluff

LISA McMANN

with webbed feet did a dance for them along the countertop. Some of the people sitting there turned to look curiously at the children standing with Mr. Today. A few waved hello.

Alex recognized one, just barely remembering her as one of last year's Unwanteds. *How strange*, he thought, and his mind began to turn.

"How many Unwanteds live here, actually?" he asked.

"Hmm," Mr. Today hummed, tapping his lips with his forefinger. "Perhaps five hundred? I lost count years ago."

"Five hundred!" Meghan said. "Where is everyone?"

"Oh, they're around. Here and there," he said. "Some are in evening classes, some practicing their art, some relaxing in the lounge, some in their rooms. You saw a few of them strolling about on the lawn, didn't you?"

Lani tapped Mr. Today's shoulder, which made him chuckle and give her his utmost attention. "Mr. Today," she said somberly, "did all the Unwanteds over the years decide not to be eliminated? Are they *all* here?"

Meghan gave Alex a wildish sort of look and gripped his arm, and he remembered that she had an older brother who had been eliminated five years before.

Alex nodded sharply, knowing what Meghan seemed speech-less to say, and the burning question rushed from his lips before he could stop it. "Yes, Mr. Today—how many years . . . ?" His face grew pale as he thought about all the Unwanteds that had been Purged from Quill since he was a boy. His mind raced, trying to remember them, but it was difficult, since Quillens had all been instructed to forget them.

Mr. Today smiled, but there was a hint of sorrow in his eyes. "Dear people, how could I forget? Yes, all the Unwanteds as far back as you can remember are here." He looked at Meghan, and his dark eyes danced again. "Meghan, your brother, Sean, is so excited to see you. He'd like you to meet him in the lounge at eight o'clock!"

Meghan squeaked in shock. "He's here . . . ?" She trailed off and gripped Alex's arm so hard it hurt him.

"Which reminds me," said Mr. Today. "I'd better show you the upstairs so you can get ready."

"Where do you suppose the lounge is?" Meghan whispered to Alex.

Mr. Today, though apparently forgetful in his old age, did not have a hearing problem. He chuckled. "You'll find instructions in your room that will tell you how to take the tube to the lounge, Meghan. Never fear! Never fear!" The magician chuckled again and rubbed his hands together, so excited to see the Unwanteds feeling a bit more comfortable as the day wore on.

"Tube?" Meghan whispered, softer now, in Alex's ear.

Alex shrugged, his eyes wide in wonder. "I have no idea."

There were several doors that led from the kitchen. Mr. Today pointed at one as they walked through the huge room and said, "Help yourself to anything in that pantry whenever you get hungry for a snack, either by coming down here or ordering up. The official mealtimes are posted on the blackboards in your rooms."

"Snacks, whenever we want?" whispered a rather thin boy at the back of the group. "Amazing."

"Where does everyone sit?" Lani asked.

"Oh, we always have room. You'll see," he said mysteriously. Mr. Today led them down another hallway and pointed out an enormous dining room, and soon they were back to the entryway and the base of the staircase.

Alex saw that Simber had once again risen to his hindquarters.

"Marrrcus," Simber said in his purr-growl voice. "I believe the young man has arrrived."

"What excellent timing," Mr. Today said. "Thank you, Sim. Wait here one moment for me, children." He went to the giant door and opened it. On the step sat Samheed, his broad shoulders curled over and his chin in his hands. Mr. Today sat next to him, and the two exchanged a few quiet words.

Alex leaned down and whispered to Lani and Meghan, "Where do you suppose the other statue went?" For now the warrior woman had disappeared.

Lani giggled. "Perhaps she needed a snack from the pantry."

"Or maybe a nap?" Meghan, who was nearly shivering in anticipation of seeing her brother, laughed a strange, high-pitched laugh and hiccupped.

Mr. Today and Samheed joined the others, and they ascended the magnificent staircase, Samheed still wearing a mildly sullen look on his face. Lani and several others sent suspicious glances his way, but Samheed made no further outbursts, and he stayed near the back of the group. The rest of them chattered excitedly now, wondering over things like the statues, the pictures on the walls, the music that floated about their ears, not

LISA McMANN

really understanding any of it but liking it all the same. They gathered at the center of the balcony.

"That hallway there," said Mr. Today, pointing toward the rightmost wing, "is where the families live." It seemed to go on endlessly. "And this hall next to it is for the other adults."

He pointed to the expanse of wall directly in front of Alex. "This one, right about here, is where the female students live—boys, you and I can't see it, and therefore we can't enter it. But we can see the one next to it—that's the boys' hall. You girls can't see that, can you?"

Meghan, Lani, and the other girls exchanged surprised looks as Mr. Today continued.

"And here we have a wing for the few creatures who prefer to lodge indoors, though you might notice creatures in your various halls, too. Some have roaming tendencies." He chuckled at the twenty pairs of wide eyes.

"Mr. Today," someone ventured from the back of the group, "does that giant turtle have a room in the mansion?"

"No," replied the man, "Jim prefers to live in the jungle, like many of the creatures. But he's welcome here if he changes his mind, just as they all are."

"Don't you ever run out of space for everyone?"

"Never," Mr. Today said with a mysterious smile. He then turned to the group and said, "Children, please find your rooms. You'll know which one is yours as you walk along the hallway because your door will call out a greeting to you when you come near it. Inside you'll find everything you need to be comfortable. Once you feel quite settled, feel free to roam about the mansion at will. This is your home now."

Most of the children dispersed. The girls watched curiously as some of the boys seemed to disappear straight through the wall, and the boys watched the girls do the same. Only a few hung back—Alex, Lani, and Meghan briefly talked over their plans to meet again before going off to find their rooms.

Samheed hesitated as well. The boy's sullen look had mostly worn off his face by now. "Mr. Today? You missed one. Where does that hallway lead?" he asked.

Mr. Today looked to where the boy was pointing, and then regarded Samheed carefully for a short moment. "Hmm," he said, scratching at his electric hair. He wore a strange, curious smile on his face. "I'm surprised you can see it, Samheed."

LISA McMANN

Magic and Art

Lani and Meghan made their way down the long hallway in search of their rooms in the mansion. Meghan's door called out to her almost immediately, as it was located near the entrance to the balcony. After a quick exchange and a reminder to meet in the lounge later, Lani continued down the hallway alone. All the other new children had found their rooms as well by now, so the hallway was eerily silent.

Lani walked slowly past more statues, who nodded to her cordially if she looked at them, and bright square things on the walls—paintings, Mr. Today had called them—of all colors

LISA McMANN

and sizes. As she neared the end, growing more and more concerned that there would be no door calling out her name, one burst open, and a smallish, yellowish, featherish figure emerged. Lani startled and nearly screamed, because it is one thing to see a magical creature when in the company of others, and quite another thing entirely to have one nearly upon you when you're alone.

But it was worry for nothing. The feathery creature—its body might have looked like a platypus if it weren't so feathery, and its beak was definitely parrotlike—seemed more frightened of Lani than Lani seemed of her. "Squee squah!" the creature cried out in a high-pitched voice.

"I beg your pardon," Lani said, stepping back.

"I beg your pardon, I beg your pardon," repeated the creature.

And Lani, feeling bold—after all, when you've been marked for elimination, everything else seems easy—bent down and held out her hand. "My name is Lani," she said.

The creature waddled up to Lani, clamped its beak lightly on Lani's finger, and then mimicked the girl, saying, "My name is Lani." And then it erupted into a puffball of giggles and ran

LISA McMANN

madly down the hallway, wings flapping, shouting, "Lani, Lani, Lani!" all the way to the end.

Lani watched in shock until the platyprot—for that is what it was—disappeared. *If her name is Lani too, then how will I know which room is mine?* Lani wondered. But the platyprot's doorway didn't beckon to Lani as she passed it.

Finally, Lani approached the end of what she had thought might be a never-ending hallway. "Good evening, Lani!" greeted the last door on the right in a very cheerful voice. The door swung open, and Lani walked inside.

And while several magical things awaited Lani inside her room, she was so overwhelmed and exhausted that it was impossible for her to do anything except sink into an overstuffed chair. Lani was amazed at its softness, for all she had ever known were harsh wooden seats and worn-out bedrolls on the floor. She leaned her head back and closed her eyes for a moment— it had been a very long day. Before anyone could say, "Jim the winged tortoise," she was asleep.

Elsewhere in the girls' hall, Meghan explored her room and was delighted to find that it was nearly as large as an entire

Quill house, with a sitting area, a bedroom, and a lovely bathroom with pretty soaps, fluffy towels, and a bubbling waterfall bathtub. In the drawers and closets was everything a girl could ask for and infinitely more, since Quillens were accustomed to living in very sparse conditions. Here all the clothes were exactly the right size, and the styles and colors complemented Meghan's personality and skin tone. The bed was not the simple rolled cot she'd known—this was soft and cushiony and raised up from the floor. The walls were decorated in soft, calm colors of blue and green that changed from bright to muted with Meghan's mood and with the passing of afternoon into evening. It was simply dreamy.

Meghan didn't know quite what to think about the spacious quarters, the design, the unusual objects that were placed about the room, yet she found the place utterly enchanting.

And indeed it was. Both enchanting . . . and enchanted. Her room had a large rectangular screen on the wall, like a black chalkboard, with information scribbled on it. It kept the time and alerted her to upcoming activities and events, and all she had to do to find out more about a particular something was to touch the word, or ask the board a question. If she didn't

LISA McMANN

wish the board to announce things randomly out loud, she just pressed a button called SHUSH on the board. If she wanted a snack and didn't feel like walking all the way down to the kitchen, there was a corner of the blackboard that was marked PANTRY. If Meghan touched it, she could view the contents of the kitchen pantry and send something up by tube.

Ah, and the tube! Each room in the mansion was equipped with a large corner tube made of glass. An opening had been cut into its side. It looked like a very tall cylinder with a platform on which to stand, and a miniature blackboard inside offered the various destinations available at that particular time.

As Meghan explored her room, she found a stack of papers with unusual lines and markings on them; they made no sense to her at all, so she put them aside. She also discovered a basket full of long metallic rods and wooden sticklike things of various sizes, all containing small holes and tiny levers. Cautiously, Meghan touched a wooden stick, and then picked it up with both hands, feeling the solid weight of it. She rolled it in her hands curiously, pushed a small metal lever near the center and released it, and then peered into the hollow end, which opened up like a big O.

"An oboe is a musical instrument."

Meghan whirled around at the voice, but saw no one.

"You place the other end in your mouth, and blow into it. Like this." Meghan's blackboard lit up, and a picture of a beautiful woman appeared. The woman wet her lips, then placed her mouth on the instrument and blew into it. She moved her fingers on the levers, and a lovely, mournful tune came out of it. "Now you try it," the woman said, looking directly into Meghan's eyes as if she were right there in the room.

"I—I—" Meghan looked at the oboe. She turned it around, and the woman in the blackboard showed Meghan how to hold it properly. Meghan copied the hand positions, and then wet her lips and blew.

"A little harder," the woman encouraged. "And keep your tongue near it."

Meghan tried again, and the oboe squeaked.

The woman smiled warmly. "Lovely. We'll work on that a little each day. Until next time, then."

The woman faded to black, and words appeared once again. Meghan quickly put the basket of instruments away when she saw that it was nearly time for her to meet her brother.

LISA McMANN

She gazed in her closet, somewhat overwhelmed by all the clothes that hung there, and after much consideration chose a pale green dress. Looking curiously in the bathroom mirror, she fussed with her hair. She stared at the clear box on the counter, clueless as to what the various ribbons and bows contained within were for. She picked them up and examined them carefully.

When it was almost eight o'clock, she went to the blackboard, not at all sure how to get to the lounge, but finding the word "lounge" in large letters written on the board, she touched it. The blackboard shimmered like liquid, and a face pressed through, as if it were wearing a black silky mask. The face smiled.

"Good evening, Meghan. My name is Evelyn, and I am your blackboard. To get to the lounge, please enter the glass tube in the corner of your room. On the miniature blackboard inside the tube, press the word 'lounge,' and you'll be there in no time."

"Um . . . thank you, Evelyn." Meghan entered the tube, biting her lip nervously, took a deep breath, and pushed the word "lounge" on the small board. She didn't even have time to close her eyes before the scene changed—it was almost as if her room *became* the lounge. She stepped out of the glass tube and looked at her surroundings.

The lounge was enormous—three times the size of the kitchen. Dozens if not a hundred people as well as a few odd-looking creatures chatted and danced and laughed with each other. A band played fast music in the corner, and in the center of the room was a large circular island counter with stools all around.

There were no gathering places like this in Quill—letting people gather during leisure time was dangerous. Everyone knew that; it just wasn't allowed. So Meghan was quite unsure of the lounge, for she could draw nothing from her memory with which to compare it.

As Meghan stood uncertainly with her back to the tube, trying very hard to remember what her brother looked like and wondering how much he might have changed in the past five years, someone tapped her on the shoulder. She whirled around.

It was Alex. "Whoa, the tube is completely wacky, isn't it, Meg? I've been all around already!"

Meghan sighed in relief. "I'm so nervous," she said. "What if I can't find my brother?"

Alex shrugged. "Well, use the blackboard, then."

"How?"

"Just go over to it and ask it to find him. I'll bet it can do that. It can do everything! What have you been doing all this time, taking a nap?" Alex took a good look at her. "What the— what's that in your hair?" He laughed and pointed at the ribbon Meghan had finally decided to tie around her ponytail. He was completely baffled.

Meghan ignored him and walked over to the blackboard. "Hello," she said uncertainly. A shimmering face pressed outward from the center of the blackboard, just as Evelyn had done in her room.

"Hello, Ms. Ranger." This blackboard had a male voice, and he stretched out the *a* sound in her last name lazily.

"I'm looking for my brother. Sean. Sean Ranger. Um . . ."

"Ohhhh, delighted to help," the board replied. It cleared its throat. Immediately the room's sound was muted, though no one seemed to notice. The band played as usual, people continued in conversation, but there was no sound at all until the blackboard spoke again. "Sean Ranger, your poor dear sister is standing here in the lounge waiting for you, you dolt." The room's volume immediately resumed its normal level.

Meghan clapped a hand over her mouth. "Good grief," she said. "You're blunt, aren't you?"

"Wouldn't you be blunt too, if you had to live in a perpetual party room?"

Meghan hadn't thought about that before. "Yes," she said, "I suppose I might be."

"Indeed. All right, here he comes. Enjoy your reunion."

"Um . . . thank you . . . um . . ."

"Earl."

"Thank you, Earl."

The board's face smiled politely before it melted and was replaced by words once again.

Meghan turned away and scanned the room, biting her fingernails. She still didn't see anyone moving toward her, besides Alex. But when she glanced at the row of tubes, someone was just stepping out, combing his fingers through his reddish-brown hair and adjusting the collar of his shirt. It was Sean.

Meghan's heart stuck in her throat. He looked so much older now. She vaguely remembered when he left the family. He was a gangly boy back then, and now he looked like a grown-up. Strange tears flooded her eyes and bubbled over as he caught sight of her.

His face lit up. He walked swiftly toward his sister, picked her up, and whirled her around. "Meggie, you—" The words caught in his throat. He set her down and hugged her gently, then pushed her shoulders back and looked at her, his eyes dancing. "You naughty, naughty thing, you," he said, teasing. "You've turned out just like your useless older brother. Poor Mother and Father." He sniffed airily. "They won't be allowed another child now. They must feel like such failures. Tch."

Meghan thought she heard a bitter twist to his words, but with all the emotions that before now she had been required to suppress, combined with all the excitement and surprises and stress of the day, Meghan couldn't be quite sure of anything.

"I—I missed you," Meghan said. She blushed. "I just can't believe you're here."

Sean grinned. "I know," he said. "It's okay. Let's grab that sofa and table in the corner so we can talk. Who's your friend?"

Sean pointed to Alex, who had been inching away to give the two some privacy.

"Oh!" Meghan said. "I'm sorry—Alex, do you remember my brother, Sean?"

Alex held out his hand awkwardly. "Hey, Sean."

Sean gave him a quizzical look and shook his hand. "I remember you—you were in our quadrant," he said. "You're one of the twins, aren't you? You boys used to come to the Commons with your father to get your milk rations from us. Where's your brother?" Sean looked over his shoulder and around the room quickly.

Alex opened his mouth, but no sound came out. The expression on his face was enough to make Meghan want to hurriedly change the subject, but it was too late.

"Oh," Sean said. His eyes narrowed. "Well. That's just rotten cruel to separate you. I'm sorry, Alex. Was he Necessary, then, like your folks?"

"He . . ." Alex gulped.

"Aaron was a Wanted," Meghan said. "Let's go sit."

Alex trailed along, feeling a little numb. He'd mostly forgotten about Aaron in the busyness of the day, but now the hurt of being Unwanted slammed into his ribs again. "It's not Aaron's fault," he said almost automatically as he slid on the cushioned sofa next to Meghan.

Sean's eyes were still narrowed. He looked like he could spit needles if he wanted to. "Of course not," he said gruffly. "Nobody blames him. Plus, I know it's probably still a weird concept for you, but we're the lucky ones."

"He's probably pretty sad tonight," Alex mused. "Well. As sad as he can be, in Quill."

Sean and Meghan nodded thoughtfully. "It seems so different already," Meghan said. "Like, once you know it's okay to—you know—*feel* something, all the feelings get stronger."

"That's the truth," Sean said. "But better to get stronger than to disappear into the Great Lake of Boiling Oil, I always say." He laughed. "So. Have you found your way around the tubes yet?"

"Alex has," Meghan said. "I stayed in my room and blew into one of the instruments. It was called 'oboe.'" She couldn't help but grin.

"Hey, listen to you already. It's 'played' an instrument. You played an oboe, just as you play all instruments, whether they have a reed or strings or keys or a bow." Sean flipped Meghan's ponytail and grinned. "Wow. You really grew up, kid."

"So did you. You're like a man."

"I'm eighteen now. Marcus asked me to think about teaching a class now that I'm through with my training and warrior classes."

"What, um—," Alex said, "what exactly do you study here?"

"Oh, all sorts of things. Art, theater, music, and the magic that goes along with them . . ." Sean trailed off when he noticed their puzzled looks. "Clearly, I'm getting ahead of things. It's funny—I sort of forgot how little I knew when I got here." He shook his head, lost in thought. "Anyway, Alex, what were your infractions?"

"I put a stick in the dirt and moved it around, and it made a—it looked like a—like a house. And other things. A tree."

"Oh, excellent. You're an artist, most likely. Did you find any pencils, sketch pads, paintbrushes—stuff like that—in your room?"

"Um . . ." All the words were foreign to Alex.

"Long, thin sticks. Some of them have a sharp point; others

have stiff hair on one end." Sean watched Alex's face until it lit up again. "Those are pencils and paintbrushes. You take them in your hand and . . ." He clapped his hand to his forehead and laughed. "Let's make this easier." Sean pulled a tiny bit of paper from his pocket and tapped it with his finger on the table, and a small sketch pad and pencil appeared in its place.

"Wow!" Meghan and Alex both said at once.

"Watch this," Sean said. He quickly sketched a simple meadow scene with a large tree and a fence.

"How'd you do that?" Alex watched the scene appear on the paper as Sean moved the pencil around.

"Getting the sketch pad and pencil here? That was magic. Drawing the picture—that's called art. Drawing. Sketching. There are lots of different words for it. And that wasn't magic at all. That was creative talent. You have it in you already, you know. Give it a try."

Alex held the pencil in his left fist, just like he'd done with the stick all those years ago. Sean pulled it out of his hand and showed him how to hold it properly. "Does it feel best in your left hand, Alex?"

"Um . . ." Alex switched the pencil to his right hand, scowled, and then switched it back. "Yeah. The left hand feels good to me." He concentrated and pressed the point to the paper.

"Not too hard or—" Sean laughed when the point snapped and flew across the table. "Or it'll break," he finished. He pinched the pencil tip, and it grew a new perfect point; then he handed it back to Alex.

Meghan watched, enthralled. "Will we get to learn magic too?" she said, inspecting the tip of the pencil. It made no sense to her at all. And she absolutely loved it.

"After a while," Sean said. He caught his sister's eye. "Work hard on your art first. Once you get really good at it, your instructor will recommend moving you up to Magical Warrior Training."

"But what is that, exactly? Mr. Today asked us all if we would do it."

"It's a class where you learn to defend yourself and to fight, using magical weapons of art. Like—"

"Maybe Quill won't want to fight us," Meghan said.

Sean laughed, although not unkindly. "Oh, yes. I'm sure

they will. They've been gearing up for a fight for fifty years! Why do you think they put their so-called best people in the Quillitary?"

"Hmm," Meghan said thoughtfully.

Alex, who had been listening all this time as he moved the pencil on the paper, said, "How do you fight with art?" He sketched awkwardly and drew a house like the one he'd drawn in the mud back in Quill.

Sean smiled, pointing to the drawing. "Good work so far, Alex. As for fighting with art, you'll find out soon enough. It'll be great! You'll learn all sorts of amazing things. I'll let your instructors tell you more, though. Hey," he said abruptly, looking more closely at Alex's scribbling. "Seriously, that's not bad. Here, let me show you how to do shading. Lighten up with your grip a little." He tapped Alex's pencil, and a second pencil fell out of the first, so they each had one.

"I can't wait for Magical Warrior Training," Meghan said, more to herself than anyone else. Her eyes shone with excitement.

As Alex and Sean worked, Alex's tongue sticking out of the corner of his mouth in concentration, Meghan slipped away from the table and went up to the blackboard. "Hello, Earl," she said.

"Hello again."

"I'm wondering if you could, you know, *gently*—I mean, nice and gently if you would—summon Lani to come down here? She was supposed to be here by now."

"Lani. Hmm. The human girl, right?"

"Um, yes . . ." *Aren't all girls human here?* Meghan wondered.

"Yes, I'll send her down for you."

"Thank you, Earl."

"You're welcome."

"Hey, Earl?"

"Yes, Ms. Ranger." He sounded bored.

"Is there anything I can get for you?"

The eyes on the blackboard blinked in silence, and the lips parted slightly. Earl's voice softened. "No, thank you."

A moment later Lani emerged wide-eyed from the tube and laughed when she saw Meghan. "That didn't feel like anything at all," she said.

"Come on—we're getting the scoop on all sorts of things from my brother." Meghan linked her arm in Lani's, and they ran over to the table, where Alex and Sean were conversing in serious tones. The sketch pad was closed, and the pencil rested on top of it.

When the girls approached, Sean looked up. "Another friend? I'm Sean Ranger," he said, rather importantly. "Who might you be?"

"Lani. Lani Haluki." Lani and Meghan sat down.

Sean's eyes narrowed yet again. "Haluki?"

"Yes." Lani looked Sean in the eye.

"The senior governor's daughter?" Sean asked incredulously.

Lani's glance didn't waver, and when she finally answered, her voice was quiet and firm. "Not anymore."

The four sat in grim silence.

"You look young to be eliminated," Sean said after a while.

"I'm twelve."

"And why . . . ?"

"Because I was influencing other children. Telling the stories in my head. Making my father look bad, I suppose. He couldn't wait to be rid of me."

"I'm sorry."

"Why?" Lani said. "I'm here, aren't I?" Her blue eyes flashed.

A million thoughts raced through her head, like how her relationship with her father had once seemed special, and why she had been so abruptly Purged before her thirteenth year. But she didn't voice her thoughts. They hurt too much.

Sean smiled kindly. "I see. I'm guessing Artimé will be quite lucky to have your talent."

Lani softened a little and blocked out the stinging thoughts. "I'm sure it will," she said.

Alex laughed. "You've certainly landed on both feet already." His voice was filled with admiration. "Have you learned the way things work yet?"

"No, I took a nap. Can somebody tell me how that tube thing works? Where are we, exactly? There aren't any doors."

Alex and Meghan looked up and scanned the room, surprised. "Weird," Alex said. "I hadn't noticed."

"Neither had I," said Meghan.

"Good observation," Sean said. "The lounge isn't attached to the mansion. It's not actually a physical building. What I mean is, you can't see it from the outside. It doesn't take up any space. Most of Artimé is like that. Remember the small, desolate plot of land when you first came through the gate? All

LISA McMANN

of Artimé is contained in that tiny area of cement and weeds and the gray, broken-down building. Yet Artimé stretches on for miles. Many years ago Marcus had just a small world hidden here behind the gates of Quill, but as more and more Unwanteds came through, he expanded as necessary and created a few artistic instructors to help him teach the children. Now it's almost as if the world runs on its own. Though certainly," he added, "it would disappear without a mage like him in control of it."

"What's a mage?" Lani asked.

"A magician. Someone who performs magic. Anyway, to answer your question, the mansion remains relatively the same size and shape now in order to keep people from getting lost, and instead of adding on and adding on like a labyrinth, Marcus created the tube so you could get to the places that aren't in constant use. This is the most frequently used room, as far as I know. I haven't kept up with some of the new places that get added to the tube board. You'll have to tube it to some of the classrooms and to the theater. But don't worry. The blackboards know everything and are there to help you if you need it." Sean chuckled. "Some of them have strong personalities, though, so be on your guard."

Meghan nodded. "You mean like Earl?"

"Well, yes. But he's all right. A bit grumpy at times."

Lani and Alex exchanged curious glances across the table as Meghan and Sean discussed Earl and the personalities of blackboards. Alex shrugged and made a face. Lani stifled a laugh.

When the brother and sister began discussing Quill and the more delicate topic of their mother and father, Lani pointed stealthily to the bar-stool area. Alex nodded, and the two slipped away to grab a snack before turning in for the night. They noticed and discussed all sorts of odd things, like creatures and students doing magic tricks with folded up bits of paper, pencils, and other things that Alex and Lani had never seen before.

What the two didn't see at first was Samheed standing with an unfamiliar, older, sneery-faced boy near the tubes. Eventually, though, Lani noticed Samheed watching Alex through narrowed eyelids, a spiteful sort of look on his face. Startled, she poked Alex. "What's his problem?" she whispered, pointing.

But by the time Alex turned to look, Samheed and his friend had disappeared inside the tubes.

School

Several weeks of school and life in Artimé flew by. There was so much to learn, like what acting was, and how to tell if music sounded happy or sad, and how to write—not a story, yet, but actually how to write numbers and letters. Alex and the others could read, of course. But they had not been permitted to write. They'd never seen pencils before. Only the governors could authorize a teacher to write out lessons in private, and even then they were very careful to monitor the sorts of things a teacher would teach. Mostly it was math formulas and equations. After all, to be successful in the Quillitary, one

LISA McMANN

needed only to know certain things, and writing wasn't one of them. The High Priest Justine warned that writing led to creativity, and creativity led to revolt, which was very bad.

But now, with this exciting world awaiting them, the Unwanteds dove into their studies. It didn't feel like school at all. And while each child took classes in all the arts, each also had one particular art to focus on. For Alex it was drawing and painting. For Meghan it was music. For Lani it was writing and storytelling, but Lani excelled in almost everything she put her mind to. And Samheed was practically born to act on the stage.

While Samheed's sharp edges had grown a little bit softer by the end of a month, his general sourpuss, angry disposition still reared up regularly. Luckily, these emotions came in handy on the theater stage when a role required it, and that seemed to diffuse much of the anger directed at others. But Samheed continued to hold some unexplained contempt for Alex, and for Artimé.

Occasionally, Samheed would be seen in the company of the same older, sneering boy. The friends found out soon enough that the boy's name was Will Blair, and that like Samheed he was a theater focus. Will's face wore a permanent scowl. Nobody seemed to like him very much. He would shove people in crowded hallways and say rude things, as if his work were more important than anyone else's.

"I think Samheed likes hanging around with Will because Will is more of an outcast, and it makes Samheed more likeable by comparison," Meghan said, crunching on an apple at lunch one day when it was just she and Alex at the table.

"Whatever," Alex said. "I think Samheed is just mean. He was mean back in Quill, and he's still mean. I have no idea what his problem is, and I don't care." Even so, Alex got an uncomfortable, prickly feeling whenever he saw the two boys hunching over in private conversation at a corner table in the lounge and stealing glances around them or studying Alex as they whispered. It was rather unsettling.

But mainly Alex absorbed himself in his art under the instruction of Artimé's finest painting teacher, Ms. Octavia, an octogator, and he had very little time to think about Samheed and Will Blair.

"Don't be afraid of me, Alex," the octogator had said when Alex first met her, face-to-face with her alligator mouth full of teeth, and half her octopus tentacles floating about, almost as if she were walking on air.

"O-okay," Alex said, noting the location of the door in case he would need to escape.

"I'm Ms. Octavia. Mr. Today created me many years ago to cover an area of instruction in which he was not particularly gifted—the fine art of drawing and painting. Wasn't it thoughtful of him to give me so many ways to excel in my craft?" She carried with her an eraser, a paintbrush, a pencil, charcoal sticks, a palette, and a cup of coffee, and could work on various tasks simultaneously.

Alex nodded. He glanced at her sharp teeth, gleaming in the brightly lit room. "I bet all your students listen to you too," he said.

"Quite right." Ms. Octavia grinned toothily.

Alex learned quickly over his first few weeks to use a pencil, charcoals, ink, and paints, experimenting with colors and depth, precision lines and vast strokes with his paintbrushes. He began by drawing and painting simple objects like a shoe, a pineapple, and a cactus, and moving on to structures and landscapes.

LISA McMANN

"You've got a special way with that brush, Alex, and a keen eye for color," Ms. Octavia said, her appendages floating about her, busy with tasks. "Your paintings are your forte. I think you're one of the most promising students I've ever had." She gave an approving nod despite her stern bulbous eyes peering through the wire half-glasses that perched on her alligator snout.

With eight appendages Ms. Octavia could create vast paintings and charcoal drawings in no time at all, and she expected perfection from her students. But she had a soft spot for Alex and praised him liberally.

With all this praise, Alex was certain he would soon be allowed to begin further training. "I can't wait to advance to Magical Warrior Training," Alex said one day. "Do you think it'll be soon?"

The odd look on Ms. Octavia's face stopped him. "All in good time," she said finally.

"Oh." Alex looked away and shoved his hands into his pockets, embarrassed, determined not to ask the question again.

» » « «

Meghan adored her instructor too: Ms. Claire Morning. Ms. Morning was a tall, striking woman of forty or so, with long, honey-colored hair and a warm complexion. She was the same person who had popped in for a chat on Meghan's blackboard on that first day to teach Meghan the lesson with the oboe. Claire Morning was full of praise, and Meghan excelled and grew increasingly confident with her music as time passed. Meghan not only enjoyed playing the oboe and piccolo, but she loved to dance and sing as well, and her voice had such a mesmerizing lilt to it that people and creatures alike often felt compelled to stop in the hallway outside the practice room just to listen to Meghan sing.

"With a voice like yours," Ms. Morning told Meghan after three months had passed, "I do believe you are quite ready to train magically with your art as a warrior now, Meghan. I will talk with Mr. Today about it this afternoon."

Meghan's face lit up. She'd been dying to start her magical training ever since she saw her brother perform magic on the day she reunited with him. "Yes!" she said. "I've been so impatient. So I'll be the first of my class to start, right?" She grinned. "Alex will be so jealous."

Ms. Morning smiled. "Your gifts are very strong, like your brother's. He was the first of his class to begin magical training as well." Her voice turned contemplative. "But you may want to ask him about how best to deal with your successes in front of your friends. I know he had quite a difficult time being the first."

"Did he?" Meghan asked. "He didn't mention it."

Ms. Morning sat down at the desk next to Meghan's. "It is because you are all so unused to expressing your emotions, and now that you're allowed to do so, sometimes they can grow wildly out of control. All of you have felt the sting of not being a Wanted or a Necessary. It's not a pain that goes away quickly, and it resurfaces sometimes without warning."

Meghan grew somber. "You're right," she said softly. "But that's why being the first feels so nice. Like I am actually . . . you know." She blushed and scraped the toe of her sandal on the marble floor. "Like I'm valuable or something." Her face burned.

Ms. Morning patted Meghan's shoulder and tipped the girl's chin up. "You are valuable, indeed," she said quietly.

"Then, why . . . ?"

"Because this will feel like another failure to your friends."

Meghan thought about that for a long moment. She sighed, and though she didn't want to say it, she did. "Maybe I should wait for them to catch up."

Ms. Morning smiled warmly. "That is a very generous thing to say, Meghan. You are a mature young woman. But we shan't wait for them. Our warriors need you, and they need you now. You must learn everything you can, as quickly as you can. The others will join you eventually—perhaps your success will drive them to succeed as well." Her smile remained warm, but her eyes became shadowed with a hint of . . . something. Was it fear?

Meghan didn't dare to ask, and after a moment the shadow passed and Ms. Morning continued on in her cheerful manner so convincingly that Meghan thought she must have imagined it.

After her private lesson Meghan left the practice room bubbling with excitement, but also a bit anxious to know how Mr. Today would respond to Ms. Morning's suggestion. She decided she would keep her news quiet until she was certain, and only discuss it privately with Sean. Hopefully, she thought, he'd have some good advice for her. She joined

LISA McMANN

the others in the last class of the day, Actors' Studio, which they all shared.

In the midst of it she was so deep into her thoughts that Alex had to poke her in the arm when it was her turn to perform, and she was so befuddled that she flubbed her lines quite horribly, which made Samheed frustrated enough that he threw his script at her.

It hit her squarely in the forehead, and as it was Shakespeare's *The Merchant of Venice*, it was thick enough to hurt.

"Hey!" she shouted. And without thinking, she flung her script at Samheed, hitting the back of his head as he stomped off the stage.

"Why, you little . . ." Samheed charged toward Meghan, his boots thumping and echoing in the auditorium.

Lani and Alex jumped up before anyone else even noticed what was happening. Alex grabbed and yanked Samheed's arm, while Lani stood in between the spitting Meghan and the growling Samheed.

At the assault from Alex, Samheed wrenched his arm from Alex's grasp and promptly slugged him in the eye, knocking Alex flat and causing quite an outrage with the other students, until the stage was crawling with thirteen-year-olds taking swipes and cuffing one another. The voices joined in crescendo, and the volume grew to such riotous proportions that the poor little instructor, Mr. Appleblossom, had to resort to standing on a chair and reciting a magical soliloquy so deathly boring that it not only sucked all the energy from the room, causing the students to fall limply on the stage, but it also put some of the smaller ones like Lani into a deep sleep.

"Oh dear, oh dear, please summon Marcus now!" Mr. Appleblossom called out to the blackboard in his typical rhyming, iambic-pentameter fashion. He wrung his hands and muttered, "And quickly, please. I swear, I don't know how . . ."

"I have done so already. He's coming through tube." The theater blackboard preferred free verse.

Immediately Mr. Today appeared and surveyed the scene, twenty students flattened, arms and legs hanging motionless off the edge of the stage or swinging lightly with what little momentum remained. "Good heavens," Mr. Today said. "Have we had a bit of a brawl, Sigfried?"

Mr. Appleblossom, pacing and muttering still, held out his hands dramatically and cried, "Oh why, oh why, this

LISA McMANN

ruthless waste on me? Am I but sand, and they the stormy sea?"

Mr. Today coughed loudly into his hand, although it might have sounded more like a laugh to anyone who was listening closely. When he could speak again, he smiled politely. "Dear, dear Sigfried, your troubles are great indeed. And yes, it's true this sort of thing rarely happens elsewhere, but surely you understand the nature of the theater and its desperate want for dramatics . . . don't you?" Mr. Today had to sort of squinch his lips together to keep from an all-out grin, which would of course lead to chuckling, which wouldn't be good at all at this moment, he knew.

"Aye," sighed Mr. Appleblossom, "'tis true, the action's in the stage. However, wishes me they'd tone the rage. For what, but spells, is there for me to do to stop the madness—'fore they slug me too?" He dropped his arms heavily at his sides and gazed imploringly at Mr. Today.

"You did the right thing, Siggy." He turned toward the stage. "Did you hear that, students? I want you all to think about your actions, because next time Mr. Appleblossom won't be quite so kind in stopping you. If you don't work out your differences in a proper manner, next time he'll use a stinging soliloquy rather than the boring one, and you'll all be really very sorry that it came to that. Is that clear?" Mr. Today didn't wait for an answer, since the children were rather unable to speak. He turned back to Mr. Appleblossom. "Let's hope that's the last of it for this group," he said quietly.

Mr. Appleblossom sighed again, but this time it was a more relaxed sort of sigh, or maybe just a simple letting out of breath that had been held. "Great thanks and more, my friend; I'll keep them here. Perhaps you'll join me later for a—"

"Cup of tea?" interrupted Mr. Today. "Of course. Just let them go when the spell wears off. Incidentally, what strength spell did you use? A temporary one, I'm assuming."

"Well . . . 'twas quite a row, you'll understand it. An hour, less or more, will sure disband it."

"Fine and good. If you need me again, please do summon." And with that, along with a hasty shaking of Mr. Appleblossom's hand, Mr. Today disappeared inside the tube before the instructor could fire off another rhyming couplet.

When the spell wore off, each child regained his full

presence at his own pace, the bigger students before the smaller ones. Samheed was first, being quite solid and muscular already for his age. He stood and looked at the scene, at Alex's face now puffing up red and purple, and he hung his head slightly, feeling a bit ashamed. "May I go?" he asked Mr. Appleblossom in a resigned voice.

The instructor didn't pause as he scratched notes in his paperwork. He merely nodded stiffly, like one of the mansion statues. But as Samheed neared the tube, Mr. Appleblossom turned and spoke a warning to the boy.

> You know, Samheed, no rival can compare
> his acting gifts to yours, but I declare:
> If you don't shake that attitude, and soon,
> I'll drop you from my program. You'll be goon.

Samheed's face burned at the reproach from his own private instructor. Yet he couldn't resist giving the little man a puzzled look. "Goon?"

Mr. Appleblossom sighed impatiently. "'Gone,' then. Oh, my stars, I hate imperfects."

Samheed dropped his gaze, entered the tube, and completed the couplet for his teacher. "I'm sorry, sir. I meant no disrespects."

When Samheed was gone, Mr. Appleblossom tapped his forefinger against his lips and, after a thoughtful moment, smiled grimly to himself.

Samheed's First Secret

The next evening, after everyone had ignored him completely due to his nasty behavior, Samheed sought and found Alex in the lounge. He slipped uneasily into the curved booth seat around the table from him, scouring Alex's face, and frowned. "All right, Stowe. I'm sorry about the black eye," he said, a bit begrudgingly.

Alex shrugged and fixed his eyes on the tube, waiting for Meghan.

Samheed rolled his eyes, as if it pained him to say it. "I mean it. I just . . . when I get mad, I just sort of go . . . a little crazy."

Alex looked down at the floor. "All right," he said, his voice cool. "It's not like I care, anyhow. And I know you're only apologizing so Mr. Appleblossom will keep you in the program. I heard what he said. You're a real jerk sometimes. And I'm not afraid to punch you back, you know."

Samheed, who stood several inches taller and weighed several pounds more than Alex, tried not to scoff. "Oh, I know," he said as seriously as he could. "You can punch me now if you want."

Alex glanced up at Samheed, a suspicious look on his face. "What's the fun in that?"

"None for me, that's for sure."

"I'd rather pound you when you're not expecting it."

"Well," Samheed said, "I can't be sure how I'd respond to a sneak attack. I might punch you again, and then we'd be right back in this stupid mess."

"That would be awkward," Alex said. He relaxed his shoulders a bit.

Samheed nodded. He looked over to the bar, squinted, and impatiently waved off his friend Will Blair. Will glowered back, his eyes like slits.

"What's with that guy, anyway?" Alex asked. "He's so . . . snarly."

"He's not so bad when you get to know him," Samheed said, sounding a little bit defensive.

"Oh, yeah?" Alex didn't believe it.

"He's just, I don't know. He's acting. I guess."

"Right."

"Seriously. That's what he said when I asked him. And he's really good. He's got some amazing spells."

"Well, why would he want to hang around with a new kid like you? Did you know him in Quill or something?"

"Yeah, I did. He lived in my column, two houses back. His father is the Quillitary general."

Alex looked shocked. "You lived in the Quillitary Sector? Your parents are Wanteds? You always walked beyond that sector from school."

Samheed's eyes flared. "I went to the Quillitary to do work with my father every day after school, to train and prepare myself for . . . Anyway. So what if my parents were Wanteds? Will's parents were Wanteds. Heck, Lani's parents were Wanteds, and her father is the senior governor! But look where that got her.

And look at you—you're Unwanted, your parents are Neces-saries, and your evil twin turned out to be Wanted. There's no pattern, Stowe." Samheed nearly spit venom with the last words.

"My brother is not evil!" Alex said, a little louder than he had planned. He hastily settled back in the seat and took a deep breath.

"Right. Sure, he's not."

"What do you know, anyway? You're just as Unwanted as I am."

"I know plenty," Samheed sniffed. "And no, I'm not as Unwanted as you or anybody else," he continued hotly. "I was supposed to join the Quillitary. I was supposed to be a Wanted—Will Blair's father told me so himself! I only had one minor offense, and they were going to let it pass. But at the last minute somebody snitched on me for something else I said. Reported me to the governors a week before the Purge."

"You're lying," Alex said, horrified. "What was the offense?"

Samheed pressed his lips together. His face was red with anger. But his answer came out quiet, even. "Dramatic Boasting."

Alex sat, stunned. "You mean . . . on the last day of school? When you and Aaron and I were walking home?"

Samheed nodded.

"But there weren't any adults around!"

Samheed just stared at Alex.

"So who . . . ?" Alex began, then turned pale. "No . . . ," he whispered. "I don't believe it."

Samheed sat excruciatingly still, his gaze never wavering.

Alex slumped back in his seat, trying to comprehend. Trying to remember if anyone else had been nearby as they left the school grounds that day. "How do you know?"

"Who else could it have been, Alex? You?" Samheed snorted.

Could it be true? Alex dropped his gaze to the table and shook his head slowly. Finally he looked up and saw that Samheed's stare had softened slightly. "If it's true, Samheed," Alex said softly, almost helplessly, "I'm . . . I'm sorry."

Samheed hastily looked away and bit his lip. His eyes glistened but remained hard. "S'all right, Stowe," he said finally. "At least we're not dead. But that doesn't mean I'll ever forget what your lousy brother did to me."

The two boys sat, saying nothing, until Meghan and

Lani arrived and slipped in the booth on Alex's side, eyeing Samheed suspiciously.

Samheed looked up. "Hey. Look, I'm sorry for the fight I caused in Actors' Studio. Forgive me?"

Alex looked away as both girls sat, slack-jawed, until Meghan murmured, "Of course, Samheed," and Lani echoed, "Of course." Hastily they all began babbling about their schoolwork in an attempt to change the uncomfortable subject. And then the next uncomfortable subject came up.

"Well, guys, I have news. I'm beginning Magical Warrior Training," Meghan said, eyes bright.

Lani shrieked and hugged Meghan. Samheed's lips parted in surprise; then he didn't even try to hide his scowl. And Alex grinned, trying to ignore the sinking feeling in his stomach for the sake of his best friend.

One by One,
the Warriors

After the initial shock Alex was truly glad for Meghan, thinking surely he'd not be far behind. After all, he was excelling in painting and drawing and had advanced to charcoals and sculpting, for which he had a special knack. The normally stern Ms. Octavia gave him the highest marks on everything and praised him until he grew red in the face. With only two hands (compared to her eight) he exceeded every assignment and finished with speed and grace. His attention to detail was well beyond his years.

"Marvelous and perfectly accurate," Ms. Octavia had said

of Alex's charcoal sketch of the sea speckled with islands in the distance.

"Simply primitive!" she'd praised when Alex showed her his stark sculpture replica of the High Priest Justine's palace.

And with all this praise, every day Alex waited anxiously for his private lesson, hoping to hear the same news that Meghan had received already: that Ms. Octavia would be talking to Mr. Today about advancing him to Magical Warrior Training. But every day, in the awkward silence at the end of each session, she merely praised him for his stunning work and sent him on without another word.

Soon Lani—and a month later Samheed—joined the ranks of student warriors, leaving Alex as the only one in his group of friends not to have earned a coveted component vest, which the others wore proudly to class. Conversations grew awkward. Alex took to brooding alone rather than share the pain of what he perceived as his failures.

Meghan was especially thoughtful about not discussing warrior classes too much in front of Alex, but there were times when even she couldn't help but show off a spell. Meghan could now lull a person or creature into a trance with her singing, and her high-pitched piccolo could cause someone to turn tail and run away screaming. When she danced the fire step, whomever she aimed her focus toward would suddenly feel his feet grow warm, then hot, then near blistering.

Samheed was a quick study in the soliloquy, and he had mastered several styles by now that all had different effects on people. His dagger spell was most impressive, for those he used it on would see and feel a magical dagger plunging into their chests, and they'd fall to the ground, stunned, though the spell did no actual damage to them. He could also "call horse," and an invisible steed would come to him and take him wherever he wanted to go. He practiced this one often on the lawn outside (although once he tried it in his room, which made a terrible mess), and he even ventured into the forest with the steed on a few occasions. But each time he quickly returned to the lawn, having gotten the wits scared out of him first by a large gray wolf, and then by Simber, the prowling winged-cheetah statue, who apparently had left his post by the mansion door and was out on a hunt for food that evening.

But Meghan and even Samheed were careful not to perform any magic on Alex, since he couldn't fight back.

Lani, on the other hand, was quickly becoming a big pain in Alex's side. She wouldn't leave him alone, and she didn't seem to understand how gut-wrenchingly awful Alex was feeling about having been passed by a twelve-year-old. And how embarrassed he'd been when she magically changed his lines in Actors' Studio as a joke, and when she made him fall asleep at dinner by using a secret phrase. One day at lunch Lani put Alex to sleep and he fell face-first into his soup.

He awoke immediately with a sputter. "What—what is your problem?" he shouted when he had his wits about him again. He grabbed his napkin and began to wipe his face, but there were noodles in his hair, and a small slice of carrot stuck to his cheek.

Lani giggled. Even Meghan had to hide a smile, and Samheed just smirked.

Alex looked down at his soiled shirt, and then he set his napkin on the table. He stood, pushed his chair in, and left without a word, without looking back.

Meghan's eyes widened, and she almost stood to go after him, but Lani waved him off. "He's just a sorehead," she said.

"You should tell him you're sorry," Meghan said.

"It was just a joke. He'll get over it."

LISA McMANN

» » « «

Lani didn't apologize to Alex, and he'd had all he could stand. From that point on, Alex withdrew from the others and took his meals in his room. And since they used the blackboards to call on him, he shut them out by putting Clive, his blackboard, on permanent "shush."

He spent his free time in his room, drawing and painting like mad, desperate to improve enough to make it to the warrior level of instruction. Late in the evenings, when his arms ached and loneliness clawed at his insides, he lay on his bed and thought about home, and about Aaron, and about what Samheed had said. Alex still had a hard time believing that his brother, Aaron, would have reported a fellow classmate. Why would Aaron do something like that? Many nights Alex chose to stand by his brother in favor of Samheed. After all, Alex knew his brother best of anyone, didn't he? And he knew from experience that Aaron was creative too—he'd just never been caught. If only Alex had known before the Purge what being Unwanted really meant, he would have reported his brother in an instant so they could be together.

"Oh, Aaron," he'd groan, feeling helpless to save him. Alex

LISA McMANN

began to miss Aaron terribly now that he felt so distanced from his friends.

And even though there was nothing that could bring Alex back together with his twin, he sometimes got a *feeling*, or a *notion*, almost like he could sense Aaron's presence and understand his thoughts. This made Alex feel even more alone. He wondered what Aaron was doing, how his studies at Wanted University were going, and what he was especially good at. And he wondered if Aaron was sad, as sad as Alex was sometimes.

"No, probably not," Alex said. He grew so lonely that recently he had begun chatting aloud, even arguing with himself. "It's impossible for Quillens to feel anywhere near as sad as we can feel here in Artimé."

"But he believes that I'm dead. That's got to make him sad," Alex argued.

"Don't forget where you came from, Alex. He's forgotten you, like he was taught to do."

And yet Alex couldn't help feeling like Aaron was somehow different because of their birth link. That maybe, just maybe, Aaron was mourning for him. Over time Alex grew convinced that Aaron belonged here in Artimé too.

LISA McMANN

Parallel Lessons

Aaron Stowe sat rigidly in the hot classroom at Wanted University as he had done every day for more months than he could recall, willing the sweat not to drip and sting his eyes. But it was no use. Droplets landed on the ancient pages of the musty-smelling book on his desk. But Aaron studied it despite that, for he knew he must let nothing distract him from the most important class in the university: Governmental History of Quill, taught by the governors themselves.

"Quill is the land of the strong," Governor Strang droned. "The strongest society that exists. We are feared, yet we are

LISA McMANN

always on the ready for attack from those who want what we have."

The class of more than twenty nodded sharply, as their instructor required of them during lectures.

The governor continued. "As your parents and instructors taught you, the land of Quill is nearly surrounded by enemies, except for the Great Lake of Boiling Oil, which lies beyond the south wall." Half the class shuddered at the mention of the deathly place, but the students kept their eyes on the books in front of them, as they had been taught to do.

Aaron scanned the worn page before him, wanting to know more about the enemies, but there was no description. He wondered how the governors knew that other lands wanted to attack, since there had been no communication outside the walls of Quill in fifty years. But he knew better than to ask. To question a governor would not only risk his quest to someday actually become a governor himself, but could risk his life as well.

"Yet Quill continues to grow as a powerful force, with the most modern fleet of tanks and all-terrain vehicles and the grandest, most intelligent military of any kingdom in all the world!" Governor Strang took a breath and wiped his brow with his handkerchief.

"Quill prevails when the strong survive!" shouted the class in unison, Aaron among the loudest, even though he wondered how they could fight so well when the Quillitary vehicles kept breaking down and falling into rusty, smoke-belching disrepair along the road that encircled Quill. *Thank the high priest that no one else can exceed the level of our poor fleet,* Aaron thought.

"And our great and fearless ruler, the High Priest Justine, has improved the people of Quill a thousand percent by eliminating the incapable among us!"

The classroom erupted again, as if on cue. "Highest honor to the High Priest Justine! Long may she rule the land of the Wanteds! May all our enemies die a thousand deaths!"

Aaron snuffed out the twinge in his belly by switching his thoughts to his daily mantra. *I am strong! May Quill prevail with all I have in me!*

On Sunday afternoons Mr. Today swept through the grounds of Artimé, his long gown flowing over the sweet-smelling grass and often dipping into the gentle waves of the sea when he walked along the narrow strand of beach. Behind him, like ducklings, trailed the most recent group of Unwanteds, eager to learn from the old man who would answer any question the young teens could think of, even the ones that seemed obvious.

"Tell us more about Quill," someone invariably asked, for that was the hottest topic. As each child spent another month in Artimé, the questions grew about Quill and how awful it was.

"What, again?" Mr. Today teased. "Perhaps you all need something that will help you remember from week to week."

For Alex this was the only time each week where he felt on the same level as the others, and he didn't have to fear Lani's magical pranks when in the presence of Mr. Today. All the Unwanteds, of all levels of training, were equally astounded by the odd and sinister practices of the land they'd never thought to question before.

Meghan spoke up. "Mr. Today, if Quill is so powerful, then why is everything so rusted and broken down?"

"Well, Meghan," Mr. Today said, climbing to the lawn and settling for a chat on the grass, "most likely it's because Quill hasn't figured out how to manufacture and produce metal products, and it no longer trades with other lands for goods. So every piece of metal in Quill is at least fifty years old, as are the vehicles. And the oil they use is some concoction of rainwater and chicken fat. Not ideal, in my opinion." The Unwanteds sat down around him.

"But why did Justine stop trading with other lands?"

The mage pressed his lips together. "Hmm. Isolationism is the root of it, I think. Fear and a suspicion of strangers is, I'm afraid, a characteristic of many humans.

"Justine wanted no outsiders to infiltrate Quill—if others were coming and going, trading goods from other lands, the traders might have spoken to the people of Quill and questioned Justine's rule. Justine would have none of that. Her idea of power is to run Quill like a puppet show—everyone doing only as she, the puppet master, demands."

The children smiled at the idea of a puppet show, for they all knew by now what puppets were, but their smiles turned to concerned looks when they realized that they, like their parents, had been the puppets.

"Mr. Today," someone else asked, "why is the gate only

locked from their side? If you are so trusted by the High Priest Justine, why does she lock you out of Quill?"

"Ah. Well, that is the way of Justine, isn't it? Protection from everything, control of everything. No one allowed even a peek outside those walls, right? Not that any Quillen dares come near our gate. And certainly, what if a group of Unwanteds, on the way to their deaths, were to revolt and overpower the Eliminators? Justine wouldn't want that mess spilling over into Quill. Alas, locking the gate was not my choice to make. And while I don't wish anyone to go back to Quill, for fear of exposing Artimé, I also don't wish to hold anyone hostage."

"Why doesn't anyone challenge the High Priest Justine?" asked Alex.

Mr. Today smiled ruefully. "They are afraid to, for of course they would be killed. And no one knows any different, my boy—without knowledge that life can be different, there can be no desire to change it. Their minds are too numb to think as we think. Therefore the thought of challenging Justine simply isn't possible."

Alex had another question too. "Mr. Today," he said rather

LISA McMANN

abruptly, "why don't *you* challenge Justine? Why don't you go into Quill and take over and teach them how to live like we do?"

The old man scratched his head and sighed wearily. He looked out over the land of Artimé, scanning the jungle, the grassy grounds, the mansion. "Because it would expose all of this. Because Justine is not a threat to us as long as she doesn't know of our existence." Mr. Today looked at the children, who gathered around him to catch his every word. "Because I don't believe that starting a war and demanding the people of Quill follow our way of life is ever going to work—they are too set in their ways to handle such an abrupt change. If Quill is to change, it will have to be on Quill's own terms. One day . . ." He sighed and trailed off. "Justine is an old woman. I await her death by natural causes. Perhaps then things will change . . . and perhaps without a war. It is what I hope for. And if I have anything in me at all, it's hope." After a moment he added very softly, "And maybe a little fear, too."

The students, quiet as the grass upon which they sat, held their breath in hopes that Mr. Today would continue. But their leader seemed lost in deep thoughts.

Alex looked out over the sea. He felt that familiar pang of loneliness for his brother, and wished he could figure out a safe way to tell Aaron how to get in without exposing Artimé.

After a while, when most of the Unwanteds had taken the long, contemplative silence as a dismissal to go and explore, Lani alone remained next to Mr. Today, a look of consternation growing on her face.

"Mr. Today," she said.

The old man startled out of his reverie. "Yes, Lani."

"What if the next ruler of Quill is worse than Justine?" Lani's face turned puce as she tried to appear nonchalant. She knew who the next ruler would be.

Mr. Today smiled ruefully at the girl. "Time holds hope for many impossible things. Let's not give up on your father just yet."

Mr. Today rose, shook the grass and wrinkles from his robe, nodded to Lani, and continued his walk alone now.

Lani lay back heavily on the grass, thinking about what would happen if Artimé were to go to war with Quill. Determined that if she ever came face-to-face in war with her father, the next in line to the high priest, she would kill him herself.

LISA McMANN

Losing Patience

Meghan leaned toward Alex during Actors' Studio and whispered, "What do you suppose Mr. Today meant last Sunday when he said it wasn't his choice to—"

"Hmm?" Annoyed, Alex looked up from the original Appleblossom script *Perseus! Perseus!* He was trying to memorize his lines. Mr. Appleblossom scurried about onstage, muttering in his typical rhyming manner, directing the actors who were in the current scene while the rest of the class sat in the auditorium, watching and going over their scripts. Lani and Samheed were onstage, in costume. *Flubbing up royally*, Alex thought.

Meghan rolled her eyes. "I said, what could it mean that Mr. Today didn't *choose* to have the gate locked from the Quill side? Doesn't Mr. Today have complete control over Artimé and all the spells that are in place? Couldn't he easily cast an illusion spell that would—"

Alex let the script fall heavily to his lap. He scowled. "How should I know? Why don't you ask your Magical Warrior instructor? I hardly know a thing about magic, as everyone here keeps reminding me."

Flinching, Meghan leaned away from him again. "Gosh, Alex." She drew her lips into a pout. "Nobody's trying to rub it in. Honestly. Why don't you ask Ms. Octavia why she hasn't recommended you yet?"

"No," Alex said, a bit too gruffly. He remembered the last time he'd asked, and how he'd vowed never to ask again.

"Are you getting all of your required work done?"

Alex stared at her, pointedly. "Not at the moment," he said, and picked up his script again. His cue was coming up, and he wanted to be ready. He rose from his seat and pushed through the door that led backstage to the props table, grabbed his sword and a pair of winged sandals, and awaited his cue.

LISA McMANN

Meghan followed him as Mr. Appleblossom set the onstage actors in motion again. "Alex," she whispered in the dimly lit hallway that led to the stage.

"What now?"

"We—all of us—especially Lani—"

"Are being horrible to me? Yes, Meg, I'm well aware of that." Alex's words were icy cold. He ignored the twinge in his gut that told him to stop talking, and continued. "You all need to grow up. Especially Lani." Alex slipped his feet into the sandals and buckled them tightly.

"That's not what I—"

"I wish you had a shush button! Now be quiet. My cue's coming up," Alex said. He turned away to focus on the stage, a gleam in his eye, his sword gripped tightly in his hand.

Meghan glared at Alex's back for a moment, then turned and flounced back out to the auditorium, muttering, "We need to grow up? We need to grow up?" under her breath.

On cue Alex entered stage left. Mr. Appleblossom waved his hand and cast a spell on the winged sandals. The white, feathery wings flapped, and slowly Alex rose in the air. He concentrated to keep his balance as the sandals propelled him to center stage, where Lani, in a tremendously large-headed costume, lay, feigning sleep.

Drawing his sword and holding it high, Alex projected his voice in a sinister tone. "Aha! You there, Medusa, your snakes betray you. I come at the bequest of King Polydectus, who has demanded your head on a platter!" Feeling a bit reckless and pent-up, Alex ad-libbed, "I see it shall take several platters to hold it all."

Lani glared. And with that, Alex shouted, "Have at you!" and brought down the sword upon the top half of Lani's ornate costumed head, sending the squirming snake portion of the costume rolling across the stage and leaving Lani trembling. Whether she trembled in fear of the sword or as part of her act, Alex wasn't sure. He grinned wickedly. That felt good.

Mr. Appleblossom stood up on his chair and applauded wildly, a pencil and his well-worn script tucked under his arm. "Bravo, Perseus! Brava, Medusa!" He stopped to scribble something, muttering, "That's it! Now, a rousing J. P. Sousa." He cued the brass band.

LISA McMANN

Lani ripped off what remained of the costume, scrambled to her feet, and glared up at Alex, her hair flying about with static from the near-suffocating Medusa head. Her eyes flashed, and she pointed. "You almost chopped my real head off, Alex! Watch it or I'll—"

Alex, who was still flying about helplessly as he waited for the distracted Mr. Appleblossom to release the spell on his sandals, glared at Lani and spat back, "Or you'll what?"

Lani whispered something under her breath.

"Knock it off—," Alex yelled, but it was too late. She had cast a spell on him as he puttered around in the flying sandals. He felt his body harden into stone and tip sideways, then upside down in the air. The sandals flapped frantically but could not hold his new stone weight, and he plunged to the stage, crashing and breaking into a thousand pieces. The winged sandals flew about the room, still holding Alex's feet. "Not funny," Alex's mouth said from stage right. "Not funny at all."

Still, everybody but Alex laughed, even as Mr. Appleblossom scurried over to put Alex back together and hand out detentions. Once Mr. Appleblossom had Alex back in one piece again, flesh and bone rather than stone, he patted the boy on the back, chuckling merrily. "You're good as new, my boy, I'll have you know. Perhaps I'll write that bit into the show!"

Alex groaned. Things couldn't get much worse.

A Big Mistake

The weather in Artimé was rarely gloomy and never too cold, though Mr. Today tossed in an occasional bit of rain or a thrilling thunderstorm to freshen things up and remind them all how much they preferred the pleasant sunshine.

On the day that marked six months of Alex's time spent in Artimé, a crisp breeze blew, and the leaves on the trees were a brilliant purplish red. Weather like this never occurred in the dry desert land of Quill.

Alex had grown tired of hiding in his room from his friends. He knew he was probably being unreasonable with them, but he just couldn't seem to deal with them these days. His mind was so occupied with *not* being in Magical Warrior Training, and the ache of missing his brother was stronger than he cared to admit—which no one else seemed to understand. So he took to wandering the grounds to keep away from everyone. He ventured into the jungle, a little farther each day, hesitantly at first but growing bolder at each attempt. There were many creatures of the jungle, but for the most part they greeted him politely and went about their business gathering nuts and roots and berries, stalking prey, feeding their young. Rarely did he witness anything that proved to be too frightening, though on several occasions he saw a huge gray wolf streaking off to find cover in the brush or resting on warm rocks near the seashore. It was almost as if the wolf were watching Alex, and the boy hoped he wouldn't become the wolf's next meal. Yet the animal never approached Alex or threatened him in any way, so Alex felt fairly safe. Today the wolf was nowhere to be seen.

Alex was quite fond of the cool darkness under the thick canopy of trees, and he was pleased to find a sparkling brook running through the jungle. There was one briny river back in Quill that the Necessaries used for transporting equipment to broken-down vehicles stranded around the community, and for delivering milk and eggs to the marketplace on large wooden rafts. But the stream here in Artimé was clear and cold, and Alex could see schools of fish now and then. On this particular boring Saturday he trekked alongside it to see where it led, and found himself, after a good deal of walking, within earshot of the gentle waves lapping the seashore in a sort of lagoon he'd never seen before. As he parted the bushes to make his way out of the jungle and onto the beach, he stopped abruptly, for there, floating in the water, was a large white boat glinting in the sunlight. He'd seen pictures of boats in his art books, but he'd never seen a real one before.

"Wow," he whispered, looking at the gleaming golden seats and shiny chrome that ran around its perimeter. "You could fit a dozen or fifteen people on that thing."

If he could have safely ventured out in the water to climb aboard, he would have, but Mr. Today had warned them that, like any large body of water, this sea contained carnivorous creatures like sharks, and so he'd advised the students to swim only in the protected waters of the cove near the mansion.

Not quite depressed enough, or desperate enough, to lose

a leg over it, Alex merely admired the boat from the shore. It didn't appear to be inhabited, and when the soft waves eased the port side of the boat toward him, he saw the craft's name painted in sleek letters on the side. CLAIRE, it read.

"That's curious," Alex said, louder than before.

"Curious. Curious. Curious," three platyprots echoed from the trees above.

Alex looked up. "Whose is it?"

The platyprots looked this way and that, and shrugged. "Whose is it?" they said to one another, before collapsing in fits of giggles.

Alex, feeling overly sensitive and wondering if the creatures were mocking him, decided it was best for him to walk away in silence. He emerged from the jungle, surprised to see no one at all walking about the grounds. Had he missed a special dinner, or a meeting? He shrugged, not really caring. He was getting used to being left out. Slowly he followed the shoreline back to the mansion and slipped inside the enormous front entrance.

The winged cheetah growled angrily. "Why arrren't you in yourrr rrroom?"

Alex stepped back in fright, for the statue had never

addressed him personally before in his comings and goings. "I—I—I was out for a walk, is all!"

Florence, the other statue, fired off a heated look at Simber. "Alex," she said, and Alex startled again and whirled around to face her. He'd never heard her speak before. "We are under lockdown. Did you forget about the governors' semiannual inspection today?"

"What? What? I don't know what you are talking about!"

"Your blackboard has been informing you for weeks! And your warrior instructor gave out the warning and the instructions yesterday," Florence said.

"I . . . don't have a warrior instructor," Alex said, and he was surprised to feel hot tears springing to his eyes. He blinked them away rapidly.

"Ah," said Florence. Her eyes narrowed. "So. You're the one."

Simber hissed sharply at Florence.

"What one?" Alex was deeply confused now, and no longer knew what anyone was talking about.

"Just go to yourrr rrroom. Don't come out until yourrr blackboarrrd tells you to." The enormous stone cheetah turned his face away in disgust, which only made Alex feel worse, having still no idea why these two were so angry with him.

"Go," said Florence. "Before I let him eat you."

Alex needed no further encouragement. He raced to the top of the stairs as fast as he could go and shot down the hallway to his room. He was halfway there before he realized that at the top of the stairs he had caught sight of a hallway that he could have sworn hadn't been there the previous day. But now was not the time to check it out.

He slipped into his room, unshushed the volume on his blackboard, and sank into the overstuffed chair, still heaving from his wild sprint up the marble staircase. "Clive," he said to the blackboard, "what's going on around here?"

Clive surfaced with a scowl and "ahemmed" several times to make sure his voice was truly back. "Oh, so now you want to talk. You shush me for weeks, ignore my messages to you, and now that you've likely messed everything up, you ask for help. Well, I'm not inclined to give it. Besides, it's too late. Here comes Marcus, and boy, are you in trouble. Ahem!"

Clive's features melted flat once again, and the screen brightened to show Mr. Today's face. He looked weary and angry, so far unlike the usual kind and humorous mage Alex knew, that for a moment Alex thought it might be someone else. The man's white hair stood up more wildly than ever, as if he'd tried recently to pull it out.

"Thank you, Clive," Mr. Today said in a defeated voice. "But all is well. No need to panic. They're gone."

Alex sat up in his chair at the sight of Mr. Today, feeling an impending sense of doom. He hadn't seen the mage in weeks, for Alex had ceased attending the Sunday chats on the lawn.

Mr. Today looked at Alex for a long moment before he spoke.

Alex swallowed hard, waiting.

"Alex," the mage said wearily, "please. Just . . ." He searched for the right words. "I don't ask much of you. Just try to respect my few requests. And pay attention. Please. I'm disabling Clive's shush button until further notice. It would be wise for you to catch up on what you've missed these past weeks, so you'll know what danger you put us all in."

"Mr. Today, I'm sorry—I didn't understand—"

Mr. Today sighed. "When the governors come, Alex, I use a very complex spell that hides Artimé, so that this place looks just like it did when you first arrived. As Artimé grows, and as I grow older, it becomes harder for me to hold that spell flawlessly and still appear to be the man they expect me to be. It takes a lot of concentration, and I need everyone in the mansion and remaining quite still during these times. Please, Alex, I know it's inevitable, but I'm not . . . quite . . . ready. . . ." He shook his head to clear his thoughts. "Listen, Alex. I'm counting on you—please don't fail me. Good night."

Alex stared openmouthed as the mage disappeared from the blackboard. And something deep inside of him, deeper than he thought anything could ever be, quivered and broke into tiny pins that stuck hard into his gut.

Secrets and Secret Places

By morning all of Artimé knew that Alex Stowe was the one who had almost gotten them discovered and killed. Of course, if Alex or anyone was anywhere inside the world of Artimé, he probably wouldn't have been detected by the governors, who merely saw the same desolate scene that the Unwanteds had seen when they first trudged through the black iron gate six months before. But Mr. Today was not usually one to take chances when it came to protecting his world, and it had been the standard protocol during all the biannual governor inspections since the beginning of Artimé to place all the

LISA McMANN

citizens on lockdown inside their magically hidden rooms.

Mr. Today, despite his creativity, was a man of order, and he liked for everyone to be in their proper places and not roaming about. For what if the spell broke? What if a chaotic fight broke out in the lounge or in the theater, or what if a student wandered off and was attacked in the jungle, and Mr. Today was unavailable to handle the situation? No, it was safest for him to know and be assured that each person and domesticated creature was secured in his appropriate place during that stressful half-day visit.

All the people and creatures that did follow the instructions would of course be very upset with the one who didn't. And so, when word got out that it was Alex Stowe who had seemingly defied their dear and faithful leader, and that it was Alex Stowe who had put them all in danger, well . . . almost no one could muster up an ounce of pity for him.

Meghan, though she had been furious early on, tried to swallow her anger when she talked to Alex at lunch. And Lani sent him pitying glances from her soulful blue eyes. But by then Alex was so utterly mortified by all the other harsh looks and pointing fingers and whispers hidden by cupped hands that he weaseled his way out of the dining room the first chance he got and closed himself in his room for the rest of the day, skipping his private lesson with Ms. Octavia, as well as Actors' Studio with Mr. Appleblossom, even though it meant missing his star performance in *Perseus! Perseus!*

Alex went into his bedroom, shut the door so he could partially block out Clive's endless yapping, and curled up on the bed, pinching his eyes shut to stop the headache that stabbed at him.

In and out he breathed, wishing with all his might that he could just go back to Quill, where he wouldn't have expectations or dreams or hopes or imagination or responsibilities at all. He could just be. Not have everyone angry with him. Not be the only one who didn't succeed. In Quill he'd be surrounded by people whose idea of success was getting up every day and picking corn or fixing the rusty, uncreative boxlike buses and Quillitary tanks, preparing endlessly, mindlessly, for a day that would never come. Indeed Alex felt like he'd become an Unwanted all over again.

He thought about his brother, which hurt even more. "Aaron would understand. Aaron would be there for me," he said, as if he were challenging anyone to deny it. "I just wish . . . at least . . . he knew I was alive."

His inner Alex didn't respond.

Eventually Alex fell into a fitful sleep. What he didn't know was that while he slept, a secret meeting of adults occurred in a very large office at the end of a mostly invisible hallway nearby.

Mr. Today's Office

Mr. Today rose from behind his desk when the two ladies arrived. "Hello, Claire, Octavia," he said.

Octavia shook Mr. Today's hand with a lithe tentacle of her own, and Claire placed a kiss on the man's cheek. "You're looking a bit less harried this evening," Claire said.

The old mage tugged absently at his whimsical hair. "The scare is over for now," he said, but his voice was grim. "But it doesn't change the situation. It was a very close call, and I'm not sure how many more times I can sustain the visits before the governors begin to suspect something. I could have sworn I saw a ripple along the edge of the Lake of Oil when Alex was out wandering." He ran his fingers over his hair now, trying to smooth it down. "Octavia, what's the latest?"

Octavia gripped the arms of a chair and slid up to the seat. Her tentacles moved about softly, one rubbing thoughtfully along the top of her long alligator snout, another adjusting her spectacles, and others dangling all around the edge of the chair like a flouncy skirt, wavering gently as if they were floating in water. "Well, Marcus. You know how I feel. The boy's growing desperate—I can see it in his drawings. He's completely brilliant, and should have been in Magical Warrior Training months ago. He skipped his private lesson today, you know. . . ." She clicked her tongue against her enormous teeth and shook her head slowly. "I'm not sure we're doing the right thing at all by holding him back."

"Claire?"

Claire sighed. "I am growing less sure of that myself every day now. Gunnar spotted him deep in the jungle before the governors arrived, and tracked him along the stream all the way to the shore, where the boat rests. Alex is spending all his

LISA McMANN

time alone—and frankly, I don't blame him. Everyone's angry with him, and he feels bad now that he's the only one not in magical training. It's only making matters worse."

Mr. Today shook his head and sank back in his chair. "Oh, oh, oh," he said quietly, "what to do? I am afraid that if Alex starts training, he will use his magic to find his brother. The powerful connection between twins . . . It's a huge risk we don't need right now, especially now that Aaron is in Justine's good graces and under her watchful eye." He pressed his two forefingers to his lips and closed his eyes, thinking hard. For several minutes he remained quite still. When he opened his eyes, they were moist. "How I wish I could have convinced Justine to eliminate both twins, but she wouldn't have it," he said. "The Wanted twin, not one infraction. Not even a hint of one. If Alex wasn't able to tempt Aaron into drawing in the dirt, I'm not sure Aaron would've been much use here, but at least we wouldn't have this potential problem on our hands."

"Marcus," Octavia said, "what we need is to get the boy to forget about his brother. Get him busy training immediately. Keep his mind occupied so he doesn't have time to dwell on it. How hard can it be? Human siblings have done it for years here without issue!"

Mr. Today's eyes narrowed sharply. He glanced at Claire, then back at Octavia. When he spoke, it was in a most serious and hushed tone. "You must understand, my dear lady, that it is very, very different with twins. There's a connection. A loyalty that exceeds all others."

Claire stared at her hands in her lap.

Octavia closed her lips over her teeth, folded several arms across her chest, and frowned. "So it's inevitable, you're saying. The connection between twins is that strong that he'll never give up?"

"That is what I believe."

"He's capable of figuring spells out on his own eventually, with or without the training," Octavia muttered, shaking her long head. "How soon before it all begins?"

"I can't say," Mr. Today said. "But I'm uneasy. I don't know what it is, but something else is brewing. Sigfried told me of some suspicious behavior on the part of a few of his actors. Costumes gone missing, fights breaking out. Something's going on."

"What?"

"I don't yet know. But I'm feeling cautious for Artimé. We may be in for some trouble."

Octavia snapped her jaw angrily. "Then we are doing Alex a great disservice by forcing him to be vulnerable, unable to protect himself."

Mr. Today regarded Octavia for a moment, and then Ms. Morning. "Claire?"

Claire, who had been biting her lip anxiously throughout the conversation, closed her eyes and opened them again slowly. "There is one other way to make Alex forget about Aaron," she said quietly.

"You know I won't do that."

"Well, then . . . I agree with Octavia," she said finally.

Mr. Today dropped his head in his hands, took a deep breath, and then looked up. His eyes were weary again. "It is decided, then. Octavia, begin the boy's training at once. And Claire . . ."

"Yes?"

A look of sorrowful understanding passed between them.

"I'm afraid it's come. It's time. Prepare our warriors for battle."

The Way It Is
with Twins

Alex tossed and turned in his sleep, his anxiety overflowing into a clutch of frightening dreams. He dreamed of Lani and Meghan taunting him, pointing their fingers; of Mr. Today's disappointment in him; of the sea turning back into the Great Lake of Boiling Oil; of the entire civilization of Artimé frogmarching him to the edge of the lake and shoving him in as he screamed.

He dreamed of Quill, only instead of the drab colorlessness and simplistic functionality of it all—from the single road that encircled the land, to the rusting Quillitary jalopies that had

LISA McMANN

been used for training on and off for the past fifty years, to the quadrant of land where crops and farm animals were raised—he dreamed that Quill was brighter than it used to be. That things were painted, and that children were allowed to laugh and make things with sticks, and that Aaron and he still shared a tiny bedroom, but now they were allowed to whisper into the night and laugh after finishing each other's sentences and tell each other about the dreams they'd had, rather than keeping them all inside and wondering.

He dreamed that Aaron was mourning for him. That Aaron missed him, just as Alex longed for Aaron. That they met again, and Aaron was so glad to see him. That Aaron wrapped his arms around his brother and said how terribly, awfully sorry he was that Alex was Unwanted, and that there had been a mistake—but that they had thought it was too late, that Alex was already dead.

In the dream Aaron couldn't believe there was a magical land where hundreds of other Unwanteds lived, and so Alex convinced Aaron to come and see for himself. And when he did, Aaron didn't want to go back.

That was a happy dream, and Alex, though he didn't know

LISA McMANN

it, smiled in his sleep. He was thrilled that Aaron knew he was still alive. And when Alex reluctantly delivered Aaron back to Quill, he whispered excitedly, "Promise not to tell anyone—not anyone. Maybe next time you can stay with me for good!"

"I won't tell," Aaron said. "I promise. You have to come back again soon!"

And just as they waved a satisfied, heartfelt good-bye, and Alex turned away to enter the gate into Artimé again, he looked back over his shoulder one last time, and his heart stopped. In place of his dear brother, Aaron, appeared the sinister face of High Priest Justine.

"ALEX!"

Alex jumped awake and shouted, "No!"

"ALEX! Please don't make me shout through your bedroom door. My voice is delicate after so many weeks of disuse."

"Clive? Is that you?" For a moment Alex didn't know where he was.

"Oh, boy," Clive said, and rolled his eyes.

Alex scrambled off the bed and opened the door to the

sitting area. "Why are you shouting at me? It's seven o'clock in the morning, for crying out sideways."

"Ms. Octavia is waiting to speak with you. Put on a shirt or something, good gracious. I'll deliver her as soon as you say you're ready."

Alex groaned as all the memories of the previous day came flooding back. More trouble, he thought, for skipping yesterday's lesson. He slid a T-shirt over his head, pulled on his shorts, and waited, breathless, in front of the blackboard. "Okay," he said.

Ms. Octavia appeared. "Hello, Alex," she said, peering down her snout at him.

Alex nodded. "Hi, Ms. Octavia," he mumbled. Waiting.

"I missed you yesterday. Were you ill?"

"N-n-not exactly, ma'am."

"I see." She adjusted her glasses. "Well, you'll be here today, won't you?"

"Y-yes, ma'am."

"Good. We're starting your Magical Warrior Training, and I wouldn't want you to miss that. I look forward to seeing you." She nodded curtly. Her picture faded to the black screen, leaving Alex standing with his jaw slacked in amazement.

LISA McMANN

Clive resurfaced and gave a patronizing smile. "Well, it's about time."

Alex scowled. "Shove a sock in it, Clive."

He showered, dressed, and headed off to classes, puzzling just a little over his dreams before pushing them back in the dark corner of his mind.

At the same time, just a few miles away, another boy who looked identical to Alex was doing the exact same things.

Aaron the Wanted

When the buzzer sounded, Aaron Stowe left his tiny gray dormitory room in Wanted University and entered the hallway as a dozen others did the same. They walked shoulder to shoulder to the cafeteria for breakfast and ate their gruel politely, in silence. Chatting at mealtimes was not permitted, so the students ate quickly and moved on to their assignments for the day.

While most students still went to their classrooms to continue their basic learning, Aaron had excelled and been promoted. He walked toward the exit, where a square, rust-

LISA McMANN

colored Quillitary Jeep pulled up. Just as Aaron reached the edge of the narrow road that encircled Quill, the vehicle belched out acrid black smoke that smelled like burning chicken grease. He got inside and nodded to the driver.

The vehicle roared and sputtered past government offices and the new Favored Farm, Aaron's own creation, where special high-quality, high-grade vegetables, fruits, grains, and animals were now raised for consumption by the High Priest Justine, the governors, and the Quillitary. The barbed-wire ceiling cast gridlike shadows that lined up almost exactly with the rows of crops. "It's looking fine," Aaron noted with a hint of satisfaction.

Since Aaron was considered to be very promising, showing not only the highest intelligence for his class but a budding strength as well, he had been chosen to train directly under the guidance of Senior Governor Haluki, a slight, graying man who was the high priest's second in command, and Governor Strang, a proven young man of twenty. Like Strang had been, Aaron Stowe was a serious boy, quiet and completely dedicated to the service of the high priest of Quill, at all costs. He was just the sort of boy who grows up to be a dangerously powerful man.

LISA McMANN

The vehicle clunked and groaned up the winding hill to the palace of the high priest, for on this day Aaron was being rewarded. First for his excellent work in solving the beef problem for the high priest, second for his insight into the matter of the Favored Farm at large, and third for his program, which outlined precisely how to run the farm most efficiently. It had been his last assignment in math class, and since all of the university students' work was checked by the governors, it did not take long for Governor Strang to notice Aaron's penchant for economics. And economics was something that the High Priest Justine was very fond of. Especially because it always benefited her.

It had been Aaron's suggestion to work the farm in the same manner as the people of the land of Quill, sorting the farm animals into three categories: Wanted, Necessary, and Unwanted. The highest quality of animals would be sequestered at the Favored Farm to breed and be fattened up, and the lower qualities of stock would be sent to the Common Farm to be bred and raised for consumption by the Necessaries. And it had been Aaron's suggestion to send the Quillitary to the Common Farm to transplant the highest quality crops to the Favored Farm as well.

Now that the Favored Farm was running without a single hitch and the process was complete, Aaron had been invited to the palace to have lunch with the governors and the High Priest Justine herself. It was an incredible honor. Aaron was pleased with his achievement so early in his instruction, but of course he didn't even smile outwardly when he heard the news. After all, his full allegiance was to Quill. And since his parents were both Necessaries, he felt he had to make extra effort to prove to the governors that he was of the highest quality and worthy of his Wanted title.

All these thoughts and more filled his mind, though at one point in the slow journey to the palace—going uphill demanded a good deal of effort from the vehicle—a nagging thought pestered his brain concerning a recurring dream he'd had lately.

It frightened him more than he cared to admit to himself, because he thought he had managed to eliminate dreams entirely from a young age, once he had learned they were wrong. But several times since the Purge he'd awakened, horrified and feeling terribly guilty, because not only had he dreamed about something, but that something was his brother,

LISA McMANN

Alex. A half year had passed since Alex had been eliminated, and Aaron admitted that he had felt a bit bad for at least an hour, until his mother had warned him to forget about it. And with his entrance to the university the day after the Purge, well, it really hadn't been difficult to forget Alex. Indeed it was rare for Aaron to think of his twin at all, but on the rare occasion he did, Alex was the sort of faint and fuzzy memory after which one wonders, *Did that really happen?*

Aaron knew better than to tell anyone about these recent dreams, though. Now that he was held in such high esteem for a young student, it would be a definite career-killing sign of weakness were he to admit that to anyone. He shuddered to think it.

Finally the vehicle came to a sputtering stop at the entrance to the palace. Aaron's mind turned swiftly back to the affairs of Quill and his luncheon with the elite. He brushed the nagging thoughts away and walked briskly and with confidence to the Quillitary guards who stood watch at the palace door.

"Your license, please."

Aaron pulled a folded document from his jacket pocket and handed it to the guard.

"Code?"

"Quill prevails when the strong survive."

"The governors await," the guard said. He opened the creaking door, and Aaron stepped inside.

Governors Haluki and Strang stood in the dimly lit entrance. "Good day, Aaron," Haluki said, looking the boy over with a trained eye. "Your first time here. Need I remind you that you're not to discuss this visit with anyone?"

"It's not necessary, sir, but I thank you nevertheless."

"Very good. Follow me." Without further comment Haluki turned and walked briskly down a dark stone corridor. Aaron clipped along behind him, keeping his eyes focused straight ahead, and Strang brought up the rear.

They entered a room with a long table, a dozen chairs around it. Three women and a man sat at the far end of the table, conversing in soft tones, their heads close together. Two of the women could not be more than twenty, and the man was quite young as well. Aaron's eyes strayed briefly to a display of potted plants in the corner of the room before he looked away hastily. He kept his expression bland, void of the surprise he felt over seeing vegetation indoors.

LISA McMANN

"Good day, Governors," Strang said to the four at the table. A round of polite good-days was exchanged in response. "This is young Aaron Stowe, the instigator of the Favored Farm plan."

"Well met, Aaron Stowe," came the even reply, though Aaron had met them all before at one point or another in the half year he'd been at university.

"Good day, Governors," he said.

Aaron, Haluki, and Strang joined the four at the table as the interrupted conversation continued once again. Aaron sat at the fringe of it, looking at his hands linked together on the table, awed that he should be allowed to listen as the governors discussed recent and long-standing issues with the quality of Quillitary vehicles, and the current state of the water shortage. When the door opened again, two Quillitary guards entered, followed by the statuesque High Priest Justine. Two additional guards trailed behind and waited at the door.

Everyone stood abruptly and turned toward the woman. Aaron swallowed hard—he'd never been this close to her before. He lowered his eyes appropriately, though not before he caught a glimpse of her structured face, etched with wrinkles around her burning black eyes and pinched mouth. She wore her hair down, as always, white streaks naturally painted into the silver. Her gown, a colorless flowing garment, was covered by a black cloak, which rested heavily on her shoulders.

Immediately following the High Priest Justine came a small entourage of service staff pushing a squeaky cart that held the luncheon.

The governors and Aaron bowed deeply before the stately woman.

Justine glanced around, her eyebrow raised slightly. She stopped at Aaron, her appraising glance apparently finding favor with the boy. "Young Mr. Stowe, I presume," she said in her powerful voice, startling the silence.

"Forever at your service, Madam High Priest," murmured Aaron, as he'd been taught. "May all Quill's enemies die a thousand deaths."

She held out her hand, her long fingers reaching limply. Aaron took her hand in his and bowed his head over it as he'd been instructed. Her fingers were as cold as barbed wire on a frosty night.

Magical  Warrior Training

Ms. Octavia was sitting at her desk, her half-glasses perched precariously on her snout and her appendages involved in a half-dozen independent activities, when Alex shuffled in.

He stopped awkwardly just inside the doorway, feeling sheepish about having missed class the previous day, watching the octogator scribble with one arm on a paper on her desk and another arm on the chalkboard behind her, while a third painted on an easel at her side. When Ms. Octavia noticed Alex, she stopped all her activities and smiled.

"Come in," she said. "Sit."

Alex sidled up to her desk and sat in the chair beside her.

"Feeling better today?" Ms. Octavia asked.

"I—yes."

"I'm a bit worried about you." Ms. Octavia's smile faded, and her voice took on a serious tone. "Would you care to talk about what's been bothering you lately, Alex?"

Alex blushed crimson. He squirmed in his seat. "I—um—"

Ms. Octavia waited patiently. Finally she patted him on the shoulder. "It's okay. Let's talk about your Magical Warrior Training instead. I am sure you are as excited as I am to start."

Alex breathed a sigh of relief. "Yes, ma'am."

"In fact you are probably wondering why I've held you back this long. It must have been excruciating for you."

"Well . . ." Alex looked at his shoes. "It sure seemed like it was fun for everybody else to pull their spell pranks on me." He thought of Lani. "I felt like I must have been really bad at this to be held back so long."

Ms. Octavia closed her eyes and sighed. When she opened her eyes, she looked to the classroom doorway and nodded. "Come in, Marcus," she said.

LISA McMANN

Alex turned in his chair. Mr. Today entered the room and closed the door behind him. "I'm afraid that I am the one to blame for your troubles, Alex," he said.

Alex didn't know what to say, and all he could think of was, "Oh."

"I do not want you to blame Ms. Octavia, for she was following my orders." Mr. Today rested his fingers on the edge of Ms. Octavia's desk, but he did not sit down. "All I can tell you right now is this: I held you back because I thought I was protecting you and Artimé, but I was wrong, my boy. You have gifts beyond compare. I look forward to watching your progress."

"I—thank you, sir." Alex desperately wanted to know how holding him back was protecting anyone, but he dared not ask.

Mr. Today nodded, and though his eyes were weary, there was a slight twinkle in them as well. "Now get to work." He smiled and left the room.

Alex blinked.

"Well, that's settled now, isn't it," Ms. Octavia said hurriedly. "Let's do get to work, shall we?"

Alex nodded swiftly, and a grin spread across his face as Ms.

Octavia pulled a component vest from her classroom closet. She handed it to him. "Congratulations," she said, her smile toothy and genuine.

Alex put it on. "Thanks," he said, too choked up to say more. *Finally*, he thought. *Finally*.

"First," Ms. Octavia said, "we'll discuss the fundamentals of magic." She opened a drawer and pulled out a handful of ordinary art supplies: a paintbrush, a pencil, a rubber eraser, several paper clips, and a piece of chalk.

Alex watched her lay them all out on the desk.

Ms. Octavia took a paper clip, unwound it, and bent it so that it looked more like a triangle, with the two ends of it crossing and sticking out prominently. With her other appendages she did the same to the other paper clips. "Everything we create here in Artimé has a little bit of magic in it already, Alex, so the true basis for these tools to work as weapons is in your mind and your ability to concentrate and direct the objects to do what they are supposed to do."

She handed five of the newly shaped clips to Alex and kept five for herself. "In this shape, we call them scatterclips," she said.

LISA McMANN

Alex soon saw why.

Ms. Octavia glided around the desk and pulled one arm back as if she were going to throw a baseball. "Right now, Alex, I'm concentrating on that picture on the wall across the room. I'm focusing on the center of it, and that is where I want to direct my throw." She threw the handful of scatterclips, and together all five soared toward the center of the portrait. At the last second they separated and veered to the edges of the canvas and stuck soundly through the wooden frame, into the wall.

"Cool," muttered Alex under his breath.

Ms. Octavia flashed him a toothy grin, but grew serious again. "Your mind must be able to focus on the center of your target, Alex, and you need to trust that the scatterclips will find the edges on their own. If you do not have faith in the clips, they will not veer properly, and they will not work correctly. So it is important to be calm and to be thinking clearly when using these items as weapons if you wish to be successful."

Alex nodded, the scatterclips in his hand becoming moist with nervous sweat. "May I try?"

"Fire away, indeed."

Alex pulled his left arm back and focused on the center of the portrait, then flung with all his might.

The scatterclips smacked into the center of the portrait and clattered to the floor.

Alex's face fell.

Ms. Octavia smiled. "If you'd managed to do it the first time, you would have been the first in Artimé's history to do it. Try again! This time, focus on throwing accurately rather than forcefully. The clips have the magical power to get there—we don't want you throwing your arm out of its socket on your first day." She chuckled as Alex scurried over to the wall to pick up his clips.

Alex's second try resulted in one clip veering off beautifully to the upper left-hand corner of the portrait, while the rest of the clips fell uselessly to the floor again. "Well done," Ms. Octavia praised. "I've a theory that left-handers pick up on the throwing spells more easily than the righties do—it was a good one to start with, and you have proven my theory worthy, my boy!"

"Thanks!" Alex said, not quite as delighted as his instructor seemed to be over the progress, but thrilled nonetheless to finally have the chance to use art as a weapon.

"Mind you," Ms. Octavia warned, "scatterclips are not to be toyed with. They can be lethal, or at least cause great harm when coupled with a verbal incantation. But for now we'll stick with the silent method. Try again."

Alex concentrated and threw again and again and again. When their hour of training was nearly over, he had succeeded in skillfully embedding the scatterclips into the edges of the portrait five times in a row.

"Now," Ms. Octavia said, "throw them at me."

"What? No, I can't!"

"Yes, you can," she said smoothly. "I trust you. You'll do fine. But I want you to see what the clips will do when you have a live enemy."

"But—"

"Alex, it's an order." Ms. Octavia stood as tall as she could against the wall and made sure all of her appendages were down at her sides and not floating about as they sometimes did when she was thinking hard.

Alex hesitated, staring helplessly at his instructor. "How can I? What if something goes wrong?"

Ms. Octavia stared at Alex. "Alex, I cannot express how

urgent it is that you get over your fear. Because one day, I expect sooner rather than later, you will have to fight. It is my job to prepare you. So concentrate, focus, and throw. Do it now."

Her stern voice echoed in Alex's ears. Finally he nodded, pulled his arm back, focused on her center of gravity, and concentrated. He threw the scatterclips, and they soared together as one bunch; then, at the last possible moment, they separated from the pack, found their marks, and stuck fast.

Ms. Octavia didn't even blink. "Good. Now, see? I'm stuck here. The clips have secured me to this wall through my clothing. They have not pierced my skin. You have succeeded in stopping me from moving, attacking, or fighting until I can manage to release myself from their grasp."

Alex, who had been holding his breath all this time, sighed in relief. He wiped the sweat off his forehead with the back of his hand.

"Release," Ms. Octavia said, and the scatterclips dropped to the floor. She stepped away from the wall and gathered them up.

"So . . . ," Alex said, thinking out loud, "the enemy has to be standing in front of a wall in order for them to work? That's not very convenient."

"Not necessarily a wall. A tree will do. But there are other ways to direct the clips." She leaned in conspiratorially. "Your friends likely haven't gotten to this in their training yet, since they learn their own focus spells first, but I will tell you if you promise not to use it on anyone but a true enemy."

Alex's eyes widened. He nodded. "I promise."

Ms. Octavia grinned. "If your target is standing in an open area, your verbal component of the spell is 'Propel!' You say it when you release the clips. The clips will then veer off as usual, but they'll continue to fly, dragging your enemy as far as necessary until they find something solid to attach to."

"Smokes," Alex said, his eyes lighting up.

"Indeed. Sometimes you can pick up another enemy or two along the way, and they'll be stacked! It's great fun to watch," she admitted. "You must be careful, though, that there are no friends in the path behind your enemy, or they could get snagged as well."

"Wow!" Alex said. "What else can they do?" He held the scatterclips in his hand and looked at them with new admiration.

"Well," Ms. Octavia said, growing serious again, "as I said before, they can cause serious injury or death. But one must know the verbal component for that."

"What is it?" Alex asked.

Ms. Octavia hesitated. She pursed her wide lips together, hiding all of her teeth. "I don't think you're quite ready for that. It's an upper-level spell. A bit too dangerous in the hands of a first year."

Alex nodded, even though he was very disappointed. "I understand," he said. He was just thankful to be learning spells at all. But his mind raced, wondering what the powerful words could possibly be.

Lessons and Warnings

Alex flew through his first weeks of Magical Warrior Training, determined to catch up to the others. Whenever he wasn't in class or in training, learning how to paint himself invisible, studying slam poetry charms, or drawing chalk outlines that would freeze a targeted person in one position indefinitely, he was in his room practicing all these things. He slipped into his classes late and left early so he wouldn't have to talk to anyone. He took most of his meals in his room, still percolating with disgust at Lani for continuing to badger him with her pranks. He didn't respond to any of his friends who left messages for him through his blackboard, though Clive of course delivered all of the messages rather loudly. Alex wished desperately to have his shush button back.

And so it was that ever since the governors' visit, Alex had completely abandoned his friends. Yet he missed the companionship they'd all had during those moments when they weren't laughing at him or disgusted by him. Finally, one morning, Alex decided to come down to the dining room to eat.

"Why won't you answer our messages?" Lani demanded over breakfast. She pouted dramatically.

"Yes, why?" Meghan said.

Alex put his breakfast on the table and sat down wearily. He was tired of being yelled at. He looked at Samheed, who simply raised an eyebrow and took another spoonful of jam for his toast.

"Hello, Samheed," Alex said pointedly.

"Awex." His mouth was too full to say more.

"It's not like we were going to yell at you. We just . . . we were worried since you haven't been around," Lani said.

"I wasn't worried," Samheed said after swallowing. "*You* were worried."

LISA McMANN

"I meant Meg and me." Lani shot Samheed a cross look.

"I wasn't worried either," offered Meghan. "Well, not much, anyway."

Lani blushed furiously and flounced in her seat. "Fine. I was worried."

"Well, get on with it, then," Alex said. "Have at me and get it over with."

"You mean the governors' inspection thing?" asked Meghan. "It's over. Hardly anybody's talking about it now."

"Yeah, right. Then why is Ms. Morning sitting over there shooting pins at me with her eyes?"

Meghan turned to look at her focus instructor and waved. Ms. Morning startled and blinked, and then her face broke into a pleasant, almost sheepish smile as she nodded hello. "See, Alex? She wasn't even looking at you."

Alex shrugged and began to respond when the giant blackboard in the dining hall came to life, and Oscar—for that was his name—spoke. "Attention, students. Please report to the theater in place of your first class this morning." The children could hear the announcement ringing in stereo throughout the mansion. Oscar melted into the screen once again, and the words he'd just spoken were written in large neon letters, sure to catch the attention of even the least aware.

"Oh, look, Alex," Samheed said. "They've added bright colors to make sure you don't miss it."

On a normal day, when Alex might have been in a better mood, he would have laughed, or fired back a reply just as snide. But there hadn't been any ordinary days for Alex in well over a month. And even though he was thrilled with his first weeks of warrior training, he was still very hurt that Lani kept knocking him off his feet with spells even though he'd asked her to stop, and he still felt bad about the mess he'd caused with the governors' visit, and he was still very lonely, missing Aaron, and probably in need of a kind word, but none of his friends seemed compelled to give it now that he'd snubbed them so much. And he didn't much care for Samheed's sarcasm this particular morning after he'd gotten a full dose of mocking from Clive already, who had laughed and laughed when Alex had failed several times to cast an invisibility-paintbrush spell on himself.

And so, instead of ignoring it, Alex shoved his chair back and leaned toward Samheed, his clenched fists on the table, a wild look in his eye. "Not funny, Burkesh."

LISA McMANN

"Geez, Alex. It was just a joke."

"I've had about enough of everybody's blasted jokes," Alex said.

"Ease up, man," Samheed said, pushing his chair back slowly. He knew Alex was no match for him, and he didn't want to have to punch him in the face again.

"Me? Ease up? Oh, that's ripe." Alex slowly moved around the table toward Samheed.

Lani stood up. "I'll take him down for you, Sam!" She began speaking an incantation.

Alex whirled around to face her. "And you! One day soon you're going to be very sorry you did th—" He stopped short and stared as Lani pointed up in the air above Alex's head and shrieked, frozen mid-spell. She fell to the floor. Immediately the dining room erupted into shouts and fearful screams.

"What—who—" Alex whipped around to see what had happened.

Samheed, a shocked look on his face, pointed upward and then dove under a nearby table, while Meghan scrambled out of her chair and ran for safety.

Alex looked up. Descending toward their table at a rapid

rate were the enormous back paws of the great winged-cheetah statue, nearly upon him. He dove off to the side, almost getting slammed across the room when the tip of the cheetah's stone wing caught him on the back.

Simber landed gracefully, though his wings flapped with such force that the wind blew the teacups right out of their saucers. "Enough!" he roared, looking at Lani. "Save yourrr spells forrr yourrr enemies!"

And after a moment of complete silence, the enormous creature ceremoniously folded in his wings, turned about carefully in the space between tables, and loped gracefully back through the dining room and down the hallway to the front entrance, where he leaped up and assumed his normal position.

Ms. Morning rushed over to the table, helping Lani sit up and checking to make sure Alex was okay. Samheed crawled back out from under the table and brushed himself off, and Meghan returned wide-eyed as well. The room remained hushed as the four stood there looking at each other. Lani was still a bit pale and shaky but otherwise unharmed . . . that is, if you didn't count the pointing and laughing from others, for

LISA McMANN

159 « The Unwanteds

days and years to come, for being the one who drove Simber just a little bit over the edge.

The four, no longer having much of an appetite, turned without further ado and made their way to the tubes, meeting again in the theater a split second later. There was no need to mention the event again; one of them wished to forget it entirely, while another hoped to remember it forever as the time the most frightening creature in all of Artimé came to his defense. Desperately Alex wished it would set in motion a better, happier time.

He bit his lip, thinking he was a big reason things weren't good now. He glanced at Lani, feeling bad about his outburst. He really needed to get a handle on things. "Sorry, guys," he said as they walked toward their seats. "I've been kind of a jerk lately."

Meghan smiled, and Samheed punched Alex lightly in the shoulder. Lani just nodded and kept her eyes on the floor. "It's okay," she said finally.

The seats in the theater filled rapidly, and one could hear murmurs through the crowd, half of them discussing the drama of the dining room, and the other half wondering what could be so important as to prompt a meeting such as this, with all of the creatures, students, instructors, families, even the little children required to attend. Simber and Florence appeared rather suddenly as well, standing elegant and tall near the back, and Meghan wondered for a moment how they could have possibly fit in the tubes. But when Mr. Today walked briskly to the stage, all stray thoughts ceased along with the buzz of the crowd.

Most of the creatures sat near the front since they were shorter than the humans. The winged creatures hovered at the ceiling, including Jim, who sort of bounced up and down like a yo-yo in his slow-flapping fashion. Each push down with his powerful wings brought him to the ceiling, and each flap up allowed him to sink several feet, sometimes more, such that the creatures sitting directly below him glanced up nervously from time to time just to make sure he wasn't about to free-fall and make feathercakes out of them.

"Good morning," Mr. Today said. The crowd was silent. Even the platyprots held their tongues whenever Mr. Today began speaking, though it was surely very difficult for them, especially when they could have had such a large audience.

"Thank you for coming on such short notice. Which reminds me, has anybody seen Alex Stowe? What's that? Oh, he's here? Tremendous!" The mage chuckled heartily and smiled in Alex's direction, and the crowd laughed as well, some feeling quite relieved that Mr. Today was making a joke out of it. Alex turned bright red and grinned reluctantly, which turned out to be the best thing he could have done; it took the pressure off him enormously. Later, when he thought about it again, Alex was quite grateful for the attention.

"To the business of the day, the task we may face," Mr. Today began in a serious tone of voice. "First of all, I do not wish to frighten anyone. We've all learned that there is enough fear of the unknown in Quill to strike us all into a panic on a whim even years later. Fear is a difficult thing to unlearn. But you know that is not my way of doing things. Rather, I called you all here this morning because I do not wish to hide anything from you." He paused, his eyes roaming the crowd.

"I have reason to believe, as I have made clear for the past several years, that we may at some point be discovered. You all know this—I've never tried to hide it. And while Artimé is magic, it was created by my flawed human hands, and therefore perfection, complete safety, isolation, is not something I have ever promised, or will ever promise you.

"Today I come before you with nothing more than a hunch, an inkling, that sometime before the next class of Unwanteds arrives a few months from now—and yes, 'sometime' could mean next week or it could mean the day of the next Purge, but I rather think it will come somewhere in between—we will be discovered by the people of Quill." A wave of whispers passed from one end of the theater to the other.

"What will happen then, you may be asking. I do not have the answer. Perhaps nothing at all. But more likely the High Priest Justine and her governors will be so completely furious that they will stop at nothing to kill us all."

In the silence that followed, no one panicked. Each member of the crowd realized that they had been preparing for a day like this to come, and while nobody wanted it, everyone knew the purpose of Magical Warrior Training and the potential danger that faced them. And since most humans in the room had faced death once before, this was not as big a shock to them as it might have been.

"And so," Mr. Today continued, "today we begin preparing in earnest, and we shall be adding more group classes to help us better learn the benefits of fighting as warriors together, rather than as individuals, each with his own plan. We will be doubling our instruction in spell casting and offering you opportunities to create spells of your own. You'll have plenty of chances to practice in class.

"Please do keep in mind that while I do not wish to tell you how to fight, for we all have our different methods and emotions involved in this issue, it is my personal policy to use nonlethal weapons and creative ingenuity to fight. Some of you will feel that it is wrong to kill another person no matter the reason, no matter that they once tried to kill you. You will no doubt create other means to protect yourselves and those around you.

"Others of you still seethe with anger and spite for what the brainwashed people of Quill have done to you, and you will not hesitate to give them the same sentence that they once gave to you—or at least the sentence they didn't stop from happening. To you, I ask only that you begin now to consider your future actions and your motivations so that you are sure of your choices. I don't wish for anyone to live to regret a hasty decision for the rest of his life." Mr. Today lowered his head for a moment, and then went on in a strong voice.

"Be assured, my dear citizens, that it takes more than strength and intelligence to win a battle—it takes creativity and skill and common sense, and Artimé is brimming with it! Let's work together now, everyone, to maximize our ingenuity and skills. To grow strong and confident. To take on any challenge that comes our way with reason and with dignity.

"My greatest hope," he said in conclusion, "is that my hunch is incorrect. But if it is not, we shall be prepared." Mr. Today folded his fingers together and bowed his head slightly. The people of Artimé hesitated, and then rallied together in cheers and applause for their beloved leader.

In the ruckus no one seemed to notice Will Blair and Samheed sneaking away to the tubes.

Together in Action

Samheed was the last to arrive at the Library of Magical Art. He plopped down in the chair next to Lani, who leaned over a large, ornate book of spells, reading intently. Alex and Meghan worked together with colorful sheets of origami paper, first following directions they had received in their group warrior class, and then branching out a little. Alex was determined not only to catch up to the others in his private warrior lessons, but also to make something of a name for himself by creating a unique charm that actually worked and was useful.

"Cute," Samheed said sarcastically. He set his scripts on

LISA McMANN

the table in front of him and peered more closely at the three-dimensional paper animals that lay strewn about the table. He picked one up, a green dragon no bigger than the palm of his hand. "What are these supposed to do again?"

"That one doesn't seem to do anything," Meghan mused in a puzzled voice. "I can't figure it out. The thing just flies around in a circle and fizzes out. What good is that?"

Samheed tried throwing it like a paper airplane. And indeed, it circled around the table, flapped its wings a few times awkwardly, and crash-landed on the table. "What gives, Alex? Isn't this in your specialty?"

"I'm trying," Alex muttered. "I have a distinct disadvantage here, you realize."

"That old crutch," Samheed said. "You'll never catch up with that attitude."

Alex made a nasty face.

"Stop it, you two. We're supposed to work together, remember?" Meghan was growing exceedingly frustrated and cross.

Lani looked up, somewhat bewildered. "Oh, you're here," she said evenly to Samheed, but he was busy studying Alex as he worked. She glanced at Alex briefly and immediately buried herself back in her book.

Alex picked up the dragon and turned it around gently in his hands, mentally going over every precise folding instruction and matching it up to the proper fold of the dragon. He shook his head. "We have it folded properly," he said. "So why . . . ?"

Samheed furrowed his brow. "Well, it hasn't got any eyes," he said. "How's it supposed to see where to go without them?"

"That's the most ridiculous—," Alex began, and then stopped short. Begrudgingly, he withdrew a handful of colored pencils from his art case. "All right. Eyes." He expertly outlined two eyes and colored them in, giving the dragon deep yellow irises and large black pupils. "There—so he can see better at night," he said dryly.

He sent the dragon afloat once more, and it circled nearly the same as before. But this time, it landed gently on the table in front of Alex. It blinked once and looked up at the boy. "Oh, hello," Alex said to the dragon, and then looked back up at his friends. "That helped the landing, at least."

Meghan grinned. "He's adorable! I want to keep him."

Samheed rolled his eyes and snorted, bringing Lani back to awareness. She blinked, taking in the mess of papers and origami animals scattered about the table, and began to watch curiously as Alex started drawing on the dragon again.

"A tongue." His own tongue poked out the side of his mouth as he drew. "And flames, of course," he said when he'd added a bright orange burst inside the dragon's mouth. When he was finished, he sent the dragon flying again. It circled just as before, landed softly in front of Alex, and blew a flame from its mouth that singed the hair on Alex's arm. "Yeowch!" he cried.

Samheed and Meghan laughed as Alex shook his arm in surprise.

Lani, still watching, said with a bored look, "You have to tell him where to go, you dolt." She'd picked up that word down in the lounge from Earl, who used it liberally. "Or else he'll keep coming back to you."

Meghan slapped her hand to her forehead. "Ugh, that's it! Of course you're right, Lani."

"Mmm-hmm." Lani nodded absentmindedly as she engaged herself with her reading again.

Alex picked up the dragon again, looking around the library.

LISA McMANN

"Attack the statue!" he said, and sent the dragon through the air.

This time, the dragon flapped its wings and raced to the statue, streaking through the air so quickly that all the children could see was a green blur. It sent flames shooting brightly from its mouth when it made contact, hovering against the statue's body for a moment until the dragon itself exploded into a little ball of fire and dropped to the floor.

The statue, a grim-looking ostrich, opened its eyes and glared at Alex. "Do you *mind*?" the bird said.

"Oh—sorry," Alex said hastily. "I thought you were one of the, um, the nonliving ones."

"We're *all* alive, thank you very much. Some of us choose not to reveal that in front of bratty, unreliable, spell-casting children, however."

"I won't do it again," Alex said with a sheepish smile.

"Sure," muttered the ostrich. She stretched out her bent leg carefully, as if she'd held that position a very long time, and then limped off to take cover behind a tall bookshelf.

The dragon had, by now, burned up completely, leaving a small heap of ashes on the floor. Samheed went to pick them up and toss them in the waste can. "Not bad, Stowe," he said. "Can you make an army of them?"

"Sure, now that I know how," Alex said.

Meghan caught Alex's eye, then looked at Lani meaningfully.

"Oh!" Alex said. "Oh, I mean, thanks to Lani."

"Hmm?" Lani said, looking up, blinking her long lashes.

Alex held her gaze for a moment before he hurriedly looked away. "Hi. I mean, thanks. Never mind," he said, suddenly feeling terribly self-conscious. In the back of his mind he began to wonder when it was that Lani had stopped acting—and looking—like a little kid.

And then he noticed her book.

"What are you reading about?" he asked.

She turned the gilded page. "Killing spells," she said.

"Seriously? Wow." He tried to imagine Lani killing someone. He thought for a moment, and his eyes narrowed. "You're not going to practice on me, are you?"

Lani laughed. "Depends," she said. She didn't tell him that there weren't any actual spells in the book, just scholarly discussions on the topic written by people with names she'd never heard before. "I guess you'd better be nice to me."

Alex felt the heat rise to his face as Lani, grinning, watched him squirm. "Okay," he said lightly, and then he scrambled to pack up his things and disappeared.

Gaining Ground

By the end of the week all the students were ready to begin practicing their fighting skills. Team Warrior class was held on the lawn, and in addition to the hundred-or-so teen students were another hundred-or-so adults and instructors, including Sean Ranger and many other recent graduates. Leading the instruction that day was none other than Florence herself. The enormous ebony stone woman glided across the lawn so gracefully that the children had to remind themselves she was actually a very heavy statue. They kept their toes tucked in whenever she walked past, just in case.

"Students, line up with your backs to the water," she boomed. "Experts, take twenty paces and face the students."

Everyone moved to the requested locations. "Experts, prepare your defenses."

The experts held up rusty shields that looked to be similar to what the Quillitary might use if attacked.

"Where'd they get those?" Alex whispered to Samheed.

"Stole them, maybe?" Samheed guessed. "Or just made them in some class."

"Stole them? How?"

"I'm not saying anybody stole them," Samheed said impatiently. "I just figured somebody went invisible in the middle of the night to the Quillitary yard, made the shields invisible too, and snagged them. It's more likely we just made them here, though."

Florence cast a withering look at the two boys. "Students! Prepare to fire. Five rounds!"

Alex hurriedly pulled five newly created weapons from his pocket and stood ready. "How would anybody be able to get out of here, anyway?" he whispered again as Florence walked down the row to inspect the weapons. "Just open the gate?"

"Nah," Samheed said. "That wouldn't work. It's locked from the outside."

"What, then?"

"I don't know." Samheed sounded irritated. "Why are you asking me? I wouldn't know anything about it." He glanced uneasily around.

"Quiet!" thundered Florence. "Students, fire five rounds on the count of three."

Alex bit his lip and prepared his first origami dragon. When Florence called out, "Three!" Alex whispered to the dragon. "Attack enemy one."

He tossed the dragon a little too hard in his excitement. It stumbled in the air and got caught in a nosedive, unable to recover. It hit the ground, exploded into a small fire, and fizzled. "Blast it," Alex muttered, as Samheed's dragon hit its mark.

"There's art in the toss, Alex," Florence said.

Alex tried again as small explosions could be heard up and down the lawn, some hitting their marks, others missing quite horribly. His second try worked better, but still fell short of the expert twenty paces away. "Blast it!" Alex said again.

He gave up on origami and instead pulled out a splatterpaint brush. Holding on to the handle, he drew his arm back over his head and, with all his force, snapped his wrist, sending a shower of brown paint toward the expert across from him. When it hit its mark, the paint spread across the expert's shield and crept over her arm, and within seconds the woman's entire body was encased in a magical mold of splatterpaint. Indeed she quite looked like she was coated in a crisp chocolate shell, good enough to eat.

"Yes!" Alex cried out. The expert across from him stood frozen in place. Alex looked down the row as students tossed, pointed, and spoke artfully at the willing adults. He watched Lani project resounding words of destruction at her partner, and slowly the adult's face grew fearful. He began to sob, and soon he turned and ran away toward the jungle.

While Samheed offered random stage-direction orders, causing his partner to run this way and that, banging into other adults and knocking over Alex's stiff chocolaty partner, Meghan pulled out her piccolo and caused her partner to fall asleep. And so it went, all the way down the line.

Soon Florence clapped her hands. The sound was like thunder. All effects of the spells vanished immediately, and the experts got up from the ground or came back to their positions, good-natured grins on their faces. "Not bad, not bad," Florence said. "For the first time, anyway. We'll do a few more rounds. This time, students, please assist the other students around you once you have successfully rendered your expert defenseless. We are a team, and working together yields the greatest rewards with the least amount of energy." The statue glanced up and down both rows. "Try different spells this time," she said.

Lani pulled a handful of paper clips from her pocket. Meghan put her piccolo away and positioned herself to do a fire step. Samheed withdrew a long black ink pen from his vest, and Alex rolled a small ball of sculpting clay between his thumb and forefinger, ready to try his very own creation. At Florence's go they all attacked and, more confident now, all succeeded within the first three attempts. The experts were immobilized.

"We're amazing," Meghan said proudly, as her partner ran off shouting, his feet growing unbearably warm.

"Yes!" Alex said. His clay had formed handcuffs and bolted the wrists and ankles of his opponent to the ground.

"Not bad at all," said Lani as her partner wriggled to get

loose from the scatterclips, which had gone right through the shield and pinned the expert's clothing to a nearby tree. "You know, there are lethal ways to use lots of these ordinary spells," she whispered to Samheed, who was next to her. "I've been reading about them."

"I wish we could start learning them now," Samheed said impatiently, as Florence released the spells and once again the experts returned.

"Very good," Florence said. "One more round and we'll dismiss for the day. At our next class I want you all to return with magic spells of your own design. Nothing lethal, remember." She paused and gave the students a weighty look. "We'll save those for another time."

Samheed's stomach flipped with anticipation.

The Mostly Secret Hallway

After weeks of intensive warrior training, Alex was so exhausted that he fell into a deep sleep immediately after dinner. It was late at night when he awoke with a start, drenched in sweat. He had been dreaming again, that same dream about Aaron, but, as always, it turned nightmarish at the end when Alex looked back at his brother. Each time he dreamed it, Aaron transformed into the High Priest Justine, who cackled evilly and came at him with a rusted trident. Alex always woke up just before the high priest skewered him.

Whenever Alex woke from this unsettling nightmare, he

LISA McMANN

couldn't get back to sleep, so he took to roaming the halls or getting a snack from the kitchen, trying to forget it. Sometimes there were other people around, but generally very few except the nocturnal creatures spent their nights moving about.

It was on one of these occasions that Alex, feeling pleasantly full and the nightmare having been extinguished from his thoughts, decided to peer down the new hallway that had been beckoning to him for weeks.

He never saw anyone enter or exit it, and no one else seemed to notice it at all. Because of this, Alex didn't dare to explore it when others were around, or it would be painfully obvious that he'd be walking through what appeared to most students as a solid, mirrored wall.

Glancing over his shoulder to make sure no one was about, he slipped quietly into the hallway and tiptoed down it. This hallway was different from the others he'd been in. It was much shorter and wider. And rather than soft carpet under his feet, this floor was deep, shiny mahogany planks. There were pillars carved of the same wood, and warm-colored paintings on the walls, giving this hallway a most comfortable feel.

Alex passed two wide, arching doorways on either side, though the doors of those four rooms were closed tightly and gave no indication of what was inside. As he walked farther down the hallway, he approached an area that appeared to be a lounge of some sort, extending far beyond the width of the hall on either side. He stopped, unsure. Straight ahead, above a sofa, was an enormous window overlooking the lawn. Alex could see stars twinkling and the shadowy trees of the jungle in the distance. Ahead and to the right he could just see into an area of gadgets and gauges, a blackboard, a tube, and a kitchenette.

Ahead and to the left he saw what appeared to be an office with a desk. Alex couldn't tell whether someone occupied that room, but it looked fairly dark in there. He moved forward slowly, trying to get a better look. On a coatrack in the corner hung a multicolored robe very much like the robes Mr. Today often wore. Alex's heart quickened, for certainly this was Mr. Today's office, and certainly students were not meant to see it. Which made it all the more enticing.

He peered more closely and saw a display of blackboards lining the wall behind the desk. On them flashed different scenes, only Alex couldn't make out what the scenes were.

They all seemed quite dark, and after a moment Alex decided that they must be pictures of the outdoors.

His breath quickened as he crept closer. He looked over his shoulder again and, seeing no one, pushed ahead toward the room. Immediately he smacked hard into something, and with a loud twang he fell to the floor, his nose and forehead throbbing painfully. "Drat it," he said, rubbing his nose. "Yeowch."

When the sharp pain faded to dull, Alex sniffed and reached his hand out tentatively until it struck something cool and slick. "Glass," he muttered. "What a nasty trick." He followed the glass wall all around, finding to his dismay that it encased the entire width of the hallway and there was no way around it that would give him access to either of the open rooms that branched out, nor the comfy-looking lounge directly in front of him.

Gingerly holding the bridge of his aching nose, he slid as close as he could to Mr. Today's office, trying to get a better glimpse of the blackboards. "What in the . . . ," he said, completely puzzled.

"Well, well, Stowe. You've found your way here too?"

Alex jumped and crashed loudly against the glass again, only this time with his shoulder, thank goodness. He whirled around, sucking in a shocked breath, and his mouth fell open in surprise.

Samheed's
Second Secret

A lex let out his held breath and grinned shakily.

"What are you doing here?"

"I could ask you the same question."
Samheed stood tall a dozen feet away, a dark look on his face. "Did I scare you? You sure jumped a mile."

"Geez, Sam. Why'd you have to do that?" Alex straightened up and dusted off his pajamas, scowling.

"I made a little noise first, but you had your nose pressed so far into the glass I wasn't sure you'd have heard a tank even if it rolled right past you. So haven't you been here before?"

"Well, I've seen the hallway for a few weeks," he said,

remembering the first time he'd seen it, on the day of the governors' inspection. "But there are always people wandering around, so I haven't had a chance to go down it until tonight."

"It's better during the daytime," Samheed said.

"Why?"

"Because you can see Quill better."

"You . . . what?"

"And," Samheed continued, "sometimes the glass barrier is down."

"So you've gone in there? And what do you mean, you can see Quill better? Through that window?"

"No, not the window. And yes, I've been in there. Well . . . only twice. But those blackboards, which I'm guessing is what you were staring at, are really live pictures of Quill."

"Live . . . ?" Alex faltered.

"You know—they're like a picture of what's happening in Quill right now. Sort of like if you were looking out the window and seeing it."

"How do you know?"

Samheed looked smug. "I've seen things," he said. "The High

Priest Justine, the governors, the Quillitary making armor and weapons. And—" He stopped short and pressed his lips together.

"And what?"

"Nothing. Never mind. Just people walking around, the fields, the nursery, a few government buildings, the palace . . . that sort."

Alex turned around and peered into Mr. Today's office again. "Are you joking?"

"Listen, Stowe, I'm getting tired of you never believing a word I tell you. It's very irritating."

"Well," Alex said, "you haven't exactly been very trustworthy, have you?" But he was not in a mood to fight, and since Samheed ignored it, he turned his face back to the glass. It grew foggy under Alex's breath. "Have you ever seen . . . you know. Your parents or anything?" Alex's voice sounded light, like he probably wasn't really asking what Samheed knew he was asking, but both of them in that room knew better, though neither would say it.

"I've only been close enough twice to really see anything at all," Samheed said, as if that explained it.

Alex didn't quite dare to ask again.

Samheed glanced over his shoulder. "What are you doing up this late, anyway?"

"I—I had a nightmare," Alex said, his face flushing guiltily now, because this was the second time he'd thought of Aaron in two minutes. "Got some milk and a snack. Decided to finally give this hallway a try . . ." He trailed off. "What about you?"

Now it was Samheed's turn to blush. "My door won't let me in. I was just on my way down to the dining room so I could take the tube when I saw you."

Alex snorted. "What did you say to it this time?"

"I told it to stop being so stupid cheerful all the time because it was driving me insane."

"That would do it," Alex said. "I suppose you could use my tube."

"Thanks."

The two boys walked back toward the balcony, hushing their voices as they neared it, and peeked around the corners, being very careful no part of their bodies showed until they were quite sure no one was around. Then together they stepped out of the hallway.

"By the way, I've always wondered," Samheed said. "What's

actually on the wall where the secret hallway is?"

"It's a gigantic mirror," Alex said, remembering.

"Ah, well, that makes sense." They continued down the boys' hall. "One day when I was standing on the balcony waiting for Lani, she came out and immediately told me I had ink on my lip. I said, 'Where?' And she looked at me like I was stupid, pointed at the secret hallway, and said, 'Well, just look in the mirror, you dolt.'"

Alex laughed quietly. "So then what?"

"I looked at the clock and said, 'We're late!'"

Alex's door sang out an overly cheerful greeting as they approached. Samheed rolled his eyes but held his tongue as the door swung open. He looked around Alex's room for a moment before sliding into the tube. "Hey, Alex, if you want to check out the"—he glanced sideways at Clive—"thing, tomorrow's a good day for it. Lunchtime."

Alex nodded. "Thanks."

"But don't get your hopes up." Samheed narrowed his eyes, studying Alex's face for a moment, and then he disappeared.

Alex stood, looking at the empty space where Samheed had been. "It's too late for that," he said.

Defense

It was rare to see Lani without a book these days. She always seemed to be reading, whether at meals or walking across the lawn or through the mansion. And while she didn't usually bump into things while reading and walking, it happened that as she left the girls' hallway on her way to breakfast, someone sort of popped out of nowhere in front of her and she ran right into him. Her book flew out of her hands and sailed over the balcony railing, causing quite a stir down below.

"Hey—watch it, shrimp!" It was Will Blair.

Lani scrambled to her feet and peered over the railing.

"Sorry," she called out to the pedestrians down below, but those assaulted by the book had moved on by now. She turned back to Will, her eyes burning. "Why do you have to be so rude?"

Will, who was a wiry boy of sixteen, snarled. "Why do you have to be such a priss?"

Lani flounced off down the stairs in a huff. When she got to the bottom, she couldn't help but look over her shoulder to see if Will was following her, but in the stream of humans and creatures all heading down the stairs for breakfast, he had disappeared. Lani rolled her eyes and picked up her book, which someone had kindly set on a hallway table to keep it from being trampled, opened it up, and began reading again as she made her way to the dining room and joined the others at their usual table.

"You're late this morning," Meghan remarked as Lani sat down next to Samheed. Both Samheed and Alex were bleary-eyed from their nighttime escapade, and they ate in silence. But Meghan was as bright as ever.

"That Will Blair," Lani grumbled, "knocked me down and blamed it on me."

"Were you reading?" Meghan asked.

LISA McMANN

"Well, yes, but he came out of nowhere and I ran right into him."

Samheed paused his chewing, turned to look at Lani, swallowed, and said, "What do you mean, he came out of nowhere? Were you standing in front of the boys' hallway or something?"

"Well, that would be a stupid place to stand, wouldn't it? Don't you think I know better than that?" Lani rolled her eyes and grabbed a jelly-filled pastry from the basket at the center of the table.

"One never knows, with you," Samheed said, not very nicely. He looked at Alex, but Alex appeared to be lost in his own thoughts and not paying attention.

Lani's eyes flared, but she held her tongue. She still stung a little from Simber's whirlwind admonishment in the dining room several weeks before.

Meghan looked around. "Where is he? I don't see him."

"He never came down the stairs," Lani said, her mouth full of pastry.

"He's not as bad as you think," Samheed said. "He's just acting."

Both girls snorted raucously at that, bringing Alex out of his trance.

"Hmm? What's that?" Alex said. He checked the clock on the wall and downed the rest of his milk in one tremendous gulp.

"Oh, never mind," Lani said. She finished her pastry, wiped her mouth on her napkin, and pushed her chair back. "Let's go."

The Team Warrior classes had been extended to two hours each morning and afternoon on the lawn. Each day it seemed more and more adult Unwanteds and mansion creatures sat in, some to brush up their fighting skills and others to observe curiously what sorts of magical items the new Unwanteds were creating.

Today Florence had them all sit on the lawn, since the first part of class was to be a lecture. The four friends sat two in front of two, and they whispered together in their little square about the new magical items they'd brought. When everyone was seated, Claire Morning came forward.

"For our lecture today," Florence boomed, "we have Ms. Morning."

While the audience applauded politely, Meghan cheered

wildly, for the musical Ms. Morning was Meghan's favorite instructor.

Alex leaned over to Samheed. "If we get an hour's worth of music lessons, I think my head might explode."

"In that case, bring on the music," Samheed muttered.

Alex scowled to hide the sting. "Whatever." He couldn't figure Samheed out.

Lani shushed them both with pokes to their ribs as Ms. Morning began to speak.

"For the next four days we will be working on defensive skills," she said. "Defensive skills are crucial to Artiméans, for if we are ever at war, we will be fighting against people with weapons very different from ours."

Samheed grew somber as he remembered how he could have been an expert with the weapons of Quill by now. He jabbed Alex with his elbow and whispered, "Defense? We need to learn how to fight to kill. It's the only way we'll win against the Quillitary."

Alex furrowed his brows. "I . . . I don't know about that. . . ."

Ms. Morning continued. "Who can give me an example of a defensive skill?" She looked around at the group of students.

"Gentlemen?" she said pointedly to Alex and Samheed, who were still whispering.

"You guys got caught," Lani whispered merrily.

"And Lani," Ms. Morning added. "The three of you come up to the front, please."

Alex and Samheed snickered at Lani's look of surprise as they went up front to join the instructor.

"Lani, you'll be the enemy, standing back here with your weapons. No magic now from you, all right?"

Lani nodded and pretended to hold a weapon.

Ms. Morning turned to the boys, who were both a bit red-faced at being the center of attention. "At my command Lani will charge at you. You should have a variety of options in mind already about what to do. But remember right now we are simply doing defensive skills, so please don't attack her with a magical item. Any questions?"

"Yeah," Alex said. "What sorts of weapons does the Quillitary have, actually?"

"Excellent question. Who has the answer?"

"Knives," Samheed said. "Shields, too."

"Pieces of horrid, rusty metal," laughed someone.

LISA McMANN

"Oooh, and slingshots," someone else hooted.

"Sticks and stones . . . and insults," said another.

Some of the Artiméans didn't laugh at that last one.

"Guns," Lani said. The word rang out.

The crowd was still.

"Yes, some guns," Ms. Morning said seriously. "Though they are not terribly powerful, they can pack a punch."

"Most of them are BB or pellet guns," Lani said with an air of authority that some might have questioned, "that could possibly kill birds, rabbitkeys, even small beavopps. But the governors all have handguns. Those are deadly to humans and large creatures."

After a long, silent pause while the crowd looked at one another, Ms. Morning nodded. "Thank you, Ms. Haluki." She turned back to face the three. "Ready?"

Alex and Samheed had been staring at Lani, not having known about the governors' weapons, but now they both snapped their attention back to Ms. Morning. Lani faced her opponents, and the three of them nodded together. "Ready."

"Go!"

Lani charged toward the boys as Alex immediately whipped

a paintbrush from his pocket and waved it in front of himself, while Samheed whispered a chant.

In a matter of seconds Alex painted himself invisible, and Samheed jumped in the air and appeared to hang suspended, then shot off like lightning toward the jungle. Lani stopped short, aimed an imaginary pistol at Samheed, and whispered, "Bam." She turned, wondering if she still had a chance to find Alex. The audience murmured while Lani studied the lush grass in front of her.

She stalked five paces, feeling a bit silly now, having no idea which direction might be correct, when she saw two dents in the grass. She charged forward as the dents moved, and then she reached out and grabbed an invisible something. But it got loose and Lani could hear Alex cackling as he reached the hard footpath, leaving her no more clues as to his whereabouts. She shrugged at Ms. Morning. "I guess I give up," she said with a half grin.

The audience roared its applause for the demonstrators as Samheed returned at a gallop, Lani clapping too, until she felt a gentle hand on her shoulder. She turned and didn't see anyone.

"You were great," Alex whispered in her ear. Her hair

smelled like mangos. He squeezed her shoulder, and not really knowing why, other than the adrenaline of the chase, or the fear of the guns, or the amazing feeling of being invisible in front of all these people, or perhaps it was the contrast of her bright blue eyes and her shiny black hair, but Alex, feeling suddenly quite daring, pulled Lani a little closer and pressed his lips against her smooth cheek.

Lani froze. "What. Are you doing."

Alex chuckled softly as the audience began looking for him. "Gotta go," he said.

Lani blushed furiously as she felt Alex's hand leave her shoulder. She turned around so her back was to the crowd and pretended to look for him. But all she could think about was that the boy with the kind brown eyes that she'd met on the Quill bus, the boy that she'd pelted with spells trying to get his attention, the boy who rarely noticed her whenever Meghan was around—that boy had just kissed her, right on the cheek.

A moment later, as the crowd's applause died down and Samheed had gone back to his seat, the sound of an aerosol spray could be heard. Soon Alex, who had now sprayed himself with visible spray, was in full view again. He sauntered back to his place next to Samheed, a goofy little grin on his lips as the audience clapped once again. He glanced sidelong at Lani, giving her a sly wink as he sat back down.

Lani's face grew hot again. She turned her attention to Ms. Morning and, trying very hard to resist touching the warm spot on her cheek, pretended quite convincingly to be enraptured by the rest of the demonstrations and lessons.

A Glimpse of Quill

At the end of class Alex, whose mind was now occupied with things other than Lani, slipped away from the others as they headed to lunch. He bounded up the marble staircase and stepped cautiously into the secret hallway, making sure no one was around. And then he crept down the hall toward Mr. Today's office, knowing that the mage always had lunch with the students on Tuesdays.

When he got to the place where the glass wall had been, he put his hands out, determined not to run into it again, but as he inched forward, it became apparent that the wall was not in place. "There's a bonus," Alex whispered under his breath.

LISA McMANN

He slipped into the office, his ears tuned for any noise, and stared at the row of blackboards on the wall.

The three on the left showed various parts of Artimé, flashing from one scene to another every ten seconds or so. Alex waited until he saw the dining room, and noted that Mr. Today was walking about cheerfully, stopping and chatting at each table.

The remaining six blackboards showed moving views of Quill. Alex was horrified by how gray and desolate it looked— it was so much worse than he remembered. He watched each blackboard, intrigued. One blackboard showed repeating views of the four quadrants, where all the houses and farms stood. He strained to pick out his parents' house from the vast expanse of rows and columns, but the picture changed too quickly for him to even come close to finding it.

He moved on and watched the Quillitary grounds for a moment. Soldiers and officers walked about mechanically, their faces expressionless. Some of them worked on tanks and other vehicles, and others toiled in a windowless room filled with sheets of rusty metal and a few cutting tools. Still others painstakingly poured liquid from a dented tin pail into a vehicle's engine, careful not to spill a precious drop.

On the last two blackboards were flashing shots of government buildings and the palace of the High Priest Justine. Alex's heart fluttered as he recognized the university grounds on one blackboard, and he waited anxiously for the scene to change, hoping against hope that he'd catch a glimpse of Aaron. *Just to see him once*, he thought. *Just to know he's okay.*

While he saw many university students sitting rigidly at lunch, he didn't see his brother. Disappointed, he turned to the palace and watched with slitted eyes as the scene showed the governors in a small meeting room, and then it flashed to the high priest herself, alone in her office. Alex scowled and turned back to the university blackboard, which now flashed from the cafeteria to an empty dormitory room to a classroom.

Alex shook his head sadly. Not only did the scenes of Quill depress him, but they also made him feel like he was so close to actually seeing Aaron, which made the results more disappointing.

Just as he was about to turn away and go down to lunch, he took one last look at the university blackboard. And there, in the once-empty dormitory room, was a dark-haired boy just entering. Alex's heart leaped—was it him? *Turn and look this way*, he pleaded silently, but he knew instinctively, whether it was the way the boy slipped his jacket off, or the way he smoothed his Quillitary haircut just so, that it was Aaron.

Alex tugged nervously at his shirt collar as he watched his brother turn and hang up his jacket, almost as if he were reaching right through the wall to Alex. He touched his shaking fingers to the blackboard and gazed at Aaron. "So serious," Alex whispered.

And then the scene flipped to the cafeteria again. Alex snapped his head up and glanced nervously at the clock, knowing he needed to get out of there before Mr. Today showed up. But he couldn't go. Twenty seconds later the dormitory room scene returned, and now Aaron lay stretched out on his cot, staring at the ceiling, hands folded behind his head. To anyone else Aaron's face might appear expressionless. But to Alex, Aaron's face looked like a troubled sea.

When the scene changed, Alex forced himself to go, leaving a little piece of himself there with his brother. He wandered down to the dining room completely preoccupied with thoughts of Aaron. Why him? Why was Mr. Today watching Aaron's room, of all places? Could it possibly be a coincidence?

Alex didn't realize that he walked right past Ms. Octavia, who called out a greeting. And he didn't notice Lani stealing glances his way, her eyes growing more hurt each moment that he didn't acknowledge her. He also didn't see Mr. Today watching him closely, a look of grave concern on the man's face.

Alex moved about quite unaware of anyone for the rest of that day. The only thing he was painfully aware of was the single question that pounded rhythmically in his head.

How?

LISA McMANN

How

Meghan and Lani were already in the lounge, slouching on a long couch, their feet propped up on the coffee table, when Alex arrived. He had spent the past two days lost in thought, dying to know more about Aaron. He was having trouble sleeping, but when he did sleep, his dream was different. After being reminded of the stark hopelessness of Quill, he no longer wanted to go back at all. It would be safer, he thought, and wiser, to rescue Aaron and take him back to Artimé. And after a while Alex began to think that Mr. Today, who seemed to know a lot about everyone in Artimé, was probably watching Aaron because Aaron should have been an Unwanted too.

Alex grunted a greeting to the girls and yawned, wildly tired. He plopped down on the couch across from them and closed his eyes, wondering if Mr. Today knew that Aaron had drawn pictures in the dirt too.

It was another hot, dry summer in the quadrant when Alex and Aaron were ten. And that day was the kind where the dust clouded up at every step, hovered around your feet and covered your shoes and legs with a thin layer of grime no matter where you walked. But late that afternoon, as Alex and Aaron dug a hole in the tiny backyard in which to bury the week's worth of unusable scraps, it began to rain. The cracked earth swallowed up the water, and both Alex and Aaron were secretly glad for it, because it not only gave their household extra water for the week, but it also made the digging easier.

Alex had the shovel—he always did the hard part now, since he knew that he would be declared Unwanted.

Aaron stood next to him, holding the bucket of scraps

and pointing out the discrepancies in the way Alex was digging.

"That's not uniform size," Aaron said.

"It doesn't matter," grumbled Alex, and he lifted the heavy shovel out of the hole and set the blade in the mud. He leaned on the handle, taking a rest and letting the rain soften the hard ground.

"It does matter," Aaron said evenly.

Alex watched the rivulets of rainwater roll across the not-quite-level square of dirt that was their backyard. He lifted up his shovel and noticed the dent it had left. And then, using the blade of the shovel in different directions, he made a triangle. And attached to the bottom of the triangle a rectangle. "Look," he whispered. "It's our house."

"Stop or I'll report you."

"What's the sense in that?" Alex said logically. "I'm already Unwanted."

Aaron frowned, and then looked at the mud drawing, tilting his head this way and that. "What? I don't see. . . ."

"Not a real house," Alex sighed. "Don't you see that it looks like our house?"

LISA McMANN

The rain muted the edges of the drawing as Aaron shook his head, puzzled.

Alex glanced over his shoulder. There was no one in sight. He grabbed the food scraps bucket, picked out a chicken bone, and pushed the shovel toward Aaron. "Here, hold this. Now watch." Aaron took the shovel as Alex sank to his haunches and made a triangle with a rectangle attached to the bottom. "See?"

Aaron shifted his eyes uneasily. "It's . . . ," he said, but it was like he was thinking so hard about what he was seeing in the mud, and how he shouldn't be thinking about it at all, that he couldn't think and speak at the same time. He dropped down to his haunches too, almost as if being smaller would protect him. The shovel's handle rested along his damp neck and the collar of his now rain-soaked shirt.

Alex glanced sidelong at his brother. He twirled the bone between his fingers, and then held it out loosely in the palm of his hand toward Aaron. The rain splashed on his forearm, shattering the air.

Slowly Aaron peered over his shoulder this way and

LISA McMANN

207 « The Unwanteds

that, then slipped his hand over the once-innocent chicken bone, which now held the power to decide his future and his fate. And shakily he lowered it to the mud. With a light hand he tried to copy Alex's house, which had now melted and was gone.

Alex watched him for a moment, trying to keep from breathing too hard in excitement and fear, and then dumped the bucket of scraps in the hole and began to push the mud back over it with his shoe to fill it.

Aaron, entranced, wiped the mud clean with his left hand and drew another house with his right. This one had almost begun to look like something when the boys heard the squelch of footsteps behind them.

"Boys," said the deep, cold voice of Mr. Stowe. The man stepped forward as Aaron wildly tossed the bone toward the hole and turned on his haunches to face his father, the shovel in his hand.

Alex stared at the bone, which had landed near his feet, and stopped pushing the mud into the hole, knowing that hiding the evidence wouldn't help his case at all. He turned around slowly, the empty bucket swinging in his hand as hard drops of rain pounded against it.

Mr. Stowe stared hard at the ground, where Aaron's house was slowly melting away. He looked at Aaron, then at Alex, then back to Aaron again. "Alex," he said to Aaron, "give your brother the shovel and come with me," he said in a horribly quiet voice.

Aaron's eyes grew wild, and then he controlled himself. He handed the shovel to Alex and followed his father to the house.

"And Aaron," Mr. Stowe said, not realizing he was actually talking to Alex, "finish up your brother's work."

What Mr. Stowe didn't see as he walked into the house was the leap of hope and the pleading glance to play along that Aaron shot to Alex over his shoulder. Nor did he see the returned look of disbelief, followed by a cool shrug of indifference from Alex, the already Unwanted. Alex turned his back on his brother, and, using the shovel as he always did, he slowly, methodically, filled in the hole.

» » « «

LISA McMANN

It was the slurping of the ice cream malts through straws that woke Alex. He opened his eyes, staring at an unfamiliar ceiling, trying to figure out where he was.

"Have a nice nap?" Meghan grinned.

Alex sat up and shook the sleep from his brain. "Yeah," he said, "actually, I did. I haven't been sleeping very well the last few nights." He rubbed his eyes. "Where's Sam?"

Meghan shrugged. "Library, maybe?"

Lani stared at the wall and didn't say anything at all.

"Lani?" Alex said. "Are you okay?"

Lani stared at the wall and said even less than nothing, if that were possible.

Meghan raised her eyebrow. "Hmm," she said. "What'd you do now, Alex?"

"I swear, I—nothing!"

Lani slurped on the dregs of her milk shake. Loudly.

Meghan looked back and forth between the two and slowly, uneasily, got up from the couch. "I'm . . . going to go find out where Samheed is," she said carefully. "I'll be right back." She hurried over to Earl, glancing back occasionally over her shoulder.

"Lani, I—"

Lani sat up and faced Alex, silencing him with her glare. She breathed evenly three or four deep breaths, her eyes flaring. Finally she spoke. "You don't just kiss a girl on the cheek and then ignore her for three days."

Alex's jaw dropped. He flushed bright red.

"Don't do it again."

"Uhh . . ." Alex whispered an oath under his breath and put his burning face in his hands, trying to think of something to say. Finally he sighed deeply, looked up, and gave Lani a helpless look.

"I said, don't do it again." Lani's voice was growing louder.

"Okay! Okay, I won't. I'm . . . sorry. I'm . . . wait a second." He tipped his head to the side. "You mean, don't . . . you know. The first thing? Or don't, um, ignore you?"

Meghan sidled back over to them, clearing her throat loudly as she approached.

Lani rolled her eyes at Alex and smiled brightly at Meghan. "Is Samheed coming down tonight?"

"Maybe later, he said. He's working on some art project in

the library with Will Blair." Both girls sneered at the mention of Will's name.

Alex sat very still, not quite sure if he was allowed to speak. And not needing to, as it turned out, since Meghan and Lani were both suddenly quite chatty.

"So, what's he working on?"

"It's some sort of drawing thing. Threety, I think he called it? Alex, you know what threety is?"

Alex cleared his throat. "Uh, what?"

Lani tilted her head. "Do you mean 3-D? Like, three-dimensional?"

"Yeah, that's it, I think. It's like he's trying to draw a closet door on the wall of his room, but it would be a 3-D doorway that led to a room you could actually go in and out of. He was thinking of it as a defensive spell—a place to hide, I guess."

"How would you keep others from coming in it once you're inside, though?" Alex asked, intrigued.

"That's what I was wondering," Meghan said. "Only Mr. Today can do that."

Lani whipped her hair behind her ear and rummaged through

her book bag. "Hold on a minute," she said. "I know I read something . . ."

Alex thought Lani's ear was just about perfect. He thought about how he'd whispered into that very same ear right before he'd kissed her, and he blushed again.

Meghan, eyeing Alex, rolled her eyes. *Ahh, now I know what's going on*, she thought. *Geez*. She coughed lightly. "I'm still trying to figure out how Simber and Florence got into the theater that one time. They're way too big to fit in the tube, and that's the only way in there."

Lani pulled out a book. "Oh, that's not too tough, Meg. I wondered the same thing. In fact Alex could probably make that happen better than either of us or Samheed."

"Who, me?"

"You're the artist, Alex," Lani said. She smiled; all traces of the earlier fire in her eyes were now extinguished.

"I don't see how that gets Simber and Florence to fit in the tube," he said. "What, did Ms. Octavia sketch 3-D pictures of them and put the picture in the tube?"

"No," Lani said, her eyes dancing now as she paged through her book. "No, it's much simpler than that."

Meghan sat up, intrigued.

Alex's brain started churning, trying desperately to come up with the answer before Lani read it, as if they were playing a game of trivia. "Let me guess," he said. "Hold on—I'm thinking." He squinched his eyes shut, picturing what elements were needed. "Okay . . . ," he said.

"Well?" Lani jiggled the book on her lap, her finger holding the place.

"She drew a bigger tube in 3-D." Alex said.

Lani blinked. "No." Lani watched Alex's shoulders fall in defeat, thinking about it. "But I think that would work too," she said thoughtfully. "Good one, Al."

Meghan frowned. "Well, what did she do, then?"

Lani smiled. "Picture the theater. Back where Simber and Florence were standing. What was right behind them? I'll give you a hint—there's something the theater has that this lounge doesn't have."

Alex looked up. "Doors," he said, puzzling. "Huge ones. But nobody ever uses them—they're just painted on for aesthetics, right?"

Meghan blinked.

Alex tapped his chin.

"Oooh," they said together. Lani grinned.

"But I still don't see . . . ," Meghan began.

Alex's eyes lit up. "So, if Ms. Octavia, or anyone good enough to draw in 3-D, painted the same set of theater doors somewhere else in the mansion, Simber and Florence could simply push them open and walk right into the theater, through those painted doors, without using the tube. Right?"

"Exactly!" cried Lani. "Just as if they were walking through any real door."

Meghan's clouded face began to clear. "But . . . why have the tubes at all, then?"

"Think about it—all those doors that would have to be painted in everybody's rooms—there would be no room for them all! We'd have to move our beds around to get to them. And this way," Lani said slyly, "Simber can't get into the lounge."

Alex sat up, his stomach twisting. "So, a 3-D magical drawing of any real doorway, anywhere in the world, would lead you into that room? No matter where you are, or where the doorway is?" He leaned forward, holding his breath.

"Yes!" Lani said. "Isn't that cool? But they're really hard to

LISA McMANN

paint. I can't understand why Samheed would think he could draw a closet of defense in a hurry—it would take hours. Days, maybe."

Alex's mind whirled. *All I have to do is learn to paint in 3-D,* he thought.

"Wow!" said Meghan. "I'm going to go tell Sam anyway. Maybe it'll help with their project." She went over to the tube and disappeared, leaving Alex and Lani quite alone in their corner of the lounge.

Alex looked up and cleared his throat. "You're really smart, Lani."

Now it was Lani's turn to blush. "Yeah," she said. "I like to read."

Alex glanced at her latest spell book. "Do you have any advanced spell books? Not like the history of killing spells like you were reading the other day at breakfast. But, like, ones with . . . with lethal spell components actually written in them?" He almost whispered the last part.

"No," Lani said.

"Oh."

"Why?"

Alex remembered what Ms. Octavia had told him about the scatterclips spell. And he thought that if he ever came across the High Priest Justine in a real battle, he wouldn't hesitate to kill her. "No reason, I guess. I mean . . ."

"Well," Lani said, "if I find one, do you want to know about it?"

"Yes. I mean, I guess so. It wouldn't hurt." Alex looked down at the carpet for a long time. "So, um, about that other thing, with the kiss?"

Lani blushed hard. "I think you're smart enough to know what I meant."

He bit his bottom lip, and then leaned forward, elbows on his knees, peering at her, remembering when they first met. "Hi," he said softly. "I'm Alex. It'll go quickly."

Lani blinked at him, surprised that he remembered that first day. "Lani," she said. "And no, it won't." They both smiled at the grim memory.

"Do you—," they both said at the same time, and laughed. "You first," said Lani.

"Do you ever think about them? Your father? Your family?" Alex asked.

LISA McMANN

Lani's eyes hardened. "Never. Only my younger brother, who Mr. Today promised me he'd try and save."

Alex regarded her thoughtfully. "Mr. Today can do that?"

"I guess he can try. He told me he helps the High Priest Justine decide who the Unwanteds will be. He said when my father wanted to send me to the Purge before I was thirteen, he helped convince Justine to do it." Her eyes clouded.

"Wow," Alex said, a bit shocked. "I didn't know. Mr. Today must have really wanted you here. . . ." He trailed off, lost in thought.

"And my father must have really wanted to get rid of me." She shrugged off the hurt. "What about you? Do you think about your parents or your brother?"

He was quiet for a long moment. "No," he said, finally. "I never think about them at all."

Windows
and Doors

One day per month the first-year students met as a group and visited various instructors for their Magical Warrior Training. It enabled them to perfect new spells based on the instructor's specialty, thereby rounding out their arsenals.

In Ms. Morning's class they had learned singing charms that could lull their targets to sleep or make them weep and collapse in misery. They had also learned slash singing, which would cause an enemy to tear himself to shreds. They each whittled a small pipe instrument that, when played, would cause the enemy to go insane. Meghan had a variety of other instruments she kept in her arsenal as well, but most of them were too difficult for those less musical to learn properly.

Mr. Appleblossom had spent his day teaching slam poetry and stunning soliloquies to the students. Both required an ability to think on one's feet, for the words uttered had to fit the situation. For example, if there was an attacker in a vehicle, one could aim an explosive slam at the tires to make them blow up, and then follow up with a singeing slam to the driver, setting his hair on fire. Lani was especially good at slams. And Samheed excelled in soliloquies—not just stunning kinds, but opposite soliloquies as well, which would make the enemy do the opposite of what he'd intended to do. Samheed planned to use that one a lot, should they go to battle. He felt that if he could get several opposite soliloquies going at once, he could make his foes turn their weapons on themselves.

Today's lesson was with Ms. Octavia, and Alex arrived in her classroom feeling chipper, despite having dreamed about Aaron yet again during the night. But he tried to push it aside and focus on the class, for Ms. Octavia was going to let Alex introduce a new spell he had created. She said he could teach everyone how to cast it. After all he'd done to catch up to the

LISA McMANN

others, Alex was proud to have this chance to prove that he had succeeded.

When all the students had arrived, Ms. Octavia called Alex to the front of the room.

"Alex, tell us about your spell," she said.

From the pocket of his component vest Alex pulled out two tiny balls of clay. He rolled them between his fingers to warm them up as he sauntered to the front of the class. "The new spell I created is called trapping clay. You aim it at the arms, legs, or neck you wish to trap, and it hardens immediately upon impact, trapping the target in place." Alex hid a wicked grin and called Lani up to be the victim.

Lani flashed him a suspicious look, but slowly made her way to the front.

"A larger ball of trapping clay can encase an entire person. Like this," he said. He picked up a larger ball, wound his arm back, and said, "Full body cast!" He flung the clay at Lani.

"No!" she squeaked, but it was too late. The clay found its mark and spread to cover her entire body, sticking her to the bulletin board. "Alex!" came a muffled cry from inside, followed by a reluctant, hollow chuckle. "I guess I deserved that."

The students laughed. Alex smiled. Revenge, at last. After a moment, though, he tapped on the hard shell cast and released the spell. Lani took a deep breath of fresh air and punched Alex playfully in the arm. "You got me," she said. "Clever."

Alex blushed. "You took that awfully well."

"That's my way of making you feel bad."

"It's working," Alex admitted. "Okay, everybody," he said to the class. "Give it a try, if you can find a willing partner. You can call out 'shackles' if you just want to chain somebody's arms and legs, or," he said, and his eyes lit up, "'dog collar' is a fun one too."

They spent the morning trying out the trapping clay, and after lunch Ms. Octavia gave them a painting lesson to calm them all down. Each student sat with his own easel and practiced defensive painting, which would allow them to quickly paint themselves out of any precarious situation.

Alex was already a professional at defensive painting, so he went to the corner of the room where he kept his easel. He picked up where he'd left off the previous day.

"May I join you back in your little corner, Alex?" Lani asked.

Alex looked at her suspiciously. "Is this a trick?"

"No. Don't be a jerk."

Alex tilted his head and narrowed his eyes. "You have a suspicious history, Ms. Haluki."

Lani rolled her eyes. "In case you haven't noticed, I haven't done anything to you in positively months. I'm done. Okay? Get over it."

"Hmm. I guess that's true." Alex was quiet. He turned back to his artwork and began daubing thoughtfully with his brush.

"What are you painting?"

"A window," he said. He shrugged in the direction of the nearest open window. "That one, there."

"Why?"

"I'm practicing my 3-D art. If I do this right, by the time I'm finished, I should be able to tear this sheet off, stick it to the wall, and put my arm straight through it to the outside."

"Cool," Lani said. "Is it hard to do?"

"Very," muttered Alex. "I haven't been able to do it yet."

"Why do you want to make a 3-D window, anyway?"

"I don't. Windows are just easier than doors. Ms. Octavia told me to start with this. I've been trying for weeks, and it's getting really boring. But I think this one might work. You

LISA McMANN

really need to shade and layer and get all the colors and textures right."

"So why do you want to make a door? Where do you want to go that you can't use the tube to get to?" Lani shook her head slightly, puzzled.

"Oh, I dunno," he said lightly.

Lani narrowed her eyes. She put her paintbrush down and gripped Alex's arm. "You want to go to Quill, don't you?" she whispered. "Why would you do that, Alex? You're going to wreck everything!"

"Shhh!" Alex said when Ms. Octavia glanced in their direction. "I don't want to wreck everything. Don't be ridiculous."

"You want to see your brother! Oh, Alex, why? He's not like us! He's evil!"

"Keep your voice down! Sheesh, Lani. Aaron is not evil. He's exactly like us. He did artistic stuff too—only I took the blame for it. He should be here!"

"It's not right! You'll put Artimé in danger. What are you thinking, Alex?" Lani shook her head in disgust. "It's too late for him. Maybe he should have been here too, but it's too late. Did you tell Mr. Today about him?"

"No! And you'd better not either."

Lani sighed and slumped in her chair. "Please don't do it, Al."

Alex sighed too and stared at his painting of the window, shaking his head. Then, he ripped it off the easel and tore it into little pieces, disgusted. "At the rate I'm going, you have nothing to worry about." He sighed and rested his head on the window ledge.

When he looked up through the glass, he saw Will Blair walking across the lawn in the distance. Will stopped and stood for a moment; then he turned toward Ms. Octavia's classroom, raised his hand impatiently, and pointed to the library. Alex's stomach clenched. Why would Will Blair want Alex to meet him at the library? Alex turned quickly to see if anybody else saw, but Lani and the rest of the class were focused on their work. All except for Samheed, that is, who stood at an easel at the back of the class, looking out the window. He nodded, his face serious. Then he packed up his things quietly, and when Ms. Octavia was involved with another student, Samheed slipped out of the room.

The Library

After several visits to Mr. Today's office, Alex had Aaron's dorm room door memorized, right down to the knots and scratches in the wood.

Every evening, as Alex worked privately in his bedroom to perfect a 3-D doorway to Aaron's room so he could save him, he couldn't stop thinking about Will and Samheed sneaking off to the library. They did it at odd times, sometimes during assemblies and sometimes during large group training. Sometimes late in the evening. Once, Alex tried to follow them, but when he tubed into the library, they had disappeared. What could they possibly be working on? At first

Alex didn't care—he was just glad that Will hadn't actually been gesturing to him that time in Ms. Octavia's room. But he grew more curious as his long, lonely nights of drawing and painting wore on with no one but Clive to talk to.

And Clive wasn't making life easy for Alex, either.

"What are you doing in there?" Clive would ask every ten minutes or so. He obviously hated that Alex worked in the cramped sleeping area between the bed and the wall, rather than out in the open living room where Clive could actually see for himself what was going on. And ever since the "episode," as Clive liked to call it, he hadn't left Alex alone.

"I'm not doing anything!" Alex would always say, growing more exasperated all the time with his nosy blackboard. "Leave me alone, will you?"

"No-o," sang Clive cheerily.

After one such episode Alex, frustrated, rolled up his paper, tucked it under his arm, and stormed out of his room, as stormy as one can be when entering a tube and pushing a button. He didn't want to give Clive the satisfaction of knowing where he was storming off to, so he pressed lounge, and then when he got to the lounge, he stayed in the tube and pressed library instead.

Out of the corner of his eye he saw Meghan and Lani at a table having milk shakes, but then he was gone again.

Inside the library he roamed to all of his usual work-stations, but all the big tables were occupied, and he needed a big table to spread out his 3-D drawing. He moved to the seldom-used stairwell and walked, rather than tubed, up to the second floor and then, seeing more stairs, up to the third, where he'd never been before. In fact there was no button for the third floor in the tube—he'd only thought there were two floors all this time. There was an old-looking sign that said ARCHIVES on the stairwell wall next to the door. Alex went in. It was dark inside, but little lights popped up as he trav-eled down the rows of books, charts, and maps. It smelled musty and old. His stomach flipped as the door clanked shut, and he ran back to make sure he wasn't locked in. He wasn't. With a sigh of relief he meandered between the shelves to a large table in the back corner, perfect for what Alex needed. His rolled-up doorway drawing bumped a seven-foot-tall tiki totem pole statue with three stacked faces. The middle face opened an eye, scowled, and then closed its eye again.

"Sorry," Alex whispered. He unrolled his paper and, when

he spread it out, said, "I wish there was more light." The table lit up with a bluish-white light that shone through the paper. Alex, surprised, looked at his drawing, each line now feeling very individual and defined, the blueness of the bright light pointing out the flaws that had kept the drawing from working the way it was supposed to work.

Alex whistled under his breath as parts of the drawing deepened before his eyes.

Inevitable

Mr. Today looked away from the long row of blackboards when he heard a growl outside his office. "Come in, Simber," he said. "Florence, welcome."

A moment later Claire Morning and Ms. Octavia arrived, and the group arranged itself comfortably around the large office. Simber sprawled on the floor, Florence eased into a sturdy-looking, grotesquely oversized floral love seat as if it had been fashioned just for her, and the two instructors sat in office chairs near Mr. Today's desk.

The mage shuffled papers on his desk and set them aside,

then looked up at his guests. "Thank you for coming," he said. "Simber, what news?"

"Alex has discoverrred this hallway," Simber began. "He's been herrre thrrree times, as farrr as I know frrrom my view at the doorrr. Once with the boy Samheed, late at night. Twice durrring Tuesday lunches."

Mr. Today nodded. "What about Will Blair?"

"I haven't seen Blairrr, but he could be using an invisibility spell to enterrr, now."

"Thank you, Simber. Octavia?"

"All seems well with Alex. Still melancholy, but such is the life of a painter. He's working on three-dimensional paintings."

"What sort?"

"Windows and doorways, that sort of thing. Quite ambitious." Octavia looked over her half-glasses and down her long snout.

"Hmm," Mr. Today said. "How close is he to getting it right?"

"Not terribly close, but he's getting better. It's a very difficult procedure, as you well know."

Florence cleared her throat. "I've spoken to the girrinos down at the gate. Arija says the Blair boy is acting suspiciously.

LISA McMANN

He's been to the gate twice in the past week. And the ostrich statue in the library reports that Blair has convinced young Samheed to help him on an art project."

"Samheed's working with Blair?" Mr. Today asked, a hint of concern in his voice.

Florence shrugged her massive shoulders. "Looks that way."

Claire interrupted. "What is Will Blair's issue? I'm afraid I don't quite understand."

"It's a bit complicated," Mr. Today said. "You see, Blair's father is the general of the Quillitary. Blair's been bitter since he arrived here three years ago, because if he had been Wanted, he'd naturally be sitting in Aaron's place right now by default of his heritage. Will has gotten more bitter since he discovered Aaron has clearly 'stolen' his seat of honor." Mr. Today pointed to the blackboard of the palace. There, in the High Priest Justine's own private office, sat Aaron, in earnest discussion with the ruler of Quill herself. "Aaron's made quite a name for himself. Gunnar reports the boy has just been appointed assistant secretary to the high priest. No one so young has ever held so high a position."

Mr. Today turned back to face the group. "Will is extremely

jealous, seething so hard he no longer sees things as they are, but as he wants them to be. When he reunited with Samheed, his former neighbor and friend, they began to talk about Quill. Will found out that Aaron was the one who reported Samheed's infraction, which put Will over the edge. He's become obsessed with watching this screen, watching Aaron in the palace having lunch with the High Priest Justine and with Will's own father, General Blair himself."

The room was silent for a moment before Claire spoke. "So he wants revenge on Aaron?"

"Yes."

"How?"

Mr. Today pursed his lips. "That, I do not yet know."

"Shouldn't we try and stop him? Can we?"

"Yes, we can stop him. You know we *can*," Mr. Today said carefully.

Claire shook her head. "I also know we won't."

"That's correct."

"But—why?" Claire sighed impatiently. "When we have the means to stop him—to stop *both* Will and Alex! Before Quill discovers and ruins Artimé. Before they put us all in danger.

Some of us are sure to be killed! Everything will change. Everything."

Mr. Today bowed his head into his hands and said nothing. His shock of white hair pointed at the wall behind his friends.

After a moment Simber responded in an uncharacteristically soft purr. "Because, Clairrre. Because neitherrr boy has brrroken the law. Because we don't punish bad ideas, orrr thoughts, orrr intentions. Because the moment we do, that's the moment ourrr worrrld takes its firrrst step towarrrd becoming like Quill."

"But if it's for our own good and safety—"

"Claire," Mr. Today said quietly, "once we start interfering with free thought, where do we stop? Believe me, I've been down this road."

"But you know yourself that you can protect our world without a war at all! You could wipe out the entire land of Quill and we could be safe forever, if you just choose to stop it."

The mage smiled sadly. "And you know, Claire, that I will not be around forever to protect Artimé from what's beyond Quill. Each person here must have something at stake in order to take ownership of our land. If our people have nothing to sacrifice, nothing to protect, what will happen to Artimé when I am gone?"

The office was stifled in heavy silence.

"Then what do we do?" Claire said, finally.

Mr. Today scratched his chin. "We prepare. And who knows, maybe something good will come of it." He took a deep breath. "Florence, have you begun the lethal-weapon training?"

"Yes."

"Very good. I want everyone to have the knowledge and ability, whether they choose to use it or not. Claire, find Gunnar in the forest and ask him to come see me. Simber, keep a close eye on Will Blair and Samheed. I'll put up a shimmer shield in the entrance to this hallway so you can tell if someone invisible walks through it."

"And the boy . . . hmm . . ." Mr. Today thought out loud. "Yes. I'll take care of Alex myself." He clasped his hands together and met the solemn eyes of his comrades. "All right, then. Let's be as ready as possible, shall we?"

Together each person, statue, and creature in the room nodded.

The Eliminators

early every night when his eyes and hand gave out from working on the doorway, Alex agonized over Aaron. "How?" he asked himself over and over after weeks of failure to produce a doorway that would lead him to his brother's dormitory room—or anywhere, for that matter. He shook his head. "I know I can rescue you. But how do I get to you? There's got to be another way."

One night Alex had had all the tossing and turning he could stand. He left his room, walked down the stairs, past the two statues, who both nodded civilly, and went outside

LISA McMANN

for a walk to clear his mind. He didn't see Simber and Florence exchange a glance, nor did he see Simber leap nimbly from his pedestal and pad up the stairs to the mage's private quarters.

Alex roamed along the seashore, and then, instead of going into the jungle, he turned back and walked diagonally in a direction almost no one cared to go because of the awful memories that accompanied it—to the giant iron gate. In the light from the stars Alex could make out the shadowy figures of the four girrinos, keeping guard as they did endlessly, seemingly without rest.

Alex cleared his throat.

"We see you, Mr. Blair," one said in a pleasant voice. "You may approach without fear."

Alex bit his bottom lip and stepped out of the shadows. "Hi—I'm, um, not Will Blair," he said, not knowing quite what else to say. "I'm Alex Stowe."

"Oh, so you are," said one whose name was Tina. "Look, ladies, a new one has come to face his fears."

The girrinos smiled. The one named Arija asked, "What brings you here tonight, Alex? Can't sleep? Feeling wonky?"

"How—how did you know?" Alex could feel the ground shiver just slightly as two of them sat down hard and turned their attention back to the door.

"We rarely get visitors. When we do, it's usually for one of two reasons. Most often someone comes to face the iron door in hopes of seeing it in a different light, from the good side of things, and thereby casting out the horrid memories of Quill."

"Does it work?"

"For some, yes."

"What's the other reason?" Alex asked presently, hoping the ladies couldn't read his mind.

Arija blinked her milky chocolate eyes solemnly. "To escape."

Alex's heart throttled, but he held his expression firm. "Oh. That seems strange," he said. His voice sounded a wee bit thin in his ears, so he tried to breathe in using his diaphragm, like Ms. Morning had taught them in choir. "I didn't think the door would work as a way out. Isn't it locked from the other side? And who would want to escape to that awful place?"

Tina grinned, her teeth like glowing rectangles in the starlight. "Right on both counts, Alex. He's a clever one, isn't he, Arija?"

"Indeed." Arija nodded. "There are two ways out of Quill, but only magical ways to get back in—we can't open the gate from our side. Unless, of course, someone from the other side unlocks it."

Alex furrowed his brow. "Two ways out of Quill? What's the second? We were told the only way out was through elimination—through this gate."

"Well, of course you were *told* that, my boy. I don't think even the governors know about the other way. And if they did, they wouldn't tell the people of Quill," said Tina.

Arija gave Tina a stern look. "Don't tease the boy, Tina. How would he know?" She turned back to Alex. "There's a secret passage from the palace to beyond the walls that the High Priest Justine and Marcus created long ago, when Justine took over the rule of the land. As far as the high priest knows, Marcus is the only other person in Quill who is aware of it."

Alex's eyes widened. "But . . . the palace," he said, thinking. "What lies beyond it? Where does the passage lead? To the great forest? To enemy territory?"

"Why . . . ," Tina began. "To the sea, of course!"

"What?" Alex asked, incredulous. "But what about the threat of the borderlands? The Quillitary? That blasted barbed-wire ceiling that protects the entire land from intruders?"

Arija stepped over to the boy. "There, now, dear," she said, and sort of nuzzled his shoulder comfortingly, as if Alex were her own son, until Alex had quite calmed down. "I'm afraid it's all a ruse to control the actions of the people of Quill." She sighed. "The land of Quill—and Artimé, attached—is an island. It's one in a chain of islands. We once traded goods with other lands, but that was before Justine had the walls constructed, I'm told."

Alex shook his head, defeated. "I can't believe it. Why would they lie to us?" he whispered. "What about the old people? Don't they remember?"

Arija shook her head, her black, silky fur catching the starlight. "No, Alex. They were made to forget."

"What, you mean . . ."

"Magic."

Alex stood there, blown away by what he was hearing.

Magic? In Quill? He shook his head in shock. "But . . . who? Who would do such an awful thing, taking people's memories?"

The ladies were silent, and then suddenly they stood at attention, peering into the shadows beyond Alex.

"Me," said a voice from the dark.

On a Dark Night

C ome, walk with me," Mr. Today said, stepping out of the shadows. "We have a lot to talk about."

Alex froze. He felt now like he had felt every time he'd been discovered committing an infraction back in Quill. His heart sank as he turned around slowly, only to find a grim look on Mr. Today's face. *Caught.*

Mr. Today waved to the girrinos and began walking across the lawn toward the mansion. He didn't appear worried that Alex would follow, and it was Mr. Today's nonchalance that compelled Alex to tag along after him rather than run away or hide. Alex hurried through the grass and caught up to the mage's brisk pace.

"It's a gorgeous night." Mr. Today breathed deeply the salty air. "I should remember to come out more often at this hour. I love the sound of the sea in the dark, when all the other creatures are quiet, don't you?"

Alex swallowed hard. "Yes," he said. And then, because it sounded funny, that word hanging out there alone, he added like a dutiful student, "It's sort of musical. Like a new kind of instrument."

"Indeed!" Mr. Today said approvingly. "My, but you've come a long way in almost a year. Can you see it in yourself, my boy?"

Alex was quiet for a moment, pleasantly confused by the turn in events, but a little suspicious all the same. "I suppose I can, sir."

"Of course you can." The old mage stopped at the shore and looked out over the sea. "Have you discovered Claire's boat in the lagoon?" he asked. "She's a real beauty."

Alex squinched his eyes shut. "Um, y-yes." Was that the right answer? Alex wasn't sure.

"One day we'll go for a cruise, maybe to one of the neighboring islands with whom we used to trade goods. I've been wanting to go back for years," Mr. Today said, almost as if to himself. "But I imagine they had hard feelings when we cut off our communications with them. . . . I wonder if anyone there would remember me." And then he roused himself from his thoughts and turned sharply, back toward the mansion. "But first we have some business to take care of."

Alex stumbled after him. "We—we do?"

Mr. Today reached the walkway, climbed the steps, opened the mansion door with a sweeping gesture, and ushered Alex inside. "To my office," he said.

"Your office?" Alex blushed as he entered the mansion. "Um, I guess I don't know where—"

Simber cocked his head at Alex and growled.

Mr. Today held up his hand and chuckled. "No need, Simber. The boy needs his dignity."

Alex stumbled up the staircase as his face burned. Without another word Mr. Today nimbly took the stairs two at a time and walked into the secret hallway. Alex hesitated, turned and looked down at Simber, and realized how stupid he had been to think no one had ever seen him go in. Simber grinned cheekily at the boy.

Alex shook his head and followed Mr. Today. "I'm such a dolt," he said.

Mr. Today laughed, and then held out a finger at the glass shield. It shimmered, splashed to the floor, and disappeared. "We all have our moments, my boy. Come, have a seat."

"Thank you," Alex said. He sat down heavily in one of the office chairs and tried with all his might not to stare at the blackboards above Mr. Today's head.

Mr. Today looked at Alex. "Let's be honest with each other, shall we?"

Alex blinked. "Okay . . ."

"Do you miss your brother?"

Alex stared. His heart quickened. "No."

Mr. Today regarded Alex for a moment. Then he turned toward the blackboard. "Alex," he said, "is it true that your brother was creative like you?"

Alex blinked. "Well, he did try to draw once." Alex remembered the time in the backyard when it rained.

"What happened?"

"My father got us mixed up. He thought Aaron was me—I was always the troublemaker, and it was pouring rain, and we're identical. It was a simple mistake," Alex said. He felt like he had to defend his father.

"And Aaron went along with it. He let you get written up for his infraction?"

Alex shifted uncomfortably. "Mr. Today, I'd already had several infractions. I knew I'd be Unwanted. One more infraction wouldn't have made a difference to me."

"And one would have made a difference for Aaron."

Alex's eyes teared up. "Yes—I mean, no. I mean . . . it's all so confusing."

Mr. Today leaned forward. "You would have done anything for him. That's the way it is with twins, isn't it?"

Alex nodded, not trusting himself to speak. Finally, he whispered, "I wish I hadn't."

"Because then he might be here, is that it?"

"Yes."

"Alex, you did a noble thing, thinking you were saving him. Believe me, I understand. And I think very highly of you for it."

Alex swallowed hard and looked at his lap.

Mr. Today shuffled some papers on his desk, and then stood. "Come. I'll walk you back."

Alex got to his feet and followed Mr. Today to the hallway.

"So, Alex," Mr. Today said, taking on a lighter tone, "How are your studies now that you're in training? All going well?" But he seemed to be searching for something deeper.

Alex thought of the dreams. The doorway. His heart ached at the thought of never seeing Aaron again. Finally he looked up at Mr. Today. "Everything's really going great. I like it here."

Mr. Today gazed at Alex as they walked, his face indecipherable. After a moment he smiled sadly. "Good," he said. "I'm very glad of that."

LISA McMANN

Where There's a Will

Where are you going?" Lani demanded, tapping her foot loudly near the library tubes, making several creatures, students, and statues scowl in her direction. "You're always sneaking around these days."

"I'm busy," Alex said.

"With what?"

"Um . . . spells. Lethal stuff. That reminds me," he said, trying desperately to think of a way to change the subject so that Lani would leave him alone—he was *so close* to finishing his doorway. "I really want to know what the incantation is for turning scatterclips lethal. Any idea?"

Lani cocked her head. "I don't know."

"Well, can you find out? I'd like to learn that one. I mean, not because I'll ever use it. I mean just in case."

Lani's eyes widened. "You mean you'd kill someone, if it came to that?"

"I'm not saying that."

"I think you are."

Alex shrugged. "Only if I had to. I don't ever want to kill anybody."

Lani was silent. She turned. "I'll see what I can find out," she said, wandering off into the rows and rows of books.

When she was out of sight, Alex slipped through the doorway to the stairwell and bounded up the steps to the third floor. He peered into the window, saw that all was dark, and went inside. Then he tiptoed back to his table to finally finish up his painting.

Before an hour had passed, he made a final stroke with his brush and stood back. The door practically grew thicker on the table, it looked so realistic. Alex grinned, certain this time it would work. He gazed at it a little longer and felt a thrill run through him as he thought about finally seeing his brother again. He glanced around, wondering if he could find a free wall in the library, but all the walls were covered with bookshelves. So he rolled it up carefully and packed up his brushes and pencils.

As he grabbed his backpack, he heard the creak of the door. Two voices spoke in hushed sounds. One of them Alex recognized. It was Samheed.

Immediately Alex tensed; then he silently took his things and stepped behind a shelf, his back up against it, facing the tiki totem pole. His breath came in a shallow, quiet flow and his skin erupted with goose bumps, and he cursed himself for not having an invisibility paintbrush with him. He could hear the two, louder now that the door had closed, settling in at a table near the front. Alex was trapped. He crept closer so he could hear them better and see them through the space between shelves.

"The hinges are all wrong. See there?" Samheed said, pointing to a door eerily similar to the one Alex had finally just perfected.

"I know! I'm trying," Will said crossly. "This isn't exactly my area of expertise."

"Let me try."

"You've tried and you can't do it either. Just be quiet. I'm concentrating."

"I could ask Alex," Samheed said.

Will laughed out loud. "Sam, you are even stupider than you look. Alex is being extremely helpful from afar already. Involving him would wreck everything. You know yourself how much he still thinks of his fink of a brother."

Samheed's eyes narrowed, but he said nothing for a moment. He pulled out a chair and sat backward on it. "Yeah, maybe I am stupid, because I don't get why you even want to go back there. I mean, sure, you can scare the skivvies off Aaron Stowe for taking your spot with the governors, but what good will that do? You'll expose Artimé, and we'll have to fight."

Will tossed his pencil, frustrated. "Look. I don't plan on anybody finding out who I really am, okay? At least not at first—not with my theatrical disguise, courtesy of your loser friend Alex and my incredible magical abilities. And believe me, when I get done with Aaron, he won't be able to tell a soul."

Alex sucked in a breath, and he nearly lost his grip on his 3-D door.

Samheed looked up as if he'd heard something, but then turned back to Will. "What do you mean? Are you going to kill him or something?" He laughed nervously.

Will Blair just shook his head and scowled. He picked up his pencil again and started working on the door.

"Seriously, Will," Samheed said when Will didn't answer. His voice grew quiet. "Are you planning to kill him?"

"I prefer the term 'eliminate,'" Will said, snarling. "You have a problem with that? Or do I have to get rid of you, too?"

Samheed's face turned green in the eerie blue light from the table. "No," he whispered. "Of course not."

Alex's heart and mind raced. How on earth was he going to get out of here, get to Aaron in time to warn him? He could only hope that Will wasn't close enough to finishing the doorway tonight before they packed up, or there would be serious problems. If he could only get to his bedroom! But no, stupid Clive would know what he was up to if he disappeared from the bedroom, and no doubt he would alert Mr. Today. Alex couldn't risk that. Where else could Alex go that no one would see him?

He slid down to the floor to sit the night out, and when he did so, his shoe crumpled the very edge of his rolled up doorway drawing.

"Did you hear something?" Samheed asked quietly.

"No."

"I think I heard something."

"So go make yourself useful and check it out, then."

Alex put a hand over his mouth and nose, as if to silence his own breath. He froze, and willed Samheed to think it was nothing.

Samheed was silent a moment, and then he got up and slowly walked through the dusky library. He rounded a row of shelves, and Alex could hear him just on the other side of the row he leaned against. He nearly exploded in fear. *No, no, no,* he kept repeating in his head. *Please, no.*

Samheed rounded the corner by the totem pole statue and stopped in his tracks when he caught sight of Alex. His eyes grew wide, scared at first, and then they narrowed. Alex, tensed and ready to run for it, silently pleaded with Samheed. Samheed stood completely still; the two boys' eyes locked on each other.

"Anything over there?" Will called.

The totem statue behind Samheed yawned in triplicate. And then it cleared its throats.

"Just a statue," said Samheed. "It's nothing." He glared at Alex for another moment, and then he turned and went back to his table.

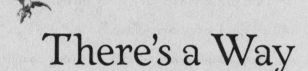

There's a Way

Alex's body ached from sitting so still in one place. He felt like a swarm of bees was trapped inside his head, thoughts going every which way. Will Blair was planning to kill Aaron—not only kill him, but actually *become* the likeness of Aaron using his theatrical spells—so that no one in Quill would know the difference. How on earth was Alex going to save his brother? He just had to get out of there!

Hours passed, with both Will and Samheed working on different parts of the door frame. Finally Samheed stretched, groaned, and said, "Can we just call it a night? We're not going to finish."

LISA McMANN

"I'm almost done. See? See how the top of the frame is rising up off the table a bit? We just need to get the rest of it perfect."

"It took us all night just to get that part done! I'm finished with this for today. I'm going to bed."

"Fine, go," Will said. "If you say anything about my plan, I will kill you. I'm not even joking."

"Okay, okay," Samheed said. His voice sounded hollow. "Relax. I'm with you."

Will stabbed his pencil into the paper and ripped a tiny hole in it. "Blast it!" he roared. "This is so frustrating!" He stood up and ran his fingers through his hair, and then began pacing around the table.

Alex froze, though he was pretty sure he no longer had control over his cramped lower half.

"All right," said Will, still pacing, but calming down. "All right. Tomorrow we're finishing it."

"Tomorrow. Good," Samheed said. He glared in the direction of Alex, but Alex could no longer see them.

They rolled the drawing and packed up their art supplies. "Back here tomorrow after lunch. We can skip training."

"But—"

"Look, Samheed, don't be an idiot. We need to get this done before the old geezer finds us out. You're making it really clear why you don't belong in the Quillitary, with all your blubbering."

"Shut it," muttered Samheed.

"What?"

"Nothing! Sheesh." Samheed fumed in silence. He slammed his chair into the library table and walked out without waiting for Will. A moment later Will followed, snickering to himself.

Alex sat for five more agonizing minutes, then slowly rose to his feet, feeling the blood rushing to his legs as they prickled mercilessly.

"Thank you," he said quietly to the statue.

The top face opened its eyes and stared at Alex. Then it nodded and went back to sleep.

When he could walk without tripping, Alex grabbed his drawing and hurried down the stairwell, avoiding the tube for fear of getting stopped by Lani. He ran around the mansion to the front entrance, where neither statue was in its usual place, and up the stairs to his room.

Samheed stood in front of Alex's door, glaring. "What did you hear?" he whispered.

Alex, breathing hard, said, "Nothing. I couldn't—hear anything. Too far."

Samheed regarded Alex, almost quivering in anger. "You're lucky I didn't tell Will."

Alex nodded wildly. "I know. I know. Thank you. You really—saved me. Thank you."

Samheed seemed to relax a little bit. "Nothing's going on," he said. "Right?"

"Right!" Alex said. "I mean, what? What are we talking about?" He gave an anxious laugh.

Samheed rolled his eyes and turned away, walked to his room, and disappeared inside.

Realizing that going inside his own room to paste up the door painting would only make Clive start asking questions, and knowing that Samheed was safe in his room, and presumably Will was too, and remembering that Simber and Florence were both out doing other things at the moment rather than standing there to spy on him, Alex looked down at his drawing and realized he knew the perfect place to put it up in secret at this time of night.

He bit his lip, checked his vest for scatterclips, and then walked nonchalantly down the boys' hallway, leaned over the balcony (still no statues below), and slipped down the secret hallway to Mr. Today's dark office. The glass shield was down, and all was dark.

Once inside the office he unrolled the door and held it against the wall, pinning it with the scatterclips. After he placed the last pin, he stepped back and watched as the door and frame grew thick and real before his eyes.

Alex hiccupped randomly and gave a shaky laugh, totally giddy and frightened that he was actually, finally, able to go see— and save—his twin. He wiped his sweaty hands on his pants, and then reached out for the doorknob, turned it, and pushed it open. He lifted his foot over the small threshold created by the space between the painting and the floor, and stepped through the opening into a dark dormitory room.

Together Again

Alex glanced over his shoulder as he pushed the 3-D door closed behind him. This door was identical to Aaron's regular door that led into the dormitory hallway—the two doors now stood side by side like twins. Alex wondered what would happen if the 3-D drawing were removed from Mr. Today's office wall. Would the magical door disappear? For a brief moment Alex felt claustrophobic. What if he couldn't get back to Artimé? He shuddered and waited for his eyes to adjust completely to the dim moonlight.

There was no way Alex could do this without scaring

Aaron—he knew that. Alex stood next to the bed, his stomach flipping, knees shaking. At first Alex tried to will Aaron awake, but that didn't work. Aaron's chest rose and fell rhythmically.

"Aaron," Alex whispered. "It's me."

The boy didn't stir.

Alex closed his eyes and breathed in a shaky breath, and then blew it out slowly and opened his eyes again. He stepped closer and touched Aaron's arm. "Aaron," he said a little louder. "Aaron. It's me, Alex."

Aaron sucked in a breath and rolled to his side. His eyes opened. Blinked.

"Aaron, wake up. It's me. It's . . . it's Alex."

Aaron reared up wildly, scrambling on his backside. He let out a shout. "Who's there?"

Alex cringed. "Shhh! Aaron, it's Alex."

Aaron's mouth fell open, a look of intense fear on his face. "No! Leave me alone!"

"What?"

Aaron blinked and scooted to the far corner of his bed, his face anguished. "Stop torturing me!"

"Aaron, please—keep your voice down before you wake

the whole dormitory. Listen, I know you're scared."

Aaron's eyes narrowed. "I'm not afraid of a dream. Alex is dead. Leave me alone." He spat out the words.

This was not the way Alex had thought the conversation would go. He hadn't known what to expect, but whatever it was, it wasn't this.

"Aaron." Alex sighed. He looked around the room in the dark, his eyes having adjusted now, and found a lamp. He lit it, and a low light filled the room. "I'm not dead. I came back to rescue you."

Aaron was silent, staring. His jaw quivered as he regained control of his emotions, and soon his face took on the old familiar serious look. His voice, controlled and cold. "You have three minutes to explain yourself before I call the guards," he said.

Alex's mouth fell open. "You're jok—," he began to say, and then he realized where he was, and that of course Aaron wasn't joking. Aaron wouldn't even know the meaning of the word. Alex closed his mouth and sighed. "Aaron, it's me, Alex. Your brother. Your twin. I'm not dead. But you will be soon if you don't listen to me. If you don't come with me. Please."

"What are you talking about? How did you get in here?"

That cold voice. Emotion was completely gone from his brother's face now. Aaron wasn't glad to see Alex. Alex's heart began to crack.

"You'd better explain."

Alex bit his lip. *Get it together.* "Aaron, please . . ." Alex couldn't help it. He reached out his hand. "Haven't you missed me? Not even a little?" Hot tears sprang to Alex's eyes. "Blast it!" He squeezed his eyes shut and turned his head away so Aaron wouldn't see, and then sank down to sit on the edge of Aaron's bed. He took a deep, shuddering breath and let it out again. "I miss you," he whispered.

Aaron's face softened, the tiniest bit. "Alex," he said, "if you aren't a dream, where have you been hiding all this time? Did you escape from the Eliminators? How could you survive this long? This is impossible."

Alex knew he had to do this right. It was his only chance. He turned back toward his brother when he had composed himself, and he spoke evenly, like he had done when he lived in Quill. "If I tell you, you must promise me you won't tell anyone."

LISA McMANN

Aaron narrowed his eyes. He was quiet for a moment. "All right."

"I live in a secret world. A wonderful, magical world of art and creativity."

Aaron stared. "Now I know for sure that I'm dreaming."

"It's a world very different from Quill. We have fun there. We paint and draw and listen to music. . . ."

"I have no idea what you are talking about. Or what you want from me."

"I want you to be with me, Aaron. Remember when we made houses in the mud with the bone? Do you? That's called drawing. You loved it, I could tell! But you were too good . . . too good to admit it, even to yourself."

Something flashed across Aaron's face and disappeared into a frown. "I had no infractions." His voice was cold again.

"You are like me, Aaron, whether you believe it or not. If you come with me right now, I will show you."

"Come with you *where*?"

"To my home in Artimé, where we will keep you safe."

"Safe from *what*? And who is 'we'?"

"We are the Unwanteds. And safe from General Blair's

son, Will, who wants to kill you and take your place."

Aaron sat for a long minute, then turned toward the wall, lay down, and closed his eyes. "Will Blair is dead. He was Unwanted three years ago."

"Aaron?"

"Stop torturing me. I am not allowed to be having all these dreams. I'm not the one who killed you—it's not *my* fault you couldn't follow the law. Now go away and never come back."

"Aaron, don't be an idiot. I'm not a dream. See?" Alex hauled off and punched Aaron in the shoulder.

"Great cats!" said Aaron. "What did you do that for?"

"To prove to you that I'm real and alive and sitting here. Why do you keep thinking I'm a dream? Have you been having the dream too? The one where we are together again, and I show you magic?"

"No," Aaron said too quickly. "I have forgotten all about you. You are dead. We don't remember the dead."

Alex stared into Aaron's eyes. "I'm not dead. And I am happy, for the first time in my life. You have no idea how happy you can be if you just come with me."

"I don't want to be happy. Happy causes infractions. I want

to be intelligent and strong. And I am. I am Wanted, assistant secretary to the High Priest Justine! Now, get off my bed, Unwanted."

"In Artimé there are no laws like in Quill. No infractions. And there, everybody has skills and talent. Everyone. You would too!" Alex felt the tears coming back again, and this time he cried openly, shoving the tears off his face as fast as they fell. "Quill is an evil place, Aaron. The High Priest Justine and the governors are telling you lies! And soon you will be killed, and I will be so sad." Alex leaned over and hugged his brother's stiff body. "I know you don't understand yet. But I'm already so sad for you." He stood up. "Will Blair is coming. He'll enter Quill and kill you. The only warning you have is mine. Please, Aaron. Please come."

Aaron sat up and shook his head. "No. Now go."

Finally, dejected, Alex convinced himself he would get nowhere with Aaron, so he turned to leave. Aaron got out of bed and stood. "Why should I believe you?" he asked, his voice dull and even. "And where did that extra door come from?" he muttered, rubbing his eyes now.

Alex turned back to face his brother, memories flooding

back to his mind. The tears poured freely down his face now, but he was not ashamed. He was proud. Proud to live in a world where people could express their feelings. "Why should you believe me?" he repeated. "Why should *you* believe *me*?" Alex's voice turned raspy. "I should be the one to ask that of you, after all you've done—you reported Samheed, didn't you?"

Aaron's eyes flickered.

Alex watched Aaron carefully. And for the first time in his life he saw the depth of the chilling hardness in Aaron's eyes. Alex broke into a cold sweat as new thoughts, new realizations surfaced. He whispered, "You reported me, too." It was not a question. For Alex there was no question anymore. He stared at his brother, forcing Aaron to either hold his gaze or look away.

Aaron's eyes filled with contempt. "Get out of my sight, you filthy, useless Unwanted." He spat the words out like icicles. "I did my duty. You failed. I hold no blame for anyone else's failures—not yours, not Samheed's, not that Ranger girl, and especially not the general's son. You are all deserving of your horrible fate."

There was a terrible pause, the identical twins standing face-to-face in the tiny dormitory room, Aaron's jaw squared harshly, his nostrils flared, and his dark eyes as lifeless as marbles, while his mirror image absorbed the insults, his deep chocolate eyes changing from anger, to hurt, to pity.

Alex spoke quietly. "You're right about one thing. We are all deserving. Thank you," he said. "You did us all a great favor."

And with that, Alex turned to the magical door and stumbled blindly through it, into the brightly lit office of Mr. Today, before the shuddering, angry sobs broke loose.

And then large, warm arms enveloped him, the arms of the mage himself, who held Alex tightly and let him snivel on his robe and then patted his back, saying, "There, there," until Alex could stop sobbing long enough to speak.

He looked at Mr. Today, all of the secrets of the past several months dancing around him, and he knew there was no way to lie around this mess.

"I'm sorry, sir," Alex whispered.

Mr. Today nodded. "I know, my boy. I know. Let's hear everything about it now, all right?" He patted a chair and urged Alex to sit, and then he moved behind the desk and sat as well.

They stayed for a moment in contemplative silence. And then the 3-D door creaked open once again, and a disheveled, dark-haired boy with eyes as round as saucers peered into Mr. Today's office.

The Visitor

Mr. Today and Alex looked up at the noise.

"Good evening," Mr. Today said, standing up rather abruptly. He flicked his wrist, and the blackboards on the wall behind him went dead. "Do come in. Care for tea?"

Aaron nearly turned around and slammed the door, but he hesitated, looking from his brother to the stranger with him. "Who are you?" he asked in a disdainful voice.

"I am commonly known to the people of Quill as the Death Farmer," Mr. Today said. "And this is my office. Please," he urged again. "Come in."

"Yes," echoed Alex in a hollow voice. "Come in, Aaron. No one will harm you."

"Why should I trust you?" Aaron's eyes were slits.

Alex looked away as his own eyes burned. *After all I've done for you, you still will not trust me.* He shook his head. "I'll get the tea."

"Mind you, don't have it sent up through *that* tube," Mr. Today said lightly. "There's a kettle on the stove in the kitchenette."

Alex nodded and walked across the hallway to the small kitchen. He glanced at the tube in the corner of the room but stayed well away from it. By the time he returned to Mr. Today's office with a tray, Aaron had stepped into the office, but he had kept the door ajar and his hand on the frame. He looked like he'd seen a ghost, and that was exactly how he felt, too.

Mr. Today invited him to sit, but Aaron shook his head.

"Well, then," Mr. Today said, taking over the conversation, for which Alex was very grateful. "I expect you want to know what this world is all about. The door onto which you are hanging for dear life is magical, as is this world you have entered.

As you can see," Mr. Today said as he poured tea and added several sugars to his own, "your brother, Alex, is not dead. He is very much alive, and quite happy, I presume. He misses you dreadfully.

"Though," Mr. Today continued as an afterthought, "it appears to me you've been quite horrible to him at times. But we'll reserve judgment, won't we, Alex?"

"Of course," Alex said softly. After nearly a year in Artimé, and facing his twin on Alex's own turf, Alex felt self-conscious and could think of nothing more to say. He remembered his own immersion into this world, and was glad now for the fairly ordinary office environment Aaron was taking in. Perhaps this would help Aaron ease into it more slowly.

Aaron glanced suspiciously from Mr. Today to Alex and back to Mr. Today again. "What do you want from me?"

Mr. Today chuckled. "Good heavens, we want nothing that you have, Aaron. But I suppose we could offer you sanctuary, so to speak. A new life, if you want it."

Alex added, "And safety from Will Blair, who wants to kill you." He glanced at Mr. Today, who raised an eyebrow at Alex. "It's true, Mr. Today. I heard him talking. He and"—Alex hesitated, and then went on—"he and Samheed. They're making a door too, like I did, and they've almost got it done. Will is going to use magic to look like Aaron and then kill Aaron and dispose of him so that no one knows what happened, and then he's going to take Aaron's place. Though I'm not sure Samheed knew all that before today," he said.

Mr. Today listened with interest and concern, and then looked back at Aaron and shrugged. "Sounds horrifying. I'd listen to your brother, if I were you," he said. "Additionally, I worry about you getting very uncomfortable standing there by that door forever. You won't get to see the grounds that way. Plus, Will Blair will find you easily enough if we leave that door up."

Aaron shook his head. "I can't even understand what you are saying."

Alex, in spite of the dire situation, could not hide the small smile that tugged at the corner of his mouth. "I know how you feel, Aaron. None of us could understand a thing until we saw it for ourselves."

"None of you could?" Aaron asked. "How many of you are there?"

273 « The Unwanteds

LISA McMANN

Alex glanced at Mr. Today, wondering how much information he should give to Aaron. Mr. Today nodded and smiled. "I'm not fond of secrets. You may tell him everything you wish to, Alex."

Alex took a deep breath. "I don't know where to start." He sighed and looked into his brother's eyes, searching for anything but the cold hardness that had filled them only moments before. "We are the Unwanteds," he began. "Hundreds of us. And this is the magical world called Artimé."

Aaron the Wanted could hardly believe his eyes or ears. Every moment he stood there, he felt more and more overwhelmed. This office was far more beautiful than even the High Priest Justine's. Everything looked shiny and new. Magic? Spells and art and all sorts of other words Aaron had never heard before? His brother certainly seemed convinced about the Will Blair character, and the old man seemed to believe him, but Aaron wasn't buying it. Still, he wondered if all of this could be true. And slowly he realized that if it were true, if all the Unwanteds were truly here, and he had been the one to discover them, he would be greatly rewarded by the High Priest Justine.

It all was too crazy to be true.

It was likely the craziest dream he'd ever had.

And he didn't like it one bit. These dreams were getting way out of control. After what felt like an hour or more, Aaron grew tired of standing by the doorway.

"Come on, Aaron, let me show you Mr. Today's mansion," Alex said.

Aaron looked at his brother and felt a small blip of something deep inside, but within a moment it was gone. "No. I've got an early appointment at the palace," he said brusquely.

Alex gripped the edge of the desk. "What?"

"I follow the law, and I do my duties. You'll never learn that, will you?"

"But—but—," Alex sputtered. "But you should stay here! You'll be safe here. Don't you understand what we're trying to tell you?"

Aaron stared at Alex, and the identical twins stood motionless, facing each other. Finally Aaron spoke. "I have never understood you, and I never will. Please leave me alone."

And with that, Aaron swiveled around and pushed open the 3-D door, stumbled a bit on the unnatural threshold that was made by the painting not quite reaching the floor, and slammed the door behind him.

Alex smashed his hand down on Mr. Today's desk. "No!"

Broken Ties

I'm sorry, sir. I—I made such a mess of everything," Alex said as he dropped into a chair. Mr. Today snapped his wrist again, and the scenes reappeared on the blackboards behind his desk. They watched Aaron shake his head and flip the light out on the blackboard that showed his room.

The old man sat behind the desk and pressed a finger to his lips, looking disappointed and perhaps angry, but saying nothing, as if he were waiting to hear more.

"I mean . . . what was I thinking? I've ruined everything." A look of pure agony washed over Alex's face as he realized the extent of the trouble he had created. "Oh," he groaned, "I should have talked to you, or Ms. Octavia, or someone. But I was so sure I could convince him to come, and that would be that, you know? Quill would wonder where he went, but they'd never guess. . . . Then I just found out tonight what Will was planning to do, and, well, I went a little crazy. I had to beat him to Aaron, and I didn't think . . . I didn't think it through. I mean, he's close, Mr. Today—really close." He rubbed his temples and let his head sink back in the chair. "And I know I shouldn't have done it. I just was so sure. I mean, we're twins! I know him. Or at least . . . I thought I did. I really thought I had him there. For a split second there was just a flicker of something—like he wanted to believe me. But back when I was in his room, he said—he said—" Alex relayed the entire conversation, starting from the beginning.

Mr. Today just listened and waited for Alex to finish. The look on his face changed as the story came out.

"And you know what?" Alex asked. "He's right. He did his duty to Quill, and I failed. And now I failed to do my duty for you, too." Alex slumped back in his chair, miserable.

They sat in silence for a moment.

"Are you quite finished?" Mr. Today asked kindly. "I don't wish to interrupt until you've gotten it all out. Every last nasty bit."

Alex looked up. "He reported me. It was him, way back when we were nine. He was already turning people in back then. Not just me. Meghan, Samheed, and Will Blair, too. I never knew anything could hurt like this."

Mr. Today nodded. "I know. You weren't the only ones. He turned in a great deal more than that."

"He did?"

"Yes. Every year before the Purge I meet with Justine and go over the reports. Aaron has had his sights set on the palace for some time now."

Alex shook his head sadly. "All this time," he said. "I had no idea. Why didn't you tell me?"

"Because it's hurtful. And you wouldn't have believed me. I guess you needed to see it for yourself." Mr. Today sighed. "And once I saw the door and figured out what had happened, I, too, hoped you might have been able to change his mind. Alas." Then his face brightened a little. "I'm glad

279 « The Unwanteds

LISA McMANN

to have *you* here, though. Aren't you glad to be here?"

"Yes," said Alex. "But it still just kills me—how could he be so horrible? How could he be so evil without me knowing it? He was my closest . . . my closest everything! And I feel so stupid. I should have known, back in the mud. . . ." He sighed. "And what happens now?" His voice grew fearful.

"We'll never know until it happens," Mr. Today said. "But it's likely that Aaron will report having seen you, even though he promised he wouldn't. And it's likely that Will Blair will succeed eventually in getting his door finished. Which one of them acts first . . . only time will tell."

"I'm really sorry."

"Come now, Alex. Let's be done with the apologies," Mr. Today said. "Let me tell you, my boy. I admit to holding out the slightest hope for the twin connection in getting him to stay here, once he walked in the door. I've witnessed that power before. But I should have known better. . . ." Mr. Today trailed off, deep in thought, and it was quiet in the room for several minutes.

Alex, who was completely spent, drifted off to sleep in the chair during the silence, but he startled awake when he heard a growl at the door. Standing there was a most enormous gray wolf.

"Hello, Marcus. Claire said you wanted to see me?" The wolf's gravelly voice was as deep as a bassoon.

Mr. Today rose to his feet and smiled warmly. "Gunnar. How good of you to come. I'm sure you recognize Alex Stowe. Alex, this is Gunnar. You may have seen him a time or two on your treks through the jungle."

"I—yes," Alex said, remembering. He was a bit nervous having the wolf so close, but he swallowed his fear and said, his voice shaking only a little, "It's nice to meet you."

The wolf nodded politely. "Marcus, is everything all right with . . . the children?" The wolf's bright blue eyes shifted toward Alex briefly, and he left the rest of his question unasked.

Mr. Today looked puzzled, and then his face brightened. "Oh! Oh, yes, quite fine. No, I wanted to speak with you about matters of Quill, which continue to change by the minute. Aaron Stowe knows of our existence now. Do what you can to keep him in sight. I fear he'll share the knowledge with Justine within days, if not immediately."

LISA McMANN

The great wolf nodded. Alex lowered his head, feeling fully responsible for it.

"And a favor, if I may," Mr. Today said.

"Of course."

"I think you should alert the jungle creatures to what's happening. If we should come to war, I will surely offer my protection for those that wish it. But if any feel inclined to fight with us . . ." Mr. Today's voice was humble. "I would be grateful for their help if it comes to that. Would you let them know?"

The wolf regarded Mr. Today thoughtfully. "It would be better, I think," he said carefully, "for them to hear it from one of their own, rather than from me."

Mr. Today tapped his lips. "So it would," he murmured. "I'll speak to Arija." He roused himself briskly and nodded, then pulled the 3-D painting from the wall. He rolled it up swiftly and touched one end, and an iron band with a lock grew around it, holding it firmly closed. Mr. Today put it in a cupboard near the door and locked that as well. Alex knew it was for the best, but it was hard to see all those hours of work get locked up in a cupboard.

"You should probably do that immediately," the wolf said.

He glanced out the big picture window in the lounge just outside Mr. Today's office.

Alex followed his gaze and saw it was nearly dawn. He yawned despite his best intentions, but it had been a long and sleepless night.

"Very well," Mr. Today said. "Alex, perhaps you'd like to catch a few hours of sleep before training begins?"

Alex jumped. "Oh—yeah, of course."

"I must go as well," Gunnar said.

Mr. Today smiled and followed the two into the hallway. Gunnar kept walking across the lounge, past the small kitchen, and into the room where all sorts of monitors and gadgets whirred softly. He hoisted himself on his hind legs and stood in the tube in the corner.

"Take care, Gunnar," Mr. Today said.

"You also." Gunnar's body shimmered and blurred before it disappeared.

Alex blinked and rubbed his eyes, not quite sure what he had just seen. "There's a tube to the jungle?"

Mr. Today put his hand on the boy's shoulder as they walked down the hall toward the balcony. "No," he said.

"That tube is quite different from any other. Please don't ever use it. It goes places you wouldn't want to go." He turned around, pointed to the ceiling, and murmured, "Glass." Liquid glass shimmered down and froze into place, sealing the area.

"Mr. Today," Alex said, "why don't you protect your office more carefully? I . . . I could still see the blackboards when the glass was in place. And sometimes the glass isn't up at all, you know."

"I know. I'm growing forgetful." The mage sighed. "Alex, I have nothing to hide. I am the same as anyone here. I hold few secrets, and those that need protecting are personal and I keep them inside me, where no one can get to them—just like everyone does." He chuckled softly. "I hesitated to put up the glass shield at all, but my most trusted friends overruled me. The glass isn't there to protect my office. It's there to protect the most creative students, like you and others, who are able to see this hallway. And to give me a little peace and quiet. My sleeping quarters are connected to my office, you know. That's how I heard you when you went through the magical door."

Alex's eyes widened. He shook his head, amazed, puzzled, not at all sure what to say. And since he was sleep-deprived after the emotional, eventful night, his thoughts were completely jumbled.

They stepped out on the balcony, and Alex turned to go down the boys' hallway to his room. "I have so many questions."

Mr. Today smiled warmly. "I have answers. But for now," he said, "you and I will be better off getting some sleep."

Alex nodded and stumbled down the hall and into his room. "Hey, Clive, you ol' curmudgeon, you," he grumbled. "Wake me up in time for breakfast."

Clive surfaced and glared. "You look like crud."

"Your mom looks like crud."

Clive's gleaming nostrils flared. He melted back into the blackboard without another word.

The Quillitary

Aaron Stowe tossed and turned on his cot, falling into fits of battered sleep. When the gray morning light pressed into his dormitory room, he gave up rest and glanced at the wall. There was only one door there. Surely it had been a nightmare. He began his morning ritual, as always.

Since water was scarce in the desertlike land of Quill, and most of the supply was needed for the crops and cattle, each student of the university was given a pail of water every week for washing up. It felt like a bonus to most students, since households in the quadrants were given two pails of water for the entire family, no matter the size. Aaron secretly felt annoyed, because that meant that some of the child-bearers who had failed by producing two Unwanteds fared the same as he, once their children had been disposed of.

But today his mind was on other things. Methodically Aaron wet his washcloth in the tepid water, being sure to squeeze the excess out of it carefully, and wiped his face. With a finger he brushed the bit of fuzz above his lip that seemed to be growing these past few weeks as he neared his fourteenth year. He was certain that it was his facial hair coming in, and he wondered what it looked like. He wondered if it looked like Alex's.

As he washed, he tried to clear his mind of the events of the previous night. He had convinced himself by now that Alex was indeed a dream, but he was terribly concerned about how weak his abilities were to control these dreams, which grew more intense each day. He ran the washcloth over his chest and arms, and nearly yelped when he pressed on the tender spot on his shoulder where his dream brother had hit him. "What in Quill . . . ?" he murmured, massaging it. "Great cats! That smarts." His dream was all too real, yet all too impossible. "It didn't happen," he told himself firmly.

LISA McMANN

Once dressed, he sat in a chair and waited until it was time to go to breakfast. He stared blankly at the door for nearly an hour, for he had gotten up early. He tried to think about his next project that the High Priest Justine had given him—perfecting the Quillitary vehicle operations. Today he would visit the Quillitary base for a tour, and he'd learn from the officers how the vehicles ran. From there he'd take the information and develop a plan. Hopefully, it would be a plan that pleased the high priest. This was his best chance at remaining in his high position as assistant secretary and moving up to secretary in a few months when the old maid had been disposed of.

Aaron knew that solidifying his post in the palace was crucial to his advancement. The current secretary to the high priest was an ancient woman, older than the high priest herself. Soon she'd be sent on to the Ancients Sector of Quill, as her sight was failing. Once there she'd never be seen again. Well—not by Wanteds, anyway. It was the job of the Necessaries to tend to the Ancients, put them to sleep, and bury them. Aaron had learned all about the burying part because his father was a burier.

Burying. Aaron shuddered. His thoughts had turned back

to Alex and the day they'd made houses in the mud. Aaron admitted to himself that he hadn't actually "seen" a house in the random markings in the mud. At the time he had wanted to see what Alex saw. But thinking back on it, he was glad that he didn't.

Alex. Aaron shook his head violently. "Stop," he said to himself. "Or I'll be forced to report you."

Aaron's thoughts turned again to his own advancement. Once the secretary was banished to the Ancients Sector, Aaron would be on an equal level with five of the six governors. There were only two people in Quill who stood in his way from that point. One was the High Priest Justine herself, who at seventy years old was not presumed to live more than five or ten years. Aaron wasn't worried about her standing in his way when the time came, and she had no heirs. But the second obstacle would be infinitely more difficult. He was the senior governor, second in command. The man watched Aaron like a dog watches a gopher hole. Almost like he knew Aaron was hot on his heels, ready to overthrow Senior Governor Haluki and become the next high priest of Quill. Almost like he knew that Aaron would stop at nothing to succeed.

A harsh clanging of metal on metal sounded outside his door. Aaron breathed a sigh of relief, got up, and strode to the doorway. When he opened the door, and indeed as all the other doors of the hall opened simultaneously, a flash of something silvery bright caught his eye on the floor of his room next to the door. It was a thin piece of metal twisted into an odd shape. But this one wasn't brown, like all the rusty metal Aaron had ever seen. This was gleaming silver, a color Aaron had never before laid eyes on, except in the dream the previous night.

Swiftly, he reached down and picked it up. He put it in his pocket to study later in private, and stepped into the line of students that would take him to the cafeteria for breakfast.

At eight o'clock Aaron slipped out of the university and into the awaiting vehicle that would take him to the Quillitary base for his tour. In the front seat, next to the driver, was Governor Haluki; in the back with Aaron, Governor Strang.

"Good day, Governors."

"Well met, Aaron," they intoned.

Now that he had an official title tied to the high priest, it bothered Aaron that they continued to call him by his first name as if he were a child. But he said nothing, and instead turned his attention to the driver, a Quillitary lieutenant. "Driver," he said curtly as the vehicle chugged and squealed along the road.

"Yes, sir, Assistant Secretary Stowe, sir!"

That made up for the previous. "What is your top speed?" Aaron asked.

"Twenty-five posts, sir."

"Sustainable?"

"Not hardly, sir."

"How long?"

"I'd say thirty minutes."

"You'd say?" Aaron sneered.

"Thirty minutes, sir!"

"What happens at thirty-one?"

"Engine locks up, Mr. Stowe. You hear the squealing now? Needs water and grease. Soon as we arrive, I'll rejuice so I can make it back."

Aaron's brow furrowed. "Water? What's the water allotment for the base? Gentlemen?"

Governor Strang spoke. "We've just increased it to thirty barrels."

LISA McMANN

"A week?"

"Thirty barrels," Strang repeated, "a day."

Aaron sat back in the seat. "Thank you, gentlemen," he said evenly, even though Senior Governor Haluki hadn't contributed a word, and even appeared to be nodding off in the front seat.

Thirty barrels a day. Aaron looked out his window, up through the barbed-wire defense ceiling, and scanned the sky for rain clouds. Seeing none, he feared for the life of his first project, the Favored Farm. With water this scarce and the Quillitary vehicles sucking up a ridiculous amount, something had to be done.

Haluki, Strang, and Aaron toured the Quillitary base, walking past new Wanted soldiers practicing the traditional Quillitary death chants that would be used in battle should Quill ever come under attack. But Aaron's focus was on transportation today. He absorbed everything he saw and heard regarding the vehicles. Then the three returned to the vehicle for the short ride to the palace to meet with the High Priest Justine. The car creaked and strained its way up the hill, and Aaron, now feeling the exhaustion from too few hours of sleep the night before, let his thoughts wander once again to the strange episode during the night. It felt distant now, but something tugged at Aaron's mind. How could it be possible that behind that great fence was an entire world full of Unwanteds? Aaron couldn't fathom it. There was no way they would fit, for one thing—not according to the accounts he'd overheard from the governors' inspection about the small plot of land. And where would they hide? It was ridiculous. There was nothing but a building, some weeds, and a—a lake. A Great Lake of Boiling Oil.

Aaron closed his eyes for a moment, telling himself to stop all thoughts of Alex forever before he did something to jeopardize his standing with the high priest. Even so, he fingered the thin piece of metal in his pocket through the fabric of his trousers, wondering where else something like that could have possibly come from.

Finally the driver pulled the vehicle up to the palace. After the customary passwords and formal greetings with the high priest, the four sat in the conference room.

Senior Governor Haluki began the briefing, updating the high priest with a status report from General Blair. Strang

LISA McMANN

continued, speaking of their tour, and then the three turned to Aaron. "And what are your findings?" Justine asked.

Throughout the briefing, something had niggled at the edge of Aaron's thoughts. He struggled to come up with something brilliant to say, but he was afraid that his comments would disappoint. He knew this was important. He knew this could prove that his first idea, the Favored Farm, was not a fluke. This could prove his brilliance. And perhaps, just perhaps, it might answer the burning question that had been plaguing him for months.

The high priest waited patiently for Aaron to answer.

Haluki and Strang eyed him carefully.

Aaron straightened his already extreme posture to a state of rigid. "If it pleases the high priest, I wish to offer a solution to the growing problem, not only of the poor quality of the Quillitary vehicles, for indeed they are in a sorry state. But also a solution that will ease Quill's looming water shortage."

Justine's gaze didn't waver. "Proceed," she said.

Aaron nodded. "I believe there is a method that, to my limited knowledge," he said humbly, "we have not explored. Perhaps you will consider it worthy." Aaron took a breath, knowing he couldn't stall much longer without actually making his suggestion, yet still trying desperately in his mind to figure out exactly how it would work.

Haluki, who sat opposite Aaron, shifted in his chair, his narrowed eyes not leaving the boy's face.

Strang nodded encouragingly, for he had an appreciation for the boy's mind.

The High Priest Justine's mouth twitched, as if she were growing impatient. "Out with it, then."

Aaron nodded again and pressed his lips together. "Very well," he said, his esophagus feeling tight enough to stop his breath. "I believe the solution to making the vehicles run more efficiently, and to freeing up the thirty barrels of water used by the Quillitary base each day, is . . ." Aaron swallowed, and continued. "The Great Lake of Boiling Oil."

The High Priest Justine knitted her brows, the look on her face growing even more intense. "And?" she prompted sharply.

"And . . ." Aaron's voice cracked, making him cringe and clear his throat. "And," he continued, "therefore, as I have never seen the Great Lake of Boiling Oil, I'd like your permission to pay a visit to the Death Farm so I might gather a sample for study and testing."

Haluki's eyes flickered for an instant before they returned to their cold steel-blue color. He shifted in his chair as the high priest and Strang grew thoughtful.

"No. It's out of the question," Haluki said.

The high priest offered Haluki a rare look of disdain. "What?" she said, her voice raised slightly as fire rose in her eyes.

"It's contaminated," Haluki said forcefully. "Polluted. Perhaps you've forgotten what goes in there."

Aaron and the young Governor Strang exchanged an uncomfortable look.

The high priest glared at Haluki. "I'll thank you to leave that decision up to me." She turned to the palace guards at the door. "Guards! Fetch a vehicle immediately, suitably large enough for the four of us."

Aaron's stomach flipped.

Haluki hesitated, and then stood abruptly and made for the door. "Make that three. I've another appointment. Good day, madam."

The three remaining at the table watched him go, and then

looked at each other, none of them bothering to hide the shock on their faces at this strange behavior. Finally the high priest had the wherewithal to call out, "Oh, for Quill's sake, Haluki. Come back here immediately!"

But the man was already gone.

Visitors

And so it was that while Mr. Today was holding a meeting on the lawn to give the most recent developments to all humans, statues, and domesticated creatures, and while Arija called to order a similar meeting of all the wild creatures in the jungle, the squeaky Quillitary vehicle containing the High Priest Justine, Governor Strang, and Assistant Secretary Stowe came to a stop outside the vast iron gate. And because no one had ever come through the gate without six months' notice, and because only one person in all of Quill had a key to the gate, and because the remaining three girrinos had trickled to

LISA McMANN

the fringe of the crowd on the lawn so that they could hear just a little more clearly, there was no one there to notice it.

Except for Simber, whose keen senses were the best of anyone's. But by the time the great winged cheetah had bounded over a row of Artiméans and thundered toward the gate, growling out a warning to Mr. Today that set the entire land of Artimé on their feet and reaching into their component vests for their magical weapons, it was too late. The gate was swinging open.

A look passed between the great old mage and the stately cheetah; it was a look only two friends who have known each other for many, many years could understand. So while Mr. Today held up his hand to silence the Artiméans, the stone cheetah stood solid, his enormous wings outstretched to their full span of twenty feet or more, and acted as a shield between the visitors and the crowd to keep the enthusiastic folk from descending on the three Quillens like a thousand Unwanted ghosts on the Eliminator.

And just as the three stepped around the iron door, an enormous gray wolf burst from the seaside entrance of the mansion and bounded toward Mr. Today, until he saw that he was already too late. But he was hardly noticed, since all eyes strained to see around or above or below the great expanse of Simber's wings.

With a soft word and a gentle hand, Mr. Today motioned to the enormous crowd to be seated, and because they trusted him, they did so, most of them realizing, after thinking about it for a moment, that the visitors would be so overwhelmed at the sight of Artimé that they would likely need no containment.

But Alex didn't notice everyone sitting. He didn't notice Lani tugging at his hand, and he didn't notice that when she was unable to pull him down, she stood back up and simply held his arm, and he didn't notice Mr. Today offering a slight nod of approval to Lani before he turned and walked slowly across the lawn to approach the guests. Alex merely stood and stared. And as he stood there, he thought that he should be feeling all sorts of emotional somethings inside his heart and his gut. But all he felt was a chilled emptiness, as if by their entrance, by their mere presence, the three Quillens had sucked all the emotion from the entire place into their cold veins and it had stuck and frozen there. Alex stared into his brother's eyes and watched Aaron stare back, until Aaron could not help but look away.

By this time Claire Morning had weaved her way through the maze of Artiméans, and she walked in step with Mr. Today. Florence joined Simber and stood with her back to him, facing the crowd and training her eye on Samheed, who looked like he wanted to disappear, and on Will Blair, who looked beyond eager to stand face-to-face with Aaron Stowe and blast him to tiny bits. But even Will saw that he would not win this challenge. Not now. He would have to save his venom for a new day, which now seemed nearer than ever.

Of the three it was Strang who was most shocked. But to say that the High Priest Justine and Aaron were not flabbergasted would be a fantastic lie, because they were quite beyond their capacities to speak. Their glances darted from the army of Unwanteds and strange creatures before them to the enormous mansion, to the sparkling blue-green sea, to the lush landscape and the forest in the distance.

The High Priest Justine, her eyes shooting fiery bits of anger and betrayal after the initial shock of it all, drew herself up to her full height and pressed her thin lips together so

LISA McMANN

tightly that they seemed to be a single white line painted on her rigid face.

Governor Strang looked as if he might pass out at the sight of Simber, whose keen eyes moved from one Quillen to the next, and whose body was tensed and ready to strike should the need arise.

And Aaron Stowe stared and stared, and inched backward, as all his nightmares came true before his very eyes. Simber caught the boy's eye and growled such a deep, low warning that it sounded more like a roll of thunder from somewhere beyond the border wall. Aaron stopped his inching and stood still as a—well, still as a statue. Mr. Today, with Claire at his side, approached the visitors.

"Greetings, Justine," said Mr. Today. He stood equally as tall but scores less rigid than the ruler of Quill. "Hello again, Aaron."

Aaron's face grew pale.

Justine's eyes flashed surprise as she glanced at Aaron, and then she turned her fury back on Mr. Today. Her voice, dripping with contempt, hissed, "Marcus."

And while Marcus Today had been preparing himself for

this moment for many years, it felt surreal. It felt beyond even the mage's own ability to imagine. It felt almost, not quite but nearly, pleasant—to finally be at this spot so that he could soon put it behind him. And while he was a gracious man, he knew that now was not the time to say another word.

The High Priest Justine stood just as still, and the two faced each other for several long, uncomfortable seconds, both their minds whirring, deciding how best to continue this conversation in the presence of the menagerie.

It was Justine who, by necessity as the time ticked, made the first move. She knew Marcus would take it as a sign of weakness, yet she saw no way around it other than to stand there until the end of time. And in the fashion of rulers throughout history, she said in a deathly voice, "I request a meeting in private."

Mr. Today nodded curtly. "That can be arranged."

"At the palace. Eight o'clock."

"Don't be ridiculous."

Justine's face flushed hotly, but she kept her voice even. "I beg your pardon?"

"Here and now will do." The old mage turned to Simber.

"Clear the lawn, please. Everyone inside so that I might have a word with the high priest and her comrades alone."

Claire glanced at Mr. Today, concerned. He nodded. She hesitated, and then left him alone with the three Quillens and began helping Simber funnel the Unwanteds into the mansion.

Within minutes nearly all of the Artiméans had streamed inside. Alex paused to cast one last cool glance at his brother. They locked eyes for a moment; volumes of things unsaid passed between them. For the first time since the incident in the mud Alex sensed his brother's true fear.

"Alex," Simber growled softly.

Alex broke the stare and slowly rounded the corner of the mansion along with the dregs of the crowd, in step with Ms. Morning, as Simber waited patiently and then followed them inside.

Alex found his friends in the lounge, where hushed conversations had taken the place of the usual music and laughter. He slumped down on the couch next to Meghan, feeling like all the wind had been knocked out of him. He buried his head in his hands, rubbed the guilt from his eyes, and then looked up and started telling Meghan and Lani the story. Soon Sean joined them, and then Samheed approached and sat down tentatively, exchanging a glance with Alex. Alex shrugged and nodded. It didn't matter now what Samheed knew, or what he could do. Artimé was exposed, and it was Alex's fault. And then he shared what had happened the night before, from the archives floor of the library to the 3-D door to the wolf—except that instead of Will Blair, Alex said "someone." He wasn't sure why, only that he thought that it might cause more problems if word got out.

"Maybe they won't want to fight," Lani said when Alex had finished.

"Are you stupid?" Samheed said. He looked uncharacter-istically anxious, and kept glancing at Alex, wondering if Alex had turned him in but not daring to ask in front of everyone. "Can you imagine how furious the high priest must be, know-ing that Mr. Today has betrayed her all these years? She's got to feel like the biggest fool ever. If she doesn't want to fight and word of us gets out to the Quillitary, they'll take her down and come after us!"

Sean nodded. "No doubt," he said.

Meghan chewed her fingernail. "I hope Mr. Today is all right out there."

"Don't worry," Sean said. "There's nothing they can do to him. He could kill them all in an instant. They didn't appear to have any weapons. But I am surprised Justine didn't arrive with her guards. She must have great confidence in Governor Strang and Aaron—or else she's grown so confident in her power that she no longer feels she needs protection."

"That won't last long," Lani said.

The five sat in silence, waiting for news. When Earl announced that everyone was to return to the lawn, they all jumped up anxiously and headed for the tubes.

Exposed

As the Unwanteds filed out to the lawn, one by one their faces reacted to the new scene in front of them. In place of the enormous iron gate was, well, nothing. Nothing but a gaping hole that exposed the most desolate part of Quill. Beside the hole stood three of the girrinos, peering curiously around the edge of the wall into Quill. Arija had gone back to the jungle to give an update.

"Hideous view, isn't it?" Mr. Today said when they had all come to order. "As it turns out, Governor Strang had a bit of a dizzy spell, and when he fainted, he pushed the gate closed

LISA McMANN

with his head. It locks upon latching, of course. Tch. Such a pity." When the crowd offered quizzical looks, he explained. "There's no other traditional way back into Quill. And with the only key to the gate in Justine's hand and no way to get over the wall, they were stuck, which put them into a bit of a panic." He chuckled quietly at the memory and went on. "So I gave Justine three options: to stay here forever, to be eliminated, or to go back to Quill through magical means. And, as I didn't think Strang's gentle heart would be able to handle the magical means I intended to use on him, I decided instead to use magic to remove the gate entirely and allow them out that way."

"But—but—" Several voices sputtered and erupted into a melee of questions. "Aren't you going to put it back?" "Can they come in here?"

Mr. Today held up his hands for silence. "I understand your concerns. Yes, they can see in, just as we can see out." After the next round of murmurs Mr. Today nodded seriously. "And yes. You may come and go as you please, now, just as the people of Quill will be able to enter and leave here. Though I doubt we'll see anyone but the Quillitary coming in. The Necessaries won't even be told about it, I'm sure."

This brought an outcry, and several Unwanteds jumped to their feet in protest. Patiently Mr. Today waited for silence, and then he waited a moment longer, as if the decision had weighed heavily on his mind. Finally he spoke.

"Friends. Hear me out, won't you?" He paused, gathered his words, and went on. "Now that we have been discovered, I loathe the idea of continuing to hide Artimé. Be assured that the Quillitary is finding out about us right now, and they will soon be on their way to attack. They wanted all of you dead once, remember? Now they want me dead most of all. Do you think they will simply say, 'What? You've been tricking us all these years? Oh, that's all right,' and leave us be?" He shook his head. "No, and I've never led you to believe that. This is the big opportunity they have been saving all their rage for. The removal of the gate gives us, the people of Artimé, more options. It allows for easy exit. And it allows us to see them coming."

A question came from the front of the crowd. "But—why not just seal us off completely from them rather than making us more vulnerable?"

Mr. Today smiled grimly, and then he turned and gazed over the beautiful blue-green sea. "They can reach us from the sea if they wish to — if Justine thinks of it. And she will, if it comes to that. Do you really want walls all the way around us, now that they know? Are we so afraid?" he asked, turning back to face them. "Just like Quill?" He waited to see if anyone would speak, and when no one did, he continued.

"I'd rather die fighting to keep us free to do as we wish, fighting to be free to come and go as we please, fighting so we no longer need to hide. Fighting the fear that all of you were programmed since birth to have. Fighting against Quill's bigotry, which says brains and brawn are better, or more important, than creativity. And now, with luck, we may have a chance. A chance to prove ourselves."

The crowd remained hushed.

"You will all be faced with two options: Fight or provide. For those of you who need or desire protection, or have medical skills, you will find protection and provisions in the mansion. Parents and families—I trust you will make your own decisions on whether to protect your children or fight. Both are noble deeds, and you must decide for yourselves what is best. Those who remain under protection will be able to assist with our soldiers through various ways: aiding the wounded, providing nourishment for those who fight, and caring for our youngest ones who need assistance.

"Most of the rest of you will likely choose to fight together to save Artimé." Mr. Today's eyes traveled to the very back of the crowd and alighted on Will Blair, who squirmed uncomfortably, and then the mage looked at Samheed, who looked at the ground. "I need not remind any of you that if you choose to enter Quill without the benefit of an organized team, you are taking your life into your own hands."

Mr. Today looked at Claire and nodded to her. "Ms. Morning is your commander in chief. You have done your drills. Keep your wits about you—you are far cleverer than they! Use your imaginations to your advantage. And please, though you owe me nothing, I ask a favor." He leaned forward in earnest. "Do not strike first. If there is to be a battle, let it be they who start it. As I often say, we do not know what will happen until it happens. Perhaps, by some miracle, they will choose—" Mr. Today stopped abruptly as Jim the winged tortoise flew in from the direction of the jungle and landed at his feet. The man bent down, and Jim whispered something in his ear, while the crowd inched forward, curious. It took a very long time for him to pass along the information, but no one expected otherwise where Jim was concerned. Will Blair took the tortoise distraction as an opportunity to make himself invisible and slip away.

After a long moment Mr. Today stood upright. "Thank you, Jim, that's perfect." He spoke again to the crowd on the lawn. "Our friends of the jungle have agreed to stand with us and fight. They, along with the statues, will help protect the mansion at night so that we might rest in safety, should the battle tarry on." He took a deep breath and smiled encouragingly at his beloved Unwanteds. "Any questions?"

Lani raised her hand. "How will we know when they are coming . . . and then what do we do?"

Mr. Today smiled warmly at the girl. "We have spies. Lookouts. They'll give us plenty of warning. You'll know almost immediately via your blackboards." The old man glanced at Alex and teased, "Everyone, please keep your blackboards on full volume."

Alex smiled weakly. He had nothing to worry about, since Clive no longer had a shush button.

"When you receive your orders, follow them. It's that

simple. Have your component vests loaded and your weapons ready."

As the crowd went back into the mansion to prepare, Mr. Today called out to Samheed. "A word, please," he said.

Samheed grabbed Alex's arm. "Did you tell him about me?" His eyes were wild.

"Yes," Alex answered truthfully. "But I said that you probably didn't know what Will was really up to."

"I didn't know," Samheed said. "You have to believe me. I thought we were just going to scare him. I didn't know."

Alex pressed his lips together. "You'd better go."

Samheed bit down on his bottom lip, his brow furled, and stared at Alex with an intensity Alex had never seen before. "Believe me," Samheed whispered. "I wouldn't do that to you." Then he released his grip and jogged slowly over to the mage. "Yes, sir?"

"There are a few things we need to talk about, and some things for you to think about," Mr. Today said. He pulled him to a quiet spot on the lawn, and the two sat down together, Samheed staring at the grass nearly the entire time.

When they had finished their conversation, Samheed walked slowly to the mansion, a stricken sort of look on his face, and went straight to his room.

And Mr. Today scoured the mansion and grounds in search of Will Blair, alerting all of his contacts to watch out for the young man. But Will was nowhere to be found.

Aaron

Well, well, well, Aaron Stowe." As they drove back to the palace, the High Priest Justine turned to eye the young man. "I understand you've met Marcus. How . . . interesting."

"High Priest Justine, I can explain—"

"Then do it!" She didn't raise her voice, yet the words boomed inside Aaron's head.

Aaron sat on his hands so the high priest would not see them trembling. His voice cracked. "I—I—Last night, they came into my room. I mean, he did. Alex. My brother. I mean, the Unwanted. I thought it was a dream!"

"And?"

"And, they tried to convince me—"

"They?"

"Alex and that man with the hair—they . . . they dragged me through the wall into the Death Farmer's office and told me they were trying to protect me." Aaron took a deep breath. "I escaped, thank Quill." He nodded emphatically, as if to prove it to himself that he had done the right thing.

The High Priest Justine's lips were pinched so tightly that they carried a faint tinge of blue. Her voice was wickedly calm. "And you chose to lie to me, and bring me there under the guise of refining oil. So that we could declare quite openly to the entire pathetic place that we were dumbfounded to discover their existence." Her glare grew even sharper, and her voice lost some of its calm. "And I thought you were intelligent, Aaron Stowe. I really thought you were bright. But all you've done is succeed in making us look like idiots! We're fools!" She spat out the last word. Aaron shrank back in his seat.

"I—I thought it was a dream," he whispered. "I've had some strange dreams lately—it was all too impossible. How could I have believed I could walk through a wall, and that my brother Alex was alive? Surely, Madam High Priest, surely you can understand. . . ."

"How dare you defy me! Dreams? Be silent!"

Governor Strang, somewhat recovered from the shock of the world, remained still as he drove the Quillitary vehicle up the winding road to the palace.

"Strang," the high priest said, her voice sickly calm again, "gather all the governors—blast it, why did Haluki have to run off like that? I need him immediately, and the rest of you. General Blair, too. Can't you make this thing go any faster?"

The boxy, rusted vehicle chugged and strained against the incline. "The pedal is to the floor. Nearly through it, Your Highness," Strang said.

At the mention of General Blair, Aaron bit his lip and cleared his throat softly. "Madam High Priest, my Unwanted brother told me that the general's own Unwanted son was planning to kill me and take my place, using something called 'magic.'" He dared not say any more.

The high priest did not acknowledge Aaron, and he sank back into the seat again.

Soon they had reached the palace. "Follow me," the High Priest Justine barked. Aaron hastened to keep up.

"Dreams," she muttered. "Grounds for dismissal and death."

Aaron's eyes opened wide with fear. He felt like he was going to throw up.

"Guards!" The High Priest Justine's shoes snapped and clicked on the stone floor of the palace. "Do not let this boy out of your sight," she said, sneering. "If he tries to run, kill him." She turned abruptly into her office and slammed the door in Aaron's face.

Aaron stood there for a moment, his shoulders sagging with remorse, and then turned and sat down on the floor, covering his face in his hands.

What Happens

After midnight Will Blair, who had been hiding in the jungle, snuck back to the campus before his invisibility spell wore off and tubed his way secretly back to his room. He sent a message to Samheed and waited impatiently for his friend to answer his blackboard, but to no avail. Finally he gave up and decided to go it alone. Abandoning his 3-D door failure, and no longer needing it, he sat in his room, surrounded by sketches of Alex Stowe, as if in a creepy sort of shrine. He concentrated for a few minutes, breathed deeply, and crossed his fingers. With all his might he focused on theatrical thoughts of becoming

LISA McMANN

his character, until his body and features transformed into the body of the person he'd been studying for nearly a year. Then he hoped against hope that he wouldn't bump into Alex on the way out of Artimé, because that would indeed ruin everything.

He strolled down the steps in the same manner as Alex would stroll, and when he passed Florence and Simber, he nodded like Alex would nod. Simber growled, "Alex," and nodded in return. Will made his way to the gaping space in the wall and nodded to the girrinos there. Tina asked in a frightened voice, "Where are you going?" Will didn't want to tell the nosy girrinos anything, so he simply waved and set out on his quest: to reach Wanted University before he was discovered.

When Mr. Today got word that Alex (or someone looking suspiciously like him) had left Artimé, he whirled around to check the blackboards and then flew to the tube across from his office, shimmered, and disappeared.

Hours later he returned, exhausted. And empty-handed.

By morning there were two announcements written on the blackboards: First, the Quillitary, which had been preparing for this moment for so long, was already on the march. And second, Alex Stowe had gone into Quill during the night and never returned.

Alex sputtered as he read the second. "What? Clive, is this your idea of a joke?"

The board rippled in shiny black waves as Clive's face pressed through. He smiled grimly. "It's tempting, but I didn't do it. I've already alerted Marcus that you are here. He mumbled something about Tina making the report down by the gate, and Will Blair using a disguise spell."

Alex clapped his hands to his forehead. "Oh no—Clive, you've got to send out a notice that it's not true." His stomach clenched as he wondered if Will had already killed Aaron, but there was no time to think about it now.

"On the way."

It popped up:

The previous message regarding Alex Stowe was inaccurate. Please disregard.

Alex sighed in relief. "Thanks, Clive. You're not half bad, you know that?"

Clive smirked. "Well, I'd hate to have you go off to battle and get killed without me at least doing one decent thing for you. You know. Karma."

"Wow. How big of you."

"Read your instructions. You don't have much time." Clive melted into the blackboard. "Don't die," he called out as his face disappeared and the announcements appeared on the screen again.

"I'll try not to," Alex whispered. He pressed the first announcement and read:

Alex Stowe,

The Quillitary is on the march. Your breakfast has been tubed up to you. Please report to your squad on the lawn immediately. Your commander is Simber. He will have your orders.

Thank you for your dedication and service to Artimé. You are a valuable part of our community.

Marcus Today

Alex picked up the tray of food from the tube and ate quickly, and then he washed and dressed. He grabbed his component vest, checked the bulging pockets for all his magical items, and slipped his arms through it. Ten minutes later he joined the throngs of Artiméans, easily found Simber, and stood near him. He felt a lot less scared knowing that Simber was there to lead his group.

Meghan joined him. "I'm so glad you're here—I thought you did something stupid," she whispered. She eyed the cheetah nervously. "And I'm really glad he's on our side."

Simber growled. "I can hearrr you, Rrrangerrr."

They were soon joined by three others: a young man named Peter, an older woman named Pauline, and a rather large white squirrelicorn named Rufus.

Across the lawn he saw Samheed and Lani under the leadership of Arija the girrino. He waved, and watched Lani's anxious face relax. She ran over to him, pressed a note in his hand, and said, "What was up with that report about you?" Alex just shrugged and shook his head. Lani glanced back at Arija and ran back to her post.

Alex caught Samheed's eye. Samheed had a strained look

on his face. He nodded slightly to Alex, and then he dropped his gaze.

"I wonder if he knows about Will," Alex whispered under his breath. "And if he's really on our side."

"He knows now," growled Simber. "As for the otherrr, I guess we'll find out soon enough."

Alex startled. "I've got to start remembering that you can see and hear so well," he said.

The great cheetah chuckled under his breath. "I prrreferrr knowing what you'rrre up to, Stowe."

At that moment Mr. Today and Claire Morning appeared on the rooftop of the mansion. Claire clapped her hands for order, and all in front turned to hush those behind and direct their attention to the leaders. "Commanders, please give your orders and take your stations. The Quillitary is in sight."

Alex and Meghan gulped simultaneously and exchanged a nervous glance. Alex quickly peeked at the note from Lani. It read, *Die a thousand deaths*. He looked up, alarmed, and searched for Lani, but she was nowhere to be found. *What a horrible thing to say*, he thought, shoving the note in his pocket. *I thought she was over being immature.*

He straightened his vest, going over the various components one more time, even though he knew their locations by heart. Peter and Pauline whispered together. Rufus rose up on his haunches as Simber faced them.

"Ourrr squad was specially designed to complement one anotherrr," he began. "Rrrufus is agile. He can both climb and fly. His eyesight is trrremendous, as is his bite and skewerrr." Simber indicated the squirrelicorn's foot-long horn, which grew from between his little squirrel ears. "Pauline was a theaterrr focus, Peterrr's a wrrriting instrrructorrr, Meghan is a musician, and Alex is a painterrr." He paused, and said wryly, "And in case you didn't notice, I'm an enorrrmous stone cheetah with wings. I come with a majorrr drrrawback—I am not easy to hide. Therrreforrre ourrr squad will be an open, moving tarrrget. But ourrr combined skills should overrrcome most obstacles.

"Please follow my instrrructions at all times, especially when we face combat. Trrrust my orrrders. Frrrom my vantage point I can see much farrrtherrr than you. And because of my experrri-ence as a prrredator you should trrrust my instincts. Any ques-tions?" He looked at the five who faced him. None had questions.

"All rrright. We'rrre the frrront line stationed at the rrroad.

LISA McMANN

In Quill." Simber turned and walked toward the opening in the wall.

The front line! A chill of fear moved through Alex as they approached the place where the gate once stood. It had been one thing to go from Mr. Today's office into Aaron's dormitory room, but it was quite another to face this ominous, fateful entrance again after nearly a year, and then to stand outside it and take the brunt of the attack—it was completely nerve-wracking.

Simber held his head high as he walked nobly, like a prince, through the wide opening. Mr. Today, who now stood at the entrance, murmured words of protection on each of their component vests as they passed through into the bleakness of Quill. "The words of protection will last the entire day. Please don't take your vests off—they will help keep you safe." The man put his hand on Alex's arm and whispered, "Do you remember the command I used for the glass wall?"

Alex, whose heart was pounding by now, nodded.

"You are capable of casting that, Alex. You are capable of a lot of things. Just be aware that it will shatter if it's struck hard enough, so it's not permanent. Above all, have confidence in yourself, and you will succeed. Control your emotions, and you will hit every time."

"Yes, sir," Alex whispered, feeling confidence from the pep talk. He nodded and followed Simber onto the dusty road to stand and wait for the Quillitary vehicles. There was nothing in this desolate part of Quill that could be used for cover except for a few scattered posts that held up the barbed-wire ceiling. Alex breathed in the stifling air of Quill, his eyes darting around, feeling very exposed.

Other squads lined up behind and alongside Simber's, and soon there were over a hundred defenders in place inside Quill, ready to face the oncoming Quillitary. Alex could hear the other squads behind him talking through their plans. The majority of the defenders remained in Artimé, spread out to protect the mansion, hidden behind the lush foliage, and grouped under cover along the edge of the jungle. It would be easier to fight in Artimé, where the Quillitary would be in unfamiliar territory and so shocked at the sight that they would have a disadvantage.

Soon the squealing and squeaking vehicles could be heard. Alex and Meghan stood tall, trying to catch the first glimpse, almost like little eager children of Artimé who could

LISA McMANN

hear a marching band but not yet see the approaching parade.

Just inside the opening into Artimé, Alex could see Samheed and Lani's squad waiting. Alex caught Lani's eye, and when she smiled, his stomach flip-flopped, despite her mean note. He mouthed the words "Be safe."

Lani bit her lip and nodded. "You too," she whispered.

They did not have long to wait.

A fleet of rust-colored vehicles, flanked on both sides by endless lines of marching soldiers, thundered closer. They raised no weapons. Slowly the vehicles came to a stop in front of the entrance to Artimé. They faced Simber head-on. When they came to a halt, a burly man stood up inside the front vehicle, his head and shoulders well above the windshield. He squinted as the colors of Artimé bled through the opening in the wall. Samheed recognized the man as General Blair.

"Attention, worthless Unwanteds! I have a message for Alexander Stowe," he yelled.

Simber growled angrily.

Alex felt his heart drop and splatter on the road.

After a moment Simber nodded to Alex and growled in

a low voice, "Step forrrwarrrd and claim it."

All the squads inside Artimé who could see through the opening watched the scene unfold. Alex's breath was shallow, and his teeth nearly chattered together. He stepped forward as bravely as he could, cleared his throat, and said in his deepest, harshest voice, "I'm Alex Stowe."

The general stared him in the eye for a long moment, his upper lip frozen in a sneer.

Alex stared back, unflinching.

"The message is from the High Priest Justine." He cleared his throat authoritatively.

Alex didn't move.

"The High Priest Justine thanks you for the warning you gave to Aaron Stowe two nights ago."

As the general spoke, two Quillitary officers in the seat behind him hoisted something long and bulky over their heads.

"She only wished that this," the General said as the officers flung the object into the grassy opening of Artimé, "had truly been you."

On the ground, inside a sheet of thin, ragged linen, was the lifeless body of the general's own son, Will Blair.

Battleground

Alex remained steady despite the gasps around him, gathered his wits, and spoke in a smooth voice. "If you live through the day, General," he said, "perhaps you'll ask the High Priest Justine why she's too afraid to come here and deliver that message herself."

"Get back!" Simber barked as the far flank of Quillitary marchers raised long, rusty metal weapons to their shoulders. Simber's wings burst open as a shield, forcing Alex behind them as loud blasts erupted from the Quillitary, followed by raining thuds of pellets against the stone statue. "Firrre!" commanded the stone beast.

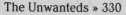

Alex regained his footing as the others in his squad sent a round of artistic fire at the Quillitary. Those soldiers who hadn't been hit rushed into Artimé and began firing on the Unwanteds within, and the vehicles roared and coughed in preparation to enter through the gateway. Alex sent off a round of blinding highlights from his fluorescent yellow pen, hitting the drivers of the first two vehicles squarely in the eyes, as well as General Blair himself. The first vehicle lurched wildly and crashed into the wall, sending the general and two others catapulting toward Samheed and Lani. The second vehicle smashed into it, causing both jalopies to hiss and shoot boiling spurts of water back at their occupants.

Samheed, still in shock at seeing his former friend lying dead, and witnessing Will's own father show absolutely no signs of emotion or remorse, realized with full certainty that the Quillitary was no longer anything he wanted to be a part of. How foolish he had been! And seeing the heartlessness all around him—it was so much worse than he remembered. He felt the old familiar rage boiling up tenfold.

With a wild yell Samheed pulled a spiked metal star from his vest and flung it with all his might at the groaning general.

LISA McMANN

It struck the man in the throat and embedded deep within. General Blair's blinded eyes widened, and then closed.

But there was no time for anyone to reflect, as Artiméans all around Samheed fell to the ground.

Another round of pellets from the enemy blasted and chinked off Simber, leaving him no worse for wear. Meghan dropped the first two officers in the far flank with sleep spells, and Peter laid down the next dozen with words of destruction. They writhed on the ground and were succinctly trampled by the Quillitary that pressed forward, trying to get into Artimé.

From the squads inside Artimé came another round of spells, causing tremendous chaos for the unsuspecting enemy. Scatterclips flew through the air, some of them dragging the enemy with them until they reached something solid enough in which to stick. Still it was all the Artiméans could do to protect themselves as the lines of vehicles and the near flank poured into the magical world.

"Rrrufus, I need numberrrs!" Simber roared.

Immediately the squirrelicorn flew up and, hovering just below the barbed-wire ceiling, counted out a quick estimate and dropped to the cheetah's back. "A thousand at least—they're backed up all the way to the nursery," Rufus reported. "More than I expected."

"How many of ourrrs down?"

Rufus flew up again to look around, and then darted into Artimé and returned. "Twelve down out here. At least two dozen down inside."

Simber roared his displeasure, which caused several nearby members of the Quillitary to hit the dirt. "Double up yourrr attacks! Make them perrrmanent!" he roared. "They arrre rrrecoverrring frrrom yourrr spells. Yourrr comrrrades arrre falling!"

Alex and Meghan pulled out their permanent power weapons. Within thirty minutes the two of them, working in beautiful tandem, rendered forty-four Quillitary members permanently frozen in odd poses using Alex's splatterpaint combined with Meghan's *Nutcracker* ice dance.

As the squads behind the fantastic Simber shield met their marks, a few of them falling back with stray pellet wounds, the squads inside nailed the enemy with fireball dragons, sting-ing soliloquies, splatterpaint, fire steps, itch glue, slam poetry, scatterclips, slash singing, blinding highlights, and the dreaded Shakespearean theater curse from those who had no qualms about inflicting mortal fencing wounds on their enemies.

Lani and Samheed weren't quite as fortunate. Samheed, though he thought he had prepared himself for this, soon found himself face-to-face with his father. And unlike with General Blair, Samheed hesitated a split second too long in this matchup, and Mr. Burkesh took advantage by slamming his son in the head and chest with a shield. Samheed groaned and fell.

Immediately Lani reacted with a paralyzing taunt at Samheed's father, but the man fell forward instead of backward, crashing on top of the young girl and trapping her under his weight. It took her several minutes to free herself, trying to cast spells at other enemies while struggling, her leg caught quite firmly underneath Mr. Burkesh. A sharp, rusty corner of the man's armor dug into her calf. With one tremendous effort she broke free, ripping a nasty gash in her leg in the process.

"Sam!" she cried, but Samheed was out cold. Blood poured from his nose, which was obviously broken. Lani dragged him with a sort of superhuman strength to a protected spot behind a tree and took a moment to rip a piece from her already shredded pant leg and wrap up her own gushing wound.

Samheed groaned and moved his head weakly. The left side of his face was rapidly swelling up and turning purple.

"Stay still!" hissed Lani.

Samheed opened the only eye that would open. He coughed, swallowed painfully, and whispered, "Kill him."

Lani gave him a wild, pleading look. "Oh, Sam. I—I can't."

Samheed looked at her for a long moment. Then he nodded weakly and tried to smile. "It's okay." He rolled to his side and spit blood, then took a deep breath and rose shakily to his feet. "I'll be right back."

"No, Sam!" Lani whispered.

Samheed staggered over to his father, released the paralyzing spell, and waited for Mr. Burkesh to stand and get his bearings again. The boy stood nearly eye to eye with the man.

"Father."

Mr. Burkesh glared. He pulled a knife from his belt and held it to Samheed's neck.

Lani ran toward them. "No!" she cried.

"Father," Samheed said again, his voice deathly calm.

Mr. Burkesh's hand trembled slightly as his face grew red.

LISA McMANN

He spoke in harsh, drawn-out words. "Don't speak to me. You are no son of mine." And then he hesitated no longer, rearing back with the knife and roaring, "Die a thousand deaths!" He plunged it through the air toward Samheed. Samheed shook, but he made no move to stop him.

Lani screamed. "No! Samheed!" She began uttering another paralyzing taunt, just as a thin voice from somewhere above her uttered a sharp rhyming curse.

Immediately Mr. Burkesh flew backward in the air and landed on the ground. His hand relaxed on the knife, and it fell in the grass.

Samheed sank to his hands and knees, shaking his head in disbelief, sobs and blood clutching at his throat. "I had to know," he choked out, "if he would really do it."

Lani tossed off a quick handful of spells at the other Quillitary nearby, and when they were all temporarily contained, she looked up to see where the voice had come from.

In the tree sat Mr. Sigfried Appleblossom. He hopped to the ground nimbly, walked over to Mr. Burkesh, and, putting a foot on his chest, tugged at something. Soon he pulled out a small, thin fencing sword, as clear as an icicle. He ceremoniously wiped it clean on the grass, gave it a quick polish with his hanky, handed it to the wounded boy, and said:

> "Your father is a beast beyond compare.
> You proved you have more dignity and grace.
> Your worth to me . . . it's more than I can share."

He paused tearfully, took a steadying breath, and continued. "Now go inside; have someone fix your face."

And with that, Mr. Appleblossom returned to his post in the tree.

Once the Quillitary's front line had turned into a magical pile of stiffs, Simber roared, "Advance!"

Inch by inch, yard by yard, Simber moved forward on the Quillitary, his squad close behind, and the other squads following in their wake.

As many Quillitary soldiers as were able to get past the great stone statue did so, easing their way into the magical world to face a new group of attackers. The afternoon wore on, Simber unwavering, though chipped in spots; Alex gaining confidence as the battle continued; Meghan temporarily set back by a melee attack that left her slashed from shoulder to elbow before she was able to stop the three attackers with a fire step that sent them running away.

It was nearing sunset on the desolate side of the wall when all those of the Quillitary who hadn't made it into Artimé had been contained in one fashion or another. Simber sent Rufus to Claire Morning with this news as the squads outside of Artimé regrouped and refueled on water and food that somehow had appeared at the gate, delivered by some brave protector.

When the squirrelicorn returned, he bore this news: "Ms. Morning is sending out the night watch. She requests the backup squads deliver the injured into the mansion at once." Rufus took a deep breath and continued. "Simber . . ." He shook his head, almost as if he were reluctant to deliver the rest of the message. "Claire wants you and Alex to meet her on the mansion roof immediately."

Alex, who was resting against the wall, blinked. "How am I supposed to get up there?"

Simber nodded. "Thank you, Rrrufus. Stowe, climb aboarrrd."

Alex didn't hesitate. He hopped on the cheetah's slick stone back, settled between the wings, and wrapped his arms around Simber's broad neck. With a power greater than any force that Alex had felt before, the cheetah flapped his wings and ascended over the carnage. Seconds later they landed on the mansion roof, Simber leaving a hearty dent in the shiny metallic shingles.

Alex stared at the property below, littered with bodies and small smoking bits of fiery weapons. His nose crinkled at the smell of smoke and blood. Nearly the entire lawn, from the giant wall on his left all the way to the jungle in front of him and to the sea on his right, was occupied by fighting pairs in hand-to-hand combat. He scanned the property for Samheed and Lani, but he couldn't find them.

"Well done, Simber." Claire Morning spoke in a smooth, firm tone. She had a bandage on her shoulder, the center of it stained with blood. "They've nearly run out of ammunition for their guns. Many thanks go to you, my friend, for rendering so many of their pellets useless."

Simber nodded. "Casualties?"

Claire tugged at her hair, deep in thought. "We have many

injured. Two of ours have died from their wounds so far."

Simber growled his dissatisfaction. "And the enemy?"

"Scores of them. It's difficult to tell who is frozen from spells and who is dead, though General Blair is most assuredly dead. Needless to say, they are hurting. And that is why I've called you here. We've word that they are sending in a second wave."

"What, tonight? In the darrrk? Fools! We'll crrrush them."

Claire nodded. "We will with this method. Gunnar reports that much of their ammunition has misfired and their guns are either clogging up, useless, or backfiring due to opposite soliloquies, so they are injuring themselves quite nicely. But there is one thing I thought of . . . and it leaves me more than a little concerned."

"What is it?"

"Justine."

The cheetah's stone forehead rippled. "I don't underrrstand."

Claire glanced at Alex and then back to Simber. "She's coming."

Simber's face softened and grew concerned, and then Alex thought for a moment that he saw a thread of fear trickling into the giant cat's marble eyes. "I see," he said gruffly. And then he added, "She'll expose herrrself if she uses any of herrr magic."

Claire nodded. "Father thinks she's growing desperate enough to risk it."

Alex had no idea what they were talking about. Justine could do magic? And who was Claire's father? Mr. Today? He hung on to every word because it seemed so terribly important.

"What do you prrropose?"

"Florence, Octavia, and I can handle Justine and the governors," Claire said, her voice bitter just saying Justine's name. "But she's leaving the palace exposed, and Father is the only one who knows the secret entrance. He wants you to accompany him. If we can disarm and seal the palace, she'll be trapped with no place to hide, and this will soon be over. Not just for us, but for the people of Quill as well."

"And the boy?"

"He's to go with you. Father doesn't want Justine anywhere near him." She turned suddenly toward the sea and put her hand to her forehead, trying to block the sheen of sunset on the waves. "There," she said, pointing to a gleaming white boat in the distance. "He's waiting."

Alex, surprised at the turn of events, hitched himself onto the cheetah's back once again. The thrill of the flight and the powerful wing strokes, a hundred feet above the vast sea, shook his ribs as he slid around on the cheetah's slippery back, trying to find a comfortable position without falling off.

Soon enough the statue reached Mr. Today. Simber closed the gap between them until he hovered just feet above the swiftly moving craft. "Now," he growled over his shoulder to Alex. "Slide off my left side."

Shivering, Alex did what he was told and dropped onto the deck. Mr. Today grasped his arm and helped him right himself as gale-force winds from Simber's immense wings blasted the boy about like an empty paper cup. Simber rose to a more comfortable altitude and easily stayed with the ship as they skimmed around the shore.

Alex stared. "It really is just an island," he said, shaking his head in disbelief. All the years the governors had lied to everyone—it was crazy. He peered ahead at the islands in the distance, growing closer as they rounded Quill.

Mr. Today glanced at Alex. "There's an entire string of islands out there, most of them inhabited by good, decent people. But we lost contact with all of them when we built the wall." The old mage stood at the helm, his hair looking perfectly normal for the occasion. He looked weary.

Alex's teeth chattered with anticipation and the cool evening sea breeze. "Where are we going, exactly?"

"Ahh," sighed Mr. Today. "I suppose we can't just enjoy the ride tonight, can we? No, indeed. Why I don't take this thing out more often is quite beyond me. I used to take Claire fishing. . . ." He shook his head, forcing his thoughts back to the threat at hand. "We're going to the palace. You know about the secret entrance into Quill, do you not?"

"Yes, er, well, Arija mentioned it, and so did Ms. Morning just now."

"Well, it's been many years since we devised it and added the magic. I think I can find it. Once we're in, we'll have a few encounters if the guards are still around, I imagine. You and I will freeze them up or some such thing; then we'll seal the palace so that if Justine makes it out of Artimé, she'll have lost her 'power,' so to speak."

"The palace is her power?"

Mr. Today furrowed his brow. "Not exactly. Her power is

the fear she instills in people. She hides behind the palace so that Quill can't see that she is afraid too."

"What is she afraid of?"

The mage laughed bitterly. "She's afraid of losing her power to make people afraid. She's afraid of not being in control. Appearing weak."

Alex thought about all of this. It was hard to imagine that the stately woman was afraid of anything. But there was another question in his mind that had been eating away at him since the night he'd gone to the gate. He hesitated, not sure if he should ask, but finally gathered up the nerve as they sped along, rounding a particularly jutting piece of the island.

"Mr. Today?"

"Yes, lad."

"You said that you made the people of Quill forget."

Mr. Today nodded thoughtfully. "Yes. I did that."

"Why?"

He scratched his chin. "To keep them from dissenting when Justine began to rule. Because back then I believed in Justine's plan when she took the title of high priest—that the best way to rule people was to protect them from everything and frighten them into obedience. I believed in it so much that I gave my full trust to Justine for years, and didn't always notice what she was up to. And because of that failure on my part, she came up with the plan to segregate the least useful in our society. I offered my services, because I was a better mage than she. It wasn't difficult to render them useless. I just had to put the Unwanteds in a splatterpaint spell, or paralyze them, or make them fall asleep, then let them stand around on the lawn outside the walls of Quill. No mess." He shook his head sadly, horrified at his own actions, as tears glistened and seeped into the wrinkles around his eyes. "But then Justine wanted to go a step further. A step too far, in my opinion, at the time. She convinced me to create the Great Lake of Boiling Oil, and then she proceeded to eliminate the Unwanteds permanently. I was horrified, but I didn't let on—she was so powerful and power hungry by then that she wouldn't have hesitated to eliminate me if I defied her. And I knew I had to stop her. So I pretended to be behind her actions fully, and I offered to take over the business of dumping all the remaining bodies, which allowed Justine to have more time to do the rest of her job." He sighed.

"So I hid them using magic and, every year, froze and hid the newest group that had been Purged."

"What . . ." Alex bit his lip. "What made you decide to make Artimé?"

"There was a little girl," he said softly. "You see, Alex, you have to understand how it all started. Fifty years ago I was young, just a little older than you, and I was foolish. I went along with Justine, disappearing every Purge day to put spells on the Unwanteds. By the time Justine wanted to actually eliminate them entirely, I had a wife, a child, some dear friends in the government—one, especially. And each year, once I took over, I pretended to eliminate the Unwanteds but merely did as I'd done before, casting spells on them and then hiding them with another spell so Justine couldn't see. But it became hard to cast these spells on children I had grown to care about. One little girl in particular. And I knew it was wrong—all of it was so, so wrong. I decided that if I were to change things and be a better man, I had to release them from these spells and let them live their lives. I had to create a secret haven for them, but I couldn't just create it and then leave them. So I did what I had to do. I left my life, my friends, my family in Quill and created Artimé.

And I sold the idea to Justine as a way to build even more fear in the hearts of the children and scare them into submission— I would hermit myself away and become the dreaded Death Farmer that no one actually saw unless they were Unwanted."

"Wow," Alex said, and took it all in. After a moment he looked up at the mage. "So originally you chose power like Justine, back when you were young, but then you changed," he said. "You became good. So maybe Aaron . . . ?"

Mr. Today smiled. "We will never lose hope, my boy."

Alex puzzled for a long moment, gazing over the water. "Were you . . . um . . . were you secretly in love with Justine or something? Is that why you went along with her?"

Mr. Today afforded a chuckle. "No, Alex. Not in the slightest. Not any more than you could be secretly in love with your twin."

Alex stared at the mage. "Wait. You mean . . ."

The old man nodded sagely. "You and I," he murmured, "have a lot in common."

They closed in on the south side of the island, where the ground grew hilly. Alex thought that they were probably near

LISA McMANN

347 « The Unwanteds

the palace, but not a thing could be seen of Quill because of the hideous wall.

"Who was the little girl?" Alex asked presently, although he thought he knew.

"My daughter, Claire. Ms. Morning."

Alex nodded. "You couldn't cast the spell."

"No." Mr. Today looked away, a wistful expression on his face.

"And so you created Artimé . . . for her."

Mr. Today nodded as he pulled the yacht closer to shore and cut the motor. "And for all of you. Best thing I've ever done. Still, it's not enough to make up for all the wrongs," he said. "Whatever I do—it'll never be enough." He scanned the rocks, muttering something to himself as he searched to remember the exact location of the magical passage. "Aha," he whispered.

Simber landed gracefully on the rocks next to the boat. Mr. Today placed the anchor spell while Alex climbed over the side of the craft, and the two embarked onto Simber's back for the short journey to dry land.

Once they reached the shore, Mr. Today put his hand on the wall and recited an incantation. A great chunk of the concrete block slid aside, and the three walked through it. They found themselves in a dark, narrow, enclosed room. Mr. Today recited a second incantation, and the wall in front of them crumbled to dust. They stepped over it and looked around the dimly lit passageway.

Everything was gray, just like all of Quill. The ceilings were very high, the hallway just wide enough for Simber to walk through without scraping his wings on the walls.

"Be ready," Mr. Today whispered in the echoing chamber. "There will be six guards, but they'll most likely be stationed at the entrance."

Alex fingered his pens and balls of clay inside his vest pocket.

They moved slowly into the heart of the palace, first Simber, then Mr. Today, and then Alex bringing up the rear. They passed doorways on the left and the right, Simber sampling the air, his ears tuned and twitching this way and that. After a moment he stopped short and pointed with a long, sharp claw. Mr. Today and Alex squeezed past Simber's body to get a look.

Four Quillitary guards stood at the windows near the palace

entrance, peering out, and two more sat, leaning against the wall, asleep.

Mr. Today gestured, Alex nodded, and together they attacked. Alex flicked his paintbrush at the first sleeping guard. The paint seeped over him entirely, and within seconds it solidified. Then he tossed two tiny balls of clay at the second sleeping guard. The clay stretched and clamped the guard's legs to the floor and his arms to the wall. Alex whispered, "Silence," as the surprised guard awoke, but the guards at the door heard the noise and whirled around. They all shrieked in terror at the sight of Simber, but two of them still had the presence of mind to pull their guns and point. One managed to get a shot off before Mr. Today simply turned all four of them to stone. The bullet pinged off the palace wall harmlessly, leaving a small chip in it.

"A souvenir for Justine," Mr. Today said.

Alex grinned and looked around. "That's it?"

Simber grumbled. "Well, that was borrring."

Mr. Today teasingly sympathized with the great beast. "Oh, Sim, I'm sorry. Say, how about you eat that one over there, hmm?"

The silenced, shackled guard's eyes widened in fear.

Simber grunted and moved back down the hallway from which they had come, anxious to get back to the action in Artimé.

"Patience," Mr. Today said. He waved a hand at the palace entrance, and the doorway became a solid wall. He turned in a circle in the large entrance, pointing all around, sealing up all the windows and doors throughout the entire structure.

There was no way into or out of the palace now, except for the secret passage.

"Well, that should do it. They won't be able to get back in. Nice work by the way, Alex," Mr. Today said. "I rather liked that clay spell. Did you create that yourself?"

"I did," Alex said proudly.

"It certainly seems solid," Mr. Today remarked, leaning over and rapping his knuckles on the frightened man's shackles. "You'll have to teach me that one sometime."

Alex beamed.

"Remind me that we'll need to come back and feed these guards in a few days, will you?" Mr. Today said lightly.

"Sure," Alex said. "So this is it? You're sure there are no more guards?"

LISA McMANN

"Only six. I've watched carefully over the years. Justine had little to fear."

"Until we came along," Alex said, a bit smugly.

Simber rolled his eyes impatiently and moved farther down the hallway. "Marrrcus."

"Oh, dear. Quite right, Sim. We should be getting back." His face turned grim, as if he had just remembered that the people of Artimé were still fighting.

Simber growled impatiently and glided back down the hallway the same way they had come. Mr. Today hurried after him, and Alex, feeling a bit relieved despite his concern over the battle in Artimé, followed them into the narrow passage, his mind overflowing with more questions for the mage.

And so it was that when a fist, like a bolt of lightning, shot out from what seemed like nowhere, Alex toppled like a toy soldier.

Severing Ties

A stunned Alex lay still for a short time until he had figured out what happened. He quickly reached for a weapon and cried out to Mr. Today for help. Mr. Today turned to see what the commotion was just as Alex pointed the highlighter at his brother and wildly shot a round of blindness spells, missing Aaron but hitting Mr. Today squarely in the eyes, causing him to double over in pain and lower himself blindly to the floor.

"Simber!" shouted the mage.

Simber, who had made it all the way to the secret passage, had to back up the entire way because nowhere was it wide enough to allow him to turn around. He roared his frustration and scuttled ungracefully in reverse.

Aaron, eyeing the others, stood near one of the palace guards. Pure hatred dripped from his features. "You useless, Unwanted piece of dirt," Aaron seethed. "You ruined my life with this! When this battle is over, Justine will dispose of me, and it's all your fault! Why couldn't you leave me alone?" In his hand he held something small and shiny.

Alex's eyes widened. "Aaron! Why—what—why won't you just believe me? You'll stoop to anything, won't you?" As he talked, buying time, he scrambled for a ball of clay, a fire dragon, a handful of scatterclips, anything! But his supplies were substantially depleted after the long day, and he had to dig deep to grasp hold of anything.

As Mr. Today hurriedly neutralized the blind spell on himself and as Simber scrambled backward, nearly trampling the mage in order to reach the wide foyer where he could turn himself around, and as Alex scooted on his backside along the cold floor, searching wildly for something with which to defend himself, and finally landing his fingers on a freezebrush, Aaron pulled his arm back and shouted, "I hope you die a thousand

LISA McMANN

deaths!" He threw the metal object with all his might.

Alex, hearing the horridly familiar words, seeing the scatterclip, suddenly realized the meaning of Lani's note. "No!" He pointed the freezebrush frantically at Aaron and uttered a curse, hitting his mark as the scatterclip whizzed toward him.

Mr. Today cried out and cast a glass-wall spell, trying to stop the scatterclip. But it was too late. The simple, innocent scatterclip, combined with the words to make it lethal, had found its mark in Alex's chest.

Simber, finally turned around, crashed through the glass wall and looked from one twin to the other, at first unsure which boy was which. Mr. Today pointed wildly at Aaron, frozen in place, and Simber immediately pounced on the frozen boy, bringing him crashing to the ground. Aaron screamed, his mouth stuck open, his eyes begging Simber not to hurt him.

Mr. Today rushed to Alex's side as the boy fell back, his eyes glazing over, a look of surprise turning to horror on his face. He grasped the air wildly, unable to get hold of the clip that had imbedded itself through his vest and into his chest, and gasped for air.

"Don't—kill—him—," Alex managed to rasp before he lost consciousness.

Lani helped Samheed into the mansion as one of the protectors met them at the door. They got Samheed settled into the newly created hospital wing alongside others with various wounds. Quickly Lani washed and bandaged her leg, and, despite the protector's protest, she went back outside as the sun was setting, just as a large shadow passed overhead. She looked up and saw Simber flying elegantly out to sea with a passenger, and she wondered briefly what that was all about. But she didn't have time to think about it. She scurried toward her commander, Arija, at their station point, pelting ten-minute sleep spells left and right along the way.

"Lani." It was Florence. "I need you at the front line."

Lani glanced over at Arija, who nodded. Lani followed Florence to the entrance just as a new line of squealing vehicles and marching Quillitary soldiers poured in, yelling wildly. These soldiers had no guns. Rather, their weapons were quite unrecognizable to anyone who had not grown up in a family that collected rusty scrap metal.

The Artiméans blasted the Quillitary as they arrived, causing a pileup of hard-shelled, stiffened bodies such that the last vehicles couldn't get through without driving over them, and even then most of the jalopies conked out.

As darkness settled and the various jungle creatures that could see quite well in the dark came out to fight, the confusion grew. Lani positioned herself behind a tree, finding it difficult to tell who was friend and who was foe.

And then a rumor spread its way to her ears. "The governors have arrived." Lani shivered. The governors.

Her mind raced back over the previous months as she had struggled with the decision: Would she use lethal weapons? She had ultimately decided that she would not, with one exception. And now, as she peered out into the darkness and confusion, that exception was slipping inside Artimé and stealing toward her, carrying a pistol in hand—the kind that only the governors owned. The pistol, Lani knew, was a hundred times stronger that the weak pellet guns that some of the Quillitary had. One shot could kill a full-grown human or beast.

Lani reached into her vest, her eyes narrowing as she glued them on her father. She took out her one and only throwing star, which Samheed had given her when she'd asked him for it months ago. She pressed the metal to her lips and whispered an incantation as her father slipped along the wall, darting between trees, his pistol gleaming whenever it caught a ray of moonlight.

She followed him to a clump of trees. *He's going to hide. Lie in wait. What a coward!* She grew angrier and angrier as all the thoughts of the Purge flooded back to her. How his shame must have been so great that he could not even acknowledge her good-bye at the gate. *A coward,* she thought, over and over again, until it became a challenge to her to make him admit it was so. *Beg me not to kill you. See how it feels.* All she knew was that she would not give her father a chance like Samheed had done for his father. She had learned her lessons well enough today.

She crept closer and watched him from ten feet away, thinking how stupid he must be not to notice he was being followed. *Your intelligence and your strength won't save you now, dear Father.*

Lani shifted to get a better view. She couldn't see what her father was doing. As she moved around the tree trunk, her vest caught on a tiny branch. It snapped off. Lani froze as Senior Governor Haluki turned sharply at the noise.

"Who's there?" he whispered sharply.

Lani held her breath. And then, because she was not a coward like her father, she stepped out from behind the tree into the shadows.

"Claire?" Senior Governor Haluki said uncertainly.

Fingering her weapon, the metal growing hot in her fingers, Lani stepped closer, her rage increasing. "No, *Father*," she spat. "It's me. Or have you forgotten me, like all the others conveniently forget their *children*?" A tiny sob caught in her throat as she twisted her arm behind her expertly, just as Samheed had taught her, and prepared to fire.

Governor Haluki sucked in a breath. "Oh, Lani," he whispered. He glanced over his shoulder in each direction, and then stepped toward his daughter, holding out his hand just as she snapped her wrist and sent the deadly star in flight.

"No! Lani—you don't understa—," he cried. The star struck him at an awkward angle. As he fell to the ground, rolling and writing wildly in pain, his body transformed into an enormous gray wolf. He took off running, tripping, limping, into the night.

The gun lay gleaming on the ground where he had stood.

Simber, with the unconscious, bleeding Alex cradled gently in his enormous jaws, and the captured, now thawed, terrorized Aaron hanging on to Simber's neck for dear life, nodded to Mr. Today and sped fluidly along the shore, leaped into the air, and flapped his powerful wings. He rose up high enough to clear the great wall and flew in a direct path this time, at his top speed, over the barbed-wire ceiling that covered the land of Quill. Aaron cried desperately in fear all the way, knowing that falling would mean certain death but that hanging on might give him another option, eventually. Mr. Today cruised around the perimeter in the boat, which could magically sense the reefs and rocks in the dark.

As the waves pounded the sides of the craft, the weary man's eyes filled with grief. He whispered constantly, pulling at his hair. "Not Alex. Please, not him. It can't happen like this. Marcus, you careless fool! How many more deaths will you be responsible for?"

When he neared Artimé, he slowed and cast the anchor spell. Simber, without either boy now, swooped to within sight in the moonlit evening, and the man climbed nimbly on the cheetah's back.

"How is he?" Marcus asked in a low voice.

"Still alive," Simber said. "Yourrr enchantment of the vest may have saved him."

"And the twin, Aaron?"

Simber roared in frustration. "He scrrreamed and pounded me the whole way. Finally he jumped as we flew overrr the inlet at the shorrre of Arrrtimé. I expect he'll have drrrowned by now, or been eaten by sharrrks. I left him—it was morrre imporrrtant to get Alex inside. He's lost a lot of blood." And indeed the blood had stained Simber's sandstone mouth and neck, making him look fiercer than ever.

"But we have otherrr trrroubles rrright now. Justine is holding a pistol on Clairrre; Gunnarrr is missing; Florrrence was hit by an out-of-contrrrol vehicle and she's lopped off at the knees. Octavia is now Septavia—she lost a tentacle, but she'll rrregenerrrate. Sean and Meghan arrre on the rrroof playing sniperrr."

LISA McMANN

"Egads."

"I'll say."

Mr. Today gazed across Artimé, counting the remaining Quillens, and then mused over his spell strengths and capabilities. "There are less than a hundred of them left," he said. "I think I can stop the remaining ones now on my own. And Quill has seen enough to know we are a strong force to be reckoned with—they'll think twice about fighting us again, which means our future is safe from further attacks. Yes, my friend, it's time. You and I both know the only spell that will end this."

"I hate to do it."

"It won't hurt them."

"That's exactly why I hate to do it," growled the cheetah. "Though you might catch Aarrron in it, which would keep him out of our hairrr forrr now."

Mr. Today patted the cheetah's smooth neck. "You had your moment of glory in the palace, Sim—you saved Alex. And you'll have another one soon. In the meantime, Claire will be all right, won't she?"

"I cerrrtainly hope so."

LISA McMANN

"Justine won't shoot her without me there. She'll want me to witness it. I'm sure she thinks it'll be symbolic." Mr. Today's voice was bitter.

"I imagine Clairrre knows that too."

"All right then, it's settled."

"Herrre we go, my frrriend." Simber took a pass along the seashore, from mansion to jungle, as Mr. Today held out his hand over the lawn. Back and forth they flew, Mr. Today keeping his hand out and concentrating very hard to hold the spell on so many people, Simber being very careful to weave just so across the property trying not to miss any of it, as if he were mowing the lawn.

When they had covered all the land up to the entrance to Quill, Mr. Today, barely holding on to the weighty spell, whispered, "Quillitary, take a dive," and snapped his fingers.

Immediately, and as one body, the remaining mobile Quillitary stopped fighting, turned, and marched their way to the seashore. The Artiméans who had a moment ago been fighting now caught their breath and watched in surprise as the Quillitary stopped and stood in the shallow water.

Simber flew over them.

"Freeze," Mr. Today said.

The water at the shore froze, trapping all the Quillitary in place, making them furious but oddly cooling off some of the hotheads nicely.

The people and creatures of Artimé looked up at their leader and broke into applause.

"All right, Simber. Take me to Claire. And then stay alert. Watch for my signal."

Lani gasped and clapped her hand to her mouth as the great gray wolf stumbled off. She was confused. "Father?" she whispered, but he was already gone.

She had seen the wolf before from a distance. And she'd thought it odd that such a wild creature would have bounded out of the mansion the previous day, only to disappear again shortly thereafter. And then it all began to make sense.

"Oh, Father, what have I done? What have *you* done?" Gingerly she picked up the gun, feeling its weight in her hand, remembering when she was ten and her father had let her hold it—had even taken her to the Quillitary range on Purge day when she was eleven to teach her how to carry it safely, and to let her shoot it when no one else was around. He had made her promise not to tell anyone. That was one secret she'd kept, because it seemed too—too—sacred a moment to work into one of her wild stories.

But to her, now, the gun represented awful things. She disarmed the gun and slid it into her vest, realizing that despite her knowledge of its workings, and all her father had taught her, perhaps even in preparation for this day, she could never, ever use it. She snuck off through the trees, growing wearier and hungrier as the evening slipped into night, and suddenly wondered what had happened to Alex, for it had been hours since she'd last seen him. She stopped short. *Hmm*, she thought, wondering if she could manage to do one of Alex's favorite spells. She withdrew a paintbrush from her pocket, whispered, "Invisible," and brushed herself up and down with it.

The last thing to disappear was the gleam in her eye.

Back at the mansion the injured Samheed had too much time to think about how his actions as Will's assistant had contributed to the battle raging. And seeing his father again— once his hero—so willing to kill his own son . . . how could

Samheed have ever wanted to go back there? Be a part of that? Now the guilt overcame him, and he could lie still no longer with this battle raging around him. He struggled to his feet, slipped his component vest on, and when the caretakers weren't looking, he limped outside.

As the entire remaining Quillitary marched into the sea, a drenched, bedraggled body finally hoisted himself up to his feet on the beach. He coughed and spit seawater, and began wiping the sand from his face and clothes. In the dark he located the looming mansion and stole quietly in that direction, limping and squishing slightly.

He stepped over bodies until he found one wearing a vest like Alex's. Aaron disrobed the fallen Artiméan and slipped the vest over his own shoulders, feeling for the one magical item he actually knew how to use.

He found a treasure of them and took one, rubbing it between his fingers, his eyes darting wildly now, looking for prey. *I'll earn my position back! I must prove myself to the high priest. I'll find the old man, and I will kill him. And then I'll finish off Alex, once and for all.*

At the corner of the mansion Aaron stood, deep in the shadows. He saw her—the great high priest, the one he would do anything for in order to regain her favor. He knew that now he must be Alex. Act like Alex. They must not suspect. He only hoped no one had yet heard what had really happened to his twin.

As he watched Mr. Today approach, he looked around at the bizarre assortment of creatures.

"Alex," someone whispered. Aaron jumped and turned sharply, coming face-to-face with a sharp-toothed alligator that had several spindly arms. He nearly screamed in fright.

"Alex," Ms. Octavia whispered again. "Be ready with your scatterclips. The lethal verbal component is 'die a thousand deaths.' If Justine makes any false moves, do your worst, my boy. She'll have to die if any of this is to be resolved. Are you comfortable with that?"

Aaron blinked, sucked in a breath, and nodded. He didn't understand half of what the creature was saying, but it was enough to know that he had accidentally stumbled upon the verbal component to the spell, which was also the mantra of the Quillitary. He held the clip, poised, appearing ready to

367 « The Unwanteds

LISA McMANN

throw in the direction of Justine, but his eyes burned into the back of the head of Mr. Today, who stood only slightly to the side of the high priest.

Samheed, seeing the high priest, crept forward behind the octogator and Alex, realizing the severity of the scene before him—Justine and Mr. Today, about to be face-to-face once again. He remained quiet, pulling a throwing star from his vest in case it was needed. If only he could take down Justine, it would prove to everyone that he was not a traitor.

Ms. Octavia readied herself as well, and then glanced more carefully at the boy beside her. She frowned. Something didn't seem right.

Samheed noticed her glance, and he took another look at Alex, at the way he stood, and at his hand that held the scatterclip. Samheed's eyes narrowed and then flashed with fire. He and Will Blair had been studying Alex for months. He knew what was wrong. This boy held the scatterclip in his right hand.

"It's not Alex!" Samheed whispered.

Aaron's eyes widened in surprise. He tried to run, but Samheed muttered, "Break a leg!" which made Aaron squeal in pain and hop on one foot.

In one swift, smooth motion four of Ms. Octavia's remaining seven appendages threaded and twisted over and under the boy's arms and around his legs, rendering his struggles useless and forcing his good leg to buckle. He dropped to the ground.

"Silence," she said in a low voice.

Aaron's cry died in his throat. He shook violently, helplessly.

"Well done, Samheed," Ms. Octavia said. "Don't move another inch, Aaron Stowe, or you're a dead man," she growled into his ear, and chomped her teeth together to keep from biting his head completely off.

"Hello, again," Mr. Today said coldly as he approached the high priest's vehicle. All around him were piles of wounded, sleeping, or splatterpainted Quillitary. On the road beyond the high priest a pileup of smoking vehicles groaned in various stages of death. The rest of Artimé's walking wounded, suddenly bereft of their enemies, picked their way around bodies and fell in behind their leader, ready to carry on if necessary for as long as they could stand and draw breath.

"Marcus, my dear," came the sarcastic reply. "I've been waiting for you."

"How terribly polite."

"Indeed," she said. The High Priest Justine sat on the seat of her vehicle with Claire Morning tucked securely under one arm, a pistol pointed at Claire's temple. Governor Strang sat beside her, his pistol trained on Meghan Ranger, who lay on the corner of the mansion roof nearest them. Four more governors stood at the entrance with their pistols, pointing randomly at anyone who dared move. Only Senior Governor Haluki was missing.

"Your young protégé, Aaron, sends his regards. Shame that you should punish him. He's the one who might have saved you all," Mr. Today said evenly.

Justine's eyes narrowed.

"Oh, come now, Justine. Why so suspicious? Have you forgotten our little secret passage to the palace?" he asked. "And, oh dear, let me see. One, two, three, four, five . . . good heavens! You're missing a governor. Pity."

The four standing governors wavered, casting sidelong glances at one another in the starlight.

"Dear me. And have you told your governors about your secret gift? You know," he whispered loudly. "Magic."

"Enough!" shouted Justine.

"You do not deny it?"

"Silence, you traitor!"

Marcus Today smiled a small smile. "Justine, honestly. Have you no secrets on me that you can reveal to my people so that they might gaze at me as suspiciously as your governors are now looking at you? Surely there must be something."

Justine glared at Mr. Today. She cocked the hammer of the pistol that grazed Claire's temple.

Claire closed her eyes reflexively, and then opened them again, granting permission to her father to do whatever it took.

"What have you done with Aaron?" Justine growled.

"Hmm? Oh, the twin? Well, there was a bit of a skirmish at the palace, you see. You know how it is with twins." He chuckled hollowly. "Best of friends, worst of enemies. All that rot. I imagine he's around here somewhere. Pity he isn't coming to your aid."

Justine snarled and looked at Claire, judging her features. "All these years, Marcus? Thirty of the last fifty years you've spent betraying me and all I've stood for. All *we've* stood for! After all I've done for you and for Quill! How could you?"

Mr. Today sighed and looked up at the sky. He shook his head slowly, and then looked back at the high priest. "The question is, dear sister, how could *you*?"

Justine's face burned. She stood up in the vehicle and wrenched Claire to her feet. "Say good-bye to your daughter, once and for all," she spat.

Mr. Today nodded amicably at the high priest and smiled warmly at Claire. "Good-bye, daughter," he said.

From the sky, a whirlwind. Simber swooped in with his powerful wings, knocking four governors across the road and the fifth headfirst into the backseat. He grabbed Claire in his jaws and sailed away.

When shots rang out in the confusion, it was the High Priest Justine who slumped over in her seat and began to deflate like a balloon, until she was nothing but a flat rubber body that flopped over and fell to the floor, only to be stepped on in the aftermath. Clearly, no bullet had done that to her.

No one could see the invisible Lani, nor could they hear her whisper "Evermore, nevermore," an irrevocable spell that she had delighted in finding in her studies. And this was the perfect use for it. Justine would forevermore be silent and useless. "Take that, you old windbag," she muttered when she saw it had worked perfectly.

Afterward Lani ran as fast as she could toward the part of the shore that remained unfrozen. She took the gun from her vest and flung it as far as she could into the sea. And then, finally, she slipped away to the forest to find her father.

LISA McMANN

And So It Happened That

When it was all over, in the wee hours of the morning, Mr. Today visited the newly created hospital wing of the mansion. There he found Lani dozing on the floor next to Alex, and discovered Meghan asleep in a chair near Samheed. The old mage roamed from bedside to bedside, offering whatever healing spells he could to the people of Artimé who had served and sacrificed for him. Eventually he took a chair, settling in near Alex, who was the most seriously injured of them all. And while he was glad for the protection spell on Alex's vest, Mr. Today couldn't stop thinking. Had he made a mistake? He buried his face in his hands as the ward tossed and turned restlessly, painfully, in the dim light around him. The old mage would not sleep that night.

By morning Gunnar Haluki had arrived. He paced anxiously with his arm in a sling, waiting for his daughter to wake up. Claire, who was quite calm despite her near-death experience of the previous evening, joined them.

Claire bent down and kissed her father on the top of the head. "Octavia's working on Florence's legs. She ought to have them solidly reattached by the end of the day, walking around good as new."

"How's Octavia's stump?"

"Oh, it's good. She's perfectly fine. Though a tad annoyed, since it was her eraser appendage. She'll have to adjust a bit until the new one grows in."

"And the twin, Aaron?"

"In custody for now. Beside himself over Justine's death but trying hard not to show it."

"How did Samheed know he wasn't Alex?"

"Alex is left-handed. Aaron was ready to throw a scatterclip, probably aiming at you, Father. He held it in his right hand."

Mr. Today pulled on his hair. "Of course," he murmured. "Identical twins—sometimes a righty and a lefty. I had forgotten that. He's brilliant to have noticed."

"Samheed knows Alex well. Perhaps now he will try to be a bit more like him."

Meghan stirred and opened her eyes. When she saw Gunnar Haluki pacing the floor, she sat up, alarmed. "What is he doing here!" she cried out, waking Lani in the process.

"It's okay, Meghan. Gunnar is on our side, and always has been," Claire told her. "We kept it a secret to protect him."

Lani sat up and looked around. Gunnar Haluki stopped in his tracks.

"Hey, you," Lani said, a sleepy smile spreading across her face. "You're pretty sneaky. I couldn't find you last night. Sorry about your shoulder."

Gunnar pressed his lips together, perhaps to stop them from quivering, and reached out his good arm to her. Lani stumbled over to him and buried her face in his shoulder.

Samheed awoke, his face throbbing, his voice hoarse. "What's going on? Good grief, what happened to Alex?" He blinked his good eye in surprise when he saw Lani embracing her father, and then glanced at his beside table, where Mr. Appleblossom's small, icelike sword gleamed in the morning light. He bit his lip, wincing at the pain but smiling inwardly as he remembered the words from his mentor, and his own ultimate save in recognizing Aaron. Perhaps it had been enough. Gingerly he rolled onto his side to watch and listen.

Mr. Today gazed over the small group with a tired half smile. *All in good time,* he thought. He rested his eyes on Alex, whose pale face set the mood for days to come. But deep down Mr. Today knew that Alex would mend and that the boy would rise up, stronger and wiser than before, preparing to take on a new role from an ailing mage. *It had to happen this way,* Marcus thought. *For him. For Artimé.*

Alex stirred and opened an eye. When he caught sight of Mr. Today, he whispered, "Don't forget . . . to go back . . . and feed the guards."

Mr. Today, overcome, nodded his assurances.

"And . . . Aaron?"

Mr. Today hesitated. "We'll take care of him, too."

Alex closed his eyes again and slept.

» » « «

Over the next days the mess of broken-down vehicles was cleared from Artimé. The remaining Quillitary, none the worse off for the dip in the ice, had been immediately freed from the sea, and those who had been attacked with permanent spells had been disarmed and released one by one, with the understanding that everything had changed, Quill had been defeated, and the war was over.

Samheed was up and around after a day or so, and he joined Lani and Meghan at Alex's side whenever the protectors would allow them to visit. "I heard what you did," Alex told Samheed. "Thank you."

Samheed smiled grimly. "I'm sorry . . . about everything," he said.

Alex smiled and held out a weak hand. "I still get to punch you, right?"

Samheed laughed and shook it. "And I still don't guarantee what will happen if you do."

Although Alex didn't know it, Mr. Today spent his nights watching over the boy until he fell into an exhausted sleep, at which time Simber took over, both of them keeping their worries to themselves. And when Alex finally came around for good, even the enormous stone beast shed a private tear, or perhaps even two.

Every day Mr. Today, Gunnar Haluki, and Simber took a trip to the palace to check on the guards. And finally, one day, seeing no reason to keep them entombed in the palace, Mr. Today removed the spell from the palace entrance and set them free. Gunnar Haluki was grateful. So were the guards. Simber . . . well, not so much.

And as it happened, no one but Lani knew for sure who had uttered the curse that had eliminated the High Priest Justine. At least, that's what Lani thought. Though she wondered deep down if her father knew it had been she. They never spoke of it.

"So, Senior Governor Haluki was the friend you mentioned to me in the boat?" Alex asked as he slurped soup, feeling decidedly better, though still keeping to his bed for the most part.

Mr. Today smiled. "Gunnar Haluki and I were fast friends back when Justine took that turn for the worse. Gunnar, a young

LISA McMANN

governor, also bought into Justine's plan at first. We desperately wanted her to be right, just as you did with Aaron," Mr. Today said.

"And though Gunnar and I kept our relationship a secret from everyone else once I moved to the Death Farm, I kept no secrets from my friend. We shared our changing thoughts whenever we met together in the wee hours of the night in my office. And that is how we formed a plan together. Gunnar worked his way up the seniority ladder until he was next in line to the high priest, putting himself into the best position to stop the madness."

The mage leaned back in his chair, reminiscing. "If Artimé could have lasted five more years without being discovered, my twin sister, Justine, would have either retired or died, for despite her strong appearance she was frail as could be. And my dear friend Gunnar would have taken over, and together we would have tried to right all the wrongs done by Justine. And," he admitted, "by me."

Alex nodded, fascinated, yet exhausted by the simple act of eating lunch. "But then I came along," he said, a bit sheepish.

Mr. Today chuckled softly. "Apparently, my plan with

Gunnar wasn't meant to be. When the now-infamous Stowe twins emerged, they caused all sorts of problems." He winked. "Gunnar, because he was loyal to me, agreed to be wolf-charmed in order to hide his identity in Artimé and keep his eye on you without looking suspicious. He used that very special tube that sits protected across the lounge from my office to go back and forth from Quill to Artimé. It leads to a variety of horrible places, like a hidden closet in Gunnar's government office, and another in his office at home, and many more."

Alex stifled a yawn. "You're really clever, Mr. Today," he said sleepily.

"And you are tired. Get some rest, my boy. I'd like to see you walking around on the lawn again soon."

"Yes, sir," Alex said, his eyes already closed. But one thing remained on his mind. "I want to talk to Aaron," he murmured.

The mage closed his eyes for a moment and sighed. "I suppose you must, eventually," he said. But Alex was already asleep.

The Way It Is with Twins, Redux

n the eve of the annual Quill Purge, Alex and
Aaron Stowe stood face to face at the entrance
to Artimé, the most neutral place they could
agree upon. "Thank you for meeting me here,"
Alex said.

Aaron nodded coolly.

"Are you well? Is your leg all right?"

"Top form," Aaron said. He folded his arms to his chest.

"Have you seen Father and Mother?"

"No, and I never plan to. They are beneath me," Aaron
said. "Have you?"

"No." Alex had no desire to see them. His sunny, all-forgiving attitude had been jaded by the war, and by circumstances, and he'd matured a lot after all he'd been through in the past year. Survival depended on shrewdness and good judgment as well as skill. He knew that now.

"So. What do you want? I don't have all day."

Alex smiled inside, knowing he'd won an invisible battle by making Aaron ask the question. "I want to know what to expect from you. Are you a friend or an enemy? Will you be a part of Artimé now that you know it is real? Or are you still set on rebuilding that mess you have in Quill?"

"I don't plan to reveal my intentions to any Unwanteds, ever." Aaron scowled, trying to look fierce, but with the desolate, bruised land of Quill behind him, it wasn't very convincing.

"I see," Alex said. Despite all he'd been through, he felt a twinge of pity in his heart for his brother, even though Aaron had tried to kill him. "I guess there's nothing more to say, then."

Aaron hesitated. "I guess not."

"Well, I'll miss what could have been." Alex gazed into the hardened eyes of his twin.

Aaron stared back and didn't waver. "You do that."

Alex stood for a moment longer, and then he nodded and turned on the ball of his foot in the gravel. He walked back into Artimé without looking back.

Aaron watched him go, and then he turned toward Quill and strode back to his old, rusted-out jalopy, one of the few that remained in working order after the battle. He got in, started it up, and chugged up the road toward the palace.

What Remained

Mr. Today, on the day of the yearly Purge, called a meeting on the lawn for all of Artimé.

"Friends," he said, "I am pleased to tell you that the new high priest of Quill, Gunnar Haluki, and I have come to an agreement: Our two lands will live separately, in peace."

The new High Priest Gunnar, standing behind the crowd in human form this time, glanced at his daughter. Lani swiveled around and flashed a smile.

LISA McMANN

"Our border will remain open," Mr. Today continued. "Residents of both places will be free to come and go as they wish, though it may be some time before anyone wishes to step into the other place. Some may never wish to.

"As this is quite an unfathomable place for many of the residents of Quill, I ask that you treat our visitors with the same respect you give me. The new high priest assures me that he will request the same."

An agreeable murmur moved through the crowd.

"We've also agreed that if Quill chooses to continue to Purge their Unwanteds each year, those Unwanteds will be welcomed here with open arms, as always, with the understanding that they will not be put to death."

Mr. Today continued earnestly as the noise died down. "For those of you who eventually wish to find your families and return to Quill, you are free to do so, though be prepared for disappointments. Likewise, for those whose ties have been severed completely, there are no demands on you. Healing is a slow process, and for some, impossible." The old mage's eyes grew misty as he looked out over the survivors, many of whom still carried visible wounds. *Even more,* he thought, catching Alex's eye, *still carry invisible wounds that no magical spell can take away.*

He continued. "And for those who wish to invite their families to Artimé, you are also free to do so. As you know," he said, and took a deep breath, tears streaming down his cheeks freely now, "we never, ever run out of room in Artimé."

Mr. Today blew his nose into his hanky. Loudly. And then he looked out over the throng of Unwanteds and said, "And with that we leave our sorrows for another day, because today is a day to celebrate."

A cheer rose up from the crowd as they began to chant, "To-DAY, To-DAY, To-DAY!"

Marcus Today raised his hand and smiled, softening the chant. He went on to say, "Friends, this is the traditional day of the Purge, and High Priest Haluki, having had little time to make changes, has carried out the Purge as usual—that is the wish of his people. And before you scowl at the practices of Quill, please remember that changes take time. Today we welcome the thirty-two new members of Artimé, seated in the front row."

A round of riotous applause burst forth, causing the fresh,

wide-eyed group of thirteen-year-olds to cover their ears in wonder. Lani poked Meghan, Samheed, and Alex and pointed out her little brother, Henry, just ten years old, sitting in the front row. "Father wasn't going to waste any more time in getting him here," she said, grinning.

The crowd buzzed, and then their voices died down as Mr. Today continued. "For now, let us welcome new friends to Artimé. Let us remember the ones we lost. And let us also remember this day as the day we have been redeemed. Wear your Unwanted title like a badge of honor, for we have prevailed!"

The crowd erupted in applause and, for those who could manage it, a standing ovation for their leader. But Alex couldn't help but recall his conversation with Aaron and wonder if everything was really going to be as easy as Mr. Today implied. In fact he knew it wouldn't be.

After the lawn had mostly cleared, Alex remained seated with his friends, not quite ready to battle the crowds. Simber nodded to the small group as he passed by. Meghan and Samheed lay back on the fresh green lawn, dozing off while listening to the platyprots chatter and giggle. When Mr. Today finished speaking privately to High Priest Gunnar and they said their good-byes, Lani hopped up, hugged her father, and bid farewell for now, promising a visit soon. She plopped down next to Alex once again and leaned back, resting her head on his arm and humming a new little song she'd learned the day before from Ms. Morning.

"So," Lani said, "what do you suppose will happen to Aaron? Do you want to see him again?"

"We talked," Alex said.

"My father says Aaron's feeling terrible—terrible about hurting you and about how he exposed Artimé. That sort of thing. Father says he seems sincere."

"I don't know about that," Alex said. "I don't believe it. He's quite an actor, no matter how much he denies his creativity." He closed his eyes and paused, thinking. "I just don't know if I can ever trust him again. I guess maybe it's like Justine and Mr. Today. They grew so far apart, there'd have been no way they could ever get back to each other again with all that junk between them. Maybe it's better if he and I don't see each other again. At least for a while."

Lani turned to look at Alex. "That's sort of sad."

LISA McMANN

Alex was quiet. "Yeah, it is."

"I think you'll know if you're ever ready to give it a try," Lani said.

Alex smiled. He reached for a strand of her hair and twirled it lazily on his finger, his eyes closed, his heart almost full, his body mostly healed. Things weren't perfect, and they never would be, he knew. But for a fourteen-year-old boy, resting on the lawn in the warm sunshine, the sea gently lapping at the shore, his friends all around . . . He sighed. At least for now, things were good.

It was more than any Unwanted could ever hope for.

Alex's and Aaron's stories continue in

THE UNWANTEDS

BOOK TWO
Island of Silence

Turn the page for a sneak peek. . . .

Exposed

The sun was low over the sea off the shore of Artimé, making the distant islands look like flaming drops of lava on the horizon. An enormous winged cheetah named Simber came into view, flying over the nearby jungle. Clinging to his stone back were four Unwanted teenagers: Alex Stowe, Meghan Ranger, Samheed Burkesh, and Lani Haluki, all slipping and sliding and shrieking while they tried desperately to hang on. As they approached the lawn, Simber dove, nearly losing Lani off his back, but at the last moment grabbing her around the waist with his tail.

Mr. Today looked up at them as he walked toward the

mansion from Artimé's entrance. An angry-faced, broken-looking woman walked alongside him. The head magician held up his hand to signal Simber, who immediately spanned his wings to catch the air, and floated to the ground in a slow, surprisingly gentle sort of way. The beast took a dozen long steps before coming to a full stop, and then he knelt to let his passengers down. The four slid off and flopped to the grass, breathless and laughing.

Simber growled. He stood again regally on all fours and started walking away. "Therrre, now leave me alone," he said, pretending like he hadn't enjoyed any of it.

"Thanks, Simber," Alex called after him. The wind had twisted Alex's dark brown hair into tangled curls. He raked his fingers through it. It was getting long, and Alex had good reason for not cutting it. He didn't want anyone to mistake him for his twin brother, Aaron, ever again. He stood up and reached out his hand.

Lani grabbed it and pulled herself to her feet. She adjusted her component vest, and then smoothed wisps of straight black hair back into her braid. "I almost died," she said matter-of-factly. "Good thing Simber caught me with his tail or I'd be completely dead right now. Not sure I'm ever doing that again, Alex."

"We would have saved you," Alex said. "Right, guys? I would have, anyway."

When Meghan and Samheed didn't answer, Lani and Alex turned to look at them. Samheed's grin was gone. His face paled and he stared past the others, toward Mr. Today and the woman who accompanied him.

Meghan reached out for Samheed's arm. "What's wrong?" she whispered. But she knew. They all knew, once they followed Samheed's gaze. It was the same thing that had happened over and over again in the past months, ever since Mr. Today had removed the gate between Artimé and Quill. Now Wanteds and Necessaries could visit and even reside in the land they never knew existed, and see the children they had once condemned to death—the family members they had thought were long gone.

The old mage, his hand on the woman's elbow, stopped her several yards from the group of teens. He turned and spoke to her with an earnest look on his face. The wrinkles around her eyes grew deeper, and then she nodded reluctantly and stood firm, crossing her arms and tapping one foot slowly on the footpath, as if she had to be somewhere. Mr. Today approached alone and stood in front of the four friends, a kindly, sympathetic look crinkling about his eyes, and he said in a gentle voice, "Samheed, my boy. Your mother has come by to see you."

Not All Tea and Roses

In the months since Artimé and Quill had opened up their border for the first time, after the deadly battle that showed Quill that creativity could hold its own in a fight, there had been many instances such as the one currently facing Samheed. In fact it was all Mr. Today could do to accomplish his normal magely duties, what with the newly installed door knocker to the mansion being clacked all the time by frightened-looking visitors, unaccustomed to the bright colors and wandering creatures of Artimé. Daily Mr. Today was met with Necessaries who wanted to escape their slavelike conditions in Quill and take up residence in the magical world of Artimé. Even a Wanted or two who felt the urge to rebel and ride the cutting edge of society joined them. Besides, the food and the landscape of Artimé were definitely more appealing than the newly fractured goings-on in Quill.

But at this moment, Samheed stared at the mage, his eyes as wide as a beavop's at the hour before dawn. "What does she want?" he asked in a quiet voice. "I have nothing to say to her." And while his tone was solid, he trembled inside, because he knew why his mother had finally come.

"She didn't say," Mr. Today said, "but I assume she'd like to talk about your father."

Samheed nodded, and then stood on tiptoe to peer over the tall mage's shoulder. "She doesn't look happy," he said. "But then, I guess she never did." He glanced tentatively at Alex, and then at the girls. "What do you think?" he asked gruffly. Samheed was not one to enjoy asking for advice.

Meghan, her expression hard, spoke up first. "I think you should say no right off." She bit her lip to keep herself from saying more, and her eyes filled with angry tears. She blinked hard to disperse them. But she couldn't contain her thoughts.

"It's not worth it, Sam. It's not. All they do is tell you how much they wish you really were dead."

Alex looked earnestly at his best friend. "Aw, Meg," he said, shoving his hands into his pockets. He didn't know what else to add—nothing seemed to comfort her these days. She and Sean had gone into Quill to approach their parents early on, hoping to be welcomed. But while their parents seemed almost pleased to see Sean again after so many years, they held some sort of bitterness toward Meghan, blaming her for their sorry lives because she was the second Unwanted they'd produced, which made them outcasts in Quill. Meghan hadn't been the same since then.

All Alex knew was that his own parents hadn't come by looking for him, and that he hadn't gone into Quill to seek them out, either. It was an easy choice. He knew his parents put their full support behind Aaron because Aaron was a Wanted. And they always would—that was just the way Mr. and Mrs. Stowe were. Alex knew better than to expect a happy reunion. Or a reunion at all.

Lani touched Samheed's arm. "You'll never know unless you talk to her. It might be okay," she said. But they all knew that hers was the rare example of things working out okay. Her mother and younger brother, Henry, were now living here in Artimé, while her father, Gunnar Haluki, the former spy and new high priest of Quill, resided in Quill's palace for the time being to govern, now that the former evil High Priest Justine was dead.

Samheed twisted the toe of his boot in the grass. "You guys don't understand," he said. "It's different for me."

"Sam, come on. You didn't have a choice," Lani said wearily, as if she'd said it more than once before. "And besides, it wasn't you. It was Mr. Appleblossom."

"Because of me."

Lani's eyes sparked. "If he hadn't done it, there'd only be three of us standing here right now."

No one could refute that, so they remained silent.

"Mr. Today?" Samheed asked, looking up. He searched the man's face for answers.

But Mr. Today had none. "The decision is yours alone," he said. "I'll stay with you if you choose to speak with your mother. And if you choose not to, I'll ask her to leave."

Samheed gazed out over the lawn to the strip of sand at the

shore, thinking, his jaw set. He muttered bitterly under his breath and turned back to seek wisdom once again from the old mage's eyes. Finally, angrily, he kicked at the ground and shook his head at Mr. Today. "Tell her no."

Blindly he broke through his circle of friends and headed toward the shore. They watched him go, but no one followed. They knew Samheed well enough by now to let him brood alone.

Aaron Stowe stepped outside the university into the hot, gray morning and scanned the road toward the palace, the peak of which he could just barely see from this distance. This tallest point of the palace was bent just slightly to one side, almost as if it had to hunch over to fit under the barbed-wire ceiling of Quill, or perhaps it helped hold up this sky border along with the forty-foot-high walls that encircled the land.

Aaron remembered the times he'd spent in the palace as assistant secretary when the High Priest Justine was alive. Only months ago he'd had so much going for him—his highly praised creation of the Favored Farm for the Wanteds, the solution to the poor Quillitary vehicle performance, and the big fix for the water shortage throughout Quill. He'd had vast plans to work his way into senior governor status and someday rule the land. But all his hopes and aspirations were shattered by former Senior Governor Haluki, who had stripped Aaron of his title and all the privileges that went with it, sending him back to university like an ordinary Wanted.

Aaron cursed the name of Artimé and all that belonged to it, for it had opened up so much chaos and insanity into his structured, regulated world. The only good thing was that Haluki was being extremely cautious about making changes, and hadn't ventured to do much of anything yet. Though, Aaron mused, if Haluki did make a drastic change and Quill rebelled, Aaron might just have the faintest chance at becoming *something* once again.

He wrinkled up his nose. The smell outside was getting worse every day. Garbage piled up along the streets, and waste of all kinds was not getting buried properly. Quill was turning into a giant cesspool now that half the Necessaries had left their duties here and flocked to Artimé. None of the Wanteds would take over such menial, dirty tasks—that was sure. It was far beneath them. So things sat as they were until the remaining Necessaries could get around to it after their regular tasks were completed. It wouldn't be long, Aaron knew, before Quill was in real trouble. The only question was how Aaron could capitalize on this latest development now that his glorious leader was dead. He pinched the bridge of his nose, remembering. Wishing. *Dear High Priest Justine . . . if you only knew what they've done to us.* He felt a rare pang in his chest at the memory of her but stifled it immediately knowing full well she'd have condemned anyone for feeling things.

Across the narrow road two men paused in their walk to look at the mess in the ditch. "I went to Haluki yesterday about this," one said to the other.

"Useless thug."

"Shh," the first said, looking over his shoulder. "He's the high priest."

"Still," said the second. "What's he doing about it? What's his big solution to this mess? S-s-songing?" He stumbled on the unfamiliar word.

"He suggested we clean it up ourselves," the first said, picking his teeth with a makeshift toothpick and then tossing it onto the pile of junk. "And milk the cows, too, while we're at it. Can you imagine that?"

A group of three walkers approached and overheard the conversation. They congregated to offer their complaints as well. "He told me to pick my own corn if I want corn," one said. "Looked me right in the eye and said it." The others shook their heads in disbelief.

Just then a group of university boys brushed past Aaron on their way into the building. "Hello," Aaron said, but the boys ignored him, as everyone had done since the battle. Ever since people found out he'd had a hand in this whole mess. Aaron kept his expression cool. He looked down at the dirt and then he closed his eyes for a moment. With a heavy sigh, he turned and followed them inside.

Aaron sat down on the edge of the meager bed in his university dorm room, elbows propped on his knees, chin resting in his hands. He stared at the bare wall across from him, where there once was a door for a short amount of time in the middle of a fateful night. But the wall held no answers to his now frequently asked questions. What was to become of him? How could this have happened? Here he sat, powerless. Stripped of his title and his access to the palace, scorned by his classmates so much that he'd begun skipping classes, hated by Unwanteds far and wide for trying to impersonate his twin brother—who was apparently so beloved by them—in the heat of the battle. And dismissed, considered worthless by all the other governors.

Aaron felt his chest tighten in fury. He closed his eyes, concentrating, willing himself to be calm but failing miserably. He felt like shouting all the vilest words he could think of at the top of his voice. He felt like stringing up Alex, High Priest Haluki, and that freakishly genteel Mr. Today, and making them suffer the way he was suffering now.

A strange growling sound began in the back of Aaron's throat, almost like a roar, and it escaped with a loud huff of air. "Garr!" He gripped the fabric edge of his flimsy mattress and twisted it, tensing all the muscles in his body, his face growing very hot. It was both frightening and liberating to let such feelings happen, and he knew he should stop, but in this case there was no turning back. "Raaah!" he said this time. And then "GRRAAH!" He flipped over on the bed, facedown now, and pounded it with his fists, trying to let out the uncontrollable noises into the thin blanket so that they were muffled. He couldn't let anyone hear him. He wasn't sure what they'd do.

Island of Silence

And then his eyes began to sting. Like giant dusty craters in the most desolate part of Quill, his eyes, unaccustomed to tears, achingly filled and threatened to spill.

But he held them in. Heaving on the bed, emotion spewing forth in every breath, Aaron brought his hands to his closed lids and pressed back the tears. His throat ached and it felt like something was stuck there. "Calm down," he whispered. "Calm down." His breaths slowed, and he wiped his face. He lay there for a moment more, realizing the grave extent of personal weakness he'd just shown.

Quickly he got off the bed, ashamed of his behavior. He went to his bucket of tepid water and dipped his hand in. He splashed the water on his face, carelessly allowing the excess to drip on the floor, wasting it.

"Great land of Quill," he muttered. He dried his face with his sleeve. "Come on. Get a grip, Stowe."

Continued in *Island of Silence!*